Rainbow Warrior

~~~

The Tale of Ares, The Battle-Lustful Son

BB CLIFFORD

A Zero Labels Book

~~~

Disclaimer: This is a work of fiction. Names, characters, places, organizations, and incidents either are products of the author's imagination or are used fictitiously. Any resemblance to actual events, places, organizations, or persons, living or dead, is entirely coincidental.

Should you have any questions about the material set out in this book, contact your clinician or doctor. If you need immediate help and you are in crisis, seek immediate, professional help. Here are your options: Call 911 (if it is available in your area), take yourself to the emergency room of your nearest hospital, call a friend or family member, and ask them to take you to the nearest emergency room, call the National Suicide Helpline at 988 or https://988lifeline.org/

Rainbow Warrior
The Tale of Ares, The Battle-Lustful Son

Print ISBN: 979-8-9851024-7-5   (Paperback)

Printed in the United States of America
First printing edition 2024
Published by Zero Labels LLC
143 E Ridgewood Ave, #1484, Ridgewood, NJ 07450

Images in cover photo used under license from Shutterstock.com

~~~

Rainbow Warrior handles some tough issues, including trauma, assault, and suicide, so it is important to include a content warning.

Should you have questions about the material set out in this book, contact your clinician or doctor. If you are in crisis, seek immediate, professional help. Here are your options: Call 911 (if it is available in your area), take yourself to the emergency room of your nearest hospital, call a friend or family member, and ask them to take you to the nearest emergency room, call the National Suicide Helpline at 988 or https://988lifeline.org/

~~~

For M, L, and W.

Contents

"He said our lives mean nothing except as a cycle of regeneration, that we are incomprehensibly brief sparks, just as the animals are, that we are no more important than they are, no more worthy of life than any living creature. That in our self-importance, in our search for meaning, we have forgotten how to share the planet that gave us life."

Charlotte McConaghy, Migrations

"Civilized life, you know, is based on a huge number of illusions in which we all collaborate willingly. The trouble is we forget after a while that they are illusions and we are deeply shocked when reality is torn down around us."

J.G. Ballard

Prologue

~~~

New beginnings

~~~

Fortresses are supposed to be impenetrable, but something was there all along, eroding it from within. Rotten to the core. Everyone who lived on Mount Pelion Way could feel it. The land looked no different, but there was something that kept them far away from the place. Not just a strangeness, but a darkness that made them dread and fear something that was hidden from view. So, when the home of the Brown family burned down, the place Eris Brown would call her *fortress*, everyone was relieved. But that was not the end of it. There were contaminants to soak the soil, as much as there were nightmares left to linger, and so the strangeness spread, along with the dread.

Whatever was so rotten seemed to regrow, through the roots and vines, up along the tree trunks. Even the blossom that flowered was parched, like aged skin, and the fruit swollen on the branches emitted a pungent aroma.

The fortress site sat alone and neglected for more than a year until a woman who had lost her job as a teacher five years ago, and couldn't afford to keep her apartment, wandered on to the land in search of food and shelter. She still regrets the way all that played out, when she saw how cruelly the principal was treating the janitor. She should have kept her mouth shut, instead of confronting the principal, because it meant that she never got tenure. So, when there were cuts made, her job was the first to go. She can still remember the look of glee on the principal's face as she was escorted from the premises, and she tried not to cry as she clutched her box of construction paper, scissors, and glitter glue.

For five years, this unemployed teacher was hounded for unpaid bills, so she found the stillness of the abandoned site to be a peaceful place to hide. And when she saw the fruit hanging in the trees, she thought the heavens had rewarded her. She never expected such red, rosy apples to rip through her gut like that, tearing apart her intestines like shiny white razor-sharp teeth.

When the people of Mount Pelion Way found her body, they dismissed this as *natural causes*. They explained to the police that the diet of a vagrant was far from healthy, and she must have eaten something spoiled from a nearby dumpster. But the police knew enough about this land that once supported a fortress. They knew how many died here before this vagrant, and they were certain that myths and legends were true all along. This land really was poisonous. But no land ever poisons itself. It's always something more, something greedy that distorts and corrupts what was once flourishing and naturally pure.

Just look at what it did to that teacher. The greed of that principal, determined to keep what power she had within her grasp, left a devoted teacher destitute. Without her apartment, the poor woman hadn't washed in months; she was starved, and she left to rot like fodder for a landfill. In the creaking limbs of the apple trees, you can still hear her croak and groan for sustenance. Her equally naïve parents always taught her to be kind and do the right thing, to work hard and keep smiling. Just look at what that did to her. Can you see her now, in the shape of the smile that stretches so wide that it splits at the seams? Is this what they wanted for her? And what about you? Would you have stood by your values or played it smart and said nothing about the janitor? I wonder.

The people of Mount Pelion Way would have kept quiet. They could never afford these nice homes on the East Coast if they always played fair. They learned from a young age to *put up and shut up if you know what's good for you, if you want this shiny object, you'll take it, no matter the pain.* So, they say nothing of the teacher they see, still appearing long after her death, and they try to ignore the pain of the terror it evokes in them. It would cause a multitude of problems if people knew of this creature, this phantom that appears. They fear most for the value of their home, should anyone find out about hauntings or cursed land. Only to their loved ones late at night, whispered in place of a nightly prayer, they say they have seen this phantom teacher in the last day or so, but the vines and roots growing around her suggest she might have been there for years, decades, even. The land, it seems, wanted to hold on to her, to show us something about our true nature. The land aches, and it wants us to ache too, it wants us to see how much pain there is, and how we are causing it all. Doesn't the teacher, tangled in the vines, remind us of the wildlife tangled in plastic and wires and other waste we discard, as recklessly, as heartlessly as we discarded that teacher? Perhaps.

But the people of Mount Pelion Way don't care about all that; they just want to maintain a well-manicured lawn. They don't care about the distortions in their bloodstream and the misshapen offspring they are bound to produce because of the contaminants building up in the soil and spreading into their water supply as much as the air they breathe. These people just want things to look nice and pretty with sharp edges and a bright gloss of green. They don't care about the talk of some people who are outside their social circle, the strange ones with dirty hair and pierced noses, who try to scare them into believing that the whole of the East Coast will disappear beneath sea level in no time at all. They don't want to see how much they will struggle as the water rushes in, and how they will fight for those final breaths, regretting too late how much trauma they have inflicted on Mother Earth. Generation after generation inflicted such violence on her, trying to conquer her and use her to build an empire, but she would never be subjugated. She was lying in wait for vengeance, the kind that Eris of Suburbia could only dream of, and the kind that creates a whole rainbow of warriors to fight this good fight.

Shortly after her death, Ralph, the teacher's brother comes, to visit Rotherwell. He wants to know what has gone on, what this town did to his sister. How can her heart just fail like that when she had no pre-existing conditions? *She was forty-eight, for Christ's sake.* Ralph rarely curses, but this was his only sister and they used to knock on the adjoining wall between their bedrooms, a morse-code form of contact that they would refer to throughout the years as a sense of connection between the two, never accepting that the connection would be severed so suddenly. It was this sister who walked this brother down the aisle when he married his husband, because their parents were too pig-ignorant to see that he wouldn't suddenly marry a woman just because they threatened to cut him out of their will. She loved her brother, no matter who he chose to marry, and she was well aware this meant she also could lose out on any inheritance. This brother and sister knew what was right, and they believed this would always keep them safe.

And now? Ralph hates such naivety, blaming it for leading her down a path of righteousness without anyone to support her, without enough food to eat, so she had to go foraging in this strange, abandoned place with the rubble of some burned down home and a lingering smell of death and foreboding.

No one will talk to him about his sister's death, because their local news outlet and Facebook group for the Rotherwell moms and dads refer to his sister as a *troubled vagrant*. They forget that she was Ellie Mary Jones, and she had beautiful long brown hair and the most wicked sense of humor. Ralph hates them for refusing to care about any of this, even after he contacted them to correct their reports. They wouldn't even use the photo he gave them, the one where she was standing on the beach and she'd seen a cute little kid playing in the sand, and afterwards she had told her brother how much she wanted children eventually, when she finally got tenure.

When Ralph walks the perimeter of the land where they found his sister's body, the vengeance that stirs in his blood seems in tune with an energy he can feel from the ground. It hums, buzzes, tickles him, even. He likes the apple trees, despite the knowledge that Ellie lay dead here, all alone and cold under the night sky. He wishes someone would tell him who found her, and what they think really happened to make her heart give out like that. The police referred to "significant injuries," but they wouldn't say any more, and they only showed Ralph her face very briefly, which made it seem like she was just sleeping.

"What did they do to you?" he asks the moonlight, certain that this will get the message to her. Ralph waits and listens, even though he never gets any reply.

"Who lived here?" he asks her, as he gestures to the smoldering rubble. "Why did you come here of all places?" Still no reply, and it is starting to get cold, so Ralph thinks he might return home. His husband has been urging him to not come here, to let it go, but he has never lost a sister, let alone so suddenly like this.

He walks on a little further, so he is now in the backyard, and Ralph stares at the row of trees that loom in the darkness. They appear to frown at him, like angry men with their arms up and trying to shoo him away. He thinks of an old neighbor who used to shout at him every time he would try to retrieve his ball, and then when he was a teenager, the neighbor would shout a gay slur at him, and his parents never said anything in reply.

"Is anyone there?" he calls out, when he sees movement on one of the tree branches. Of course Ralph wants it to be his sister, that she returns and laughs about a case of mistaken identity, even though he knows this to be impossible.

One of his footsteps cracks a twig beneath his shoe, and it makes him jump, so he looks back to the smoldering rubble, and that's when he sees something reaching from within the bricks.

"No," Ralph says, "I'm seeing things."

He sees a gap where a door must have been, and there are gaps where there might have been windows, in the parts of the lower level that did not fully collapse. From those gaps, Ralph hears something sweet and melodic, a voice, not his sister's but still something intriguing, that is urging him to come closer. This siren call is luring him to his destruction, promising this will be the most certain way for him to reunite with his sister.

Ralph shakes himself free of this thought and instead he looks beyond, to the small houses up and down the street. He winces when he sees himself breaking into one of them, and rampaging through any bodies that are there, the helpless souls he would find hunched over a laptop or slumped on a sofa staring at a cell phone. He thinks of knife blocks, and shards of glass, and baseball bats, and gun cases. It shocks him because he was never a violent man. But it is the land telling him that he deserves to do this. That they deserve to feel the pain.

She was your sister, after all.

Chapter One

~~~

Dylan

~~~

Most nights, I hear that siren as it lures me back to the fortress site. That sweet melodic disembodied voice promises I will find a home, some sort of family again, if I could just return to Mount Pelion Way. As soon as I wake, I remember the fire and how quickly it consumed Eris, my mother, and the body of my sister. So, there is no home or family to return to.

A pungent smell of rotting flesh brought me gasping to consciousness, and I quickly realize that I am in the bed of a stranger, some guy I met at the club last night. My breathing slows when I've snorted too much or taken too many pills. I'm probably not taking in enough oxygen, so the siren might have been trying to save me, pulling me to the surface for one more fight against fuck knows what. I'm tired of fighting like a warrior. Even this dude from the club wanted to fight last night when we'd stepped into the hallway of his apartment block, and I'd asked him about the weird smell. *What ya sayin', I live in a dump?* he'd snapped at me. I couldn't make out the accent; it wasn't the kind of British I've heard on those crime dramas on Netflix. He said *dump* as *doomp*, and he pouted until I suggested we do some of the stuff he'd offered me at the club. He had it in a gold vial that was hanging round his neck, and I'd been tempted, but I'd already taken one of his pills from the tip of his tongue, so I was already in the zone. But the journey home in the back of some cab had been long, and the smell of his apartment block was bringing me too acutely to my senses, so I needed something else. When he cracked open the vial, I hoped for coke to make me loved-up and horny, but when I snorted it from his chest, I realized it was the mind-bending ketamine. Quickly, his face stretched before my eyes, so his jowls dragged on the ground as he walked over to open a window. When he turned back to face me, I saw insects crawling inside his gaping mouth, and I backed away, saying I needed a moment in the bathroom. That wasn't much better because the sink became a grotesque face of startled tap eyes, a hooked spout nose, and a plughole mouth that was ready to devour me if I turned my back for a moment.

I don't know what happened after that, although I have flashes of something involving the guy and this bed that I'm now lying in. One of us, both of us, slamming each other against this headboard. Only now, in the morning or afternoon after, I can't quite tell which, I see that it isn't a headboard at all but a folded over bit of foam covered in a bedsheet. As temporary and makeshift as this little arrangement that we silently agreed upon, because keeping it at surface level is all I can cope with at the moment.

I hear him in the bathroom that is right behind the makeshift headboard. I hear him grunting, and there's a clatter of something, maybe a toilet seat, a plunger, or even a weapon to finish me off. *Fuck knows.* My head swims like I'm in a fucking goldfish bowl. I think of what he might do to me as my body cools, and then I remember the smell of something putrefying, and it starts to thicken in my nose. I can't avoid it now, images of a body in a bathtub, in the very bathroom that is behind my head. I watch as the body starts to dissolve in acid or lime or whatever else they use to get rid of bodies here in London. I heard there was a particularly powerful drain cleaner that did the job, but I don't know where I heard that, or why someone would say that. There's also the River Thames, a swirling brown and black mouth just waiting to devour your unwanted items. I've seen shopping carts and trash bags and Styrofoam in there, and even a baby doll drifting with the current when I've been walking home from another one-night stand. I assumed it was a baby doll, but then people do all sorts of horrible things, and just because the victim is a baby or a child, doesn't make them want to hurt them any less. *Hurt people hurt people*, isn't that what they say? There's no point denying it, any more than you would deny that the victims who end up in the swirling water of the Thames are often the people who want to remain invisible to the world, who need to avoid even the most tenuous of an attachment. Usually, these victims are people who have witnessed trauma and violence, and so they don't want to get attached to anyone in case they have to witness that violence again, and then the severance of that attachment can feel even more painful. Does this mean I am like those people, the ones more likely to be found floating in the Thames? Perhaps.

While I listen to the man who is pulling on the roll of toilet paper hanging on the wall behind my head, I imagine him returning to his bed, where I am now, and panicking. Perhaps he has a wife or a husband, and he was too drugged up to realize what he was doing last night. But now, as he sobers up, he might panic as he thinks of ways to dispose of me, turning me into the next victim of London's dark underbelly.

Victim.

I roll the word around in my head and then form it in my mouth. After all that Eris accused me of, it doesn't feel right to call myself a victim. She spent years painting me as the villain to sharply contrast with Ania, her innocent daughter, and when my sister died, Eris pursued me relentlessly, accusing me of all manner of malevolence. She changed her mind at the end of her life, when she discovered the truth about Paris, my father. I still hear the hiss and pop of burning flesh, and I still see the fear in his eyes when he realized I wasn't going to save him. If there is a hell or underworld, he is waiting for me there, and as he waits and watches me in this strange man's bed, his disgust tells me that I deserve to be in the underworld with him. Every day, I fight this thought, that I am already, or destined to be, anything like my father.

The apple never falls far from the tree.

This might have hastened my resolve to lose the male label as much as Paris' surname, changing from Dylan Brown, son of Paris Brown, to Dylan Gall, the non-binary offspring of Eris Gall. But some things are harder to achieve than a change of name, and even now I have travelled as far away from Rotherwell as London, still I know the ghosts are trailing me.

Above my head there is a flimsy-looking white shelf with the remnants of a dying plant spilling over the edge. It's the only sign of life amongst coffee cups and Styrofoam containers from takeout, and piles of textbooks that are still encased in their plastic film wrapping. The guy from the club might be a student like me, and we might even be on the same course. The trouble is, his face is pixelated in my mind right now. All that is coming back to me are his big muscles, and the way they flexed when he lifted me as soon as we got through his front door. It hurt when he slammed me against the wall, but there was something about the danger that excited me. Suicidal. Some might call it that. Passively suicidal because I am numb to living or the prospect of dying at the hands of some random hookup. I could drift off to sleep again, let him do whatever he needed to, but the stench keeps me alert.

The sound of the toilet flush startles me, and my awareness widens to more of the surrounding room. I see that the window is covered in condensation, a fine film of moisture that seems to dampen everything in London. It helps me to forget the bright, almost surreal colors of falls in New Jersey, and instead I think about spores of mold multiplying in my lungs with every breath.

A solitary droplet snakes its way down the flimsy-looking

glass, and a memory of Ania creeps in before I can stop it with a line or pill or shot of something. She didn't deserve any of it. Eris, my mother, was vengeful and battle-worn; she gave as good as she got, but my sister never wanted to fight with anyone. Ania's only fault was her birth into a family of violence and rage.

I want to believe that the siren who keeps calling me back to Rotherwell is my sister. She wants to protect me from something, from things I cannot yet see. But the dead might not see everything, so she might not see the dangers that remain in Rotherwell, that made me flee that place.

There is something glinting on the shelf above my head. It is small and round, and the light from the solitary bulb in the middle of the ceiling catches its glassy surface. I sit up and reach for the object, its cool surface bringing me a little more into the present, so I notice the scratchy coarse sheets beneath my naked body.

Realizing the glass ball is a snow globe, I shake it, and I watch glitter explode in the water. It looks like ice-white ash falling.

Or like tiny shards of glass.

I can't be sure whose voice that is. Sometimes I like to believe it is my mother, sometimes it is Ania. I imagine that they linger somewhere just out of sight, clutching their unfinished business like a deck of cards. Ghosts do this, especially when their death comes suddenly, before they are ready, or with the kind of violence that leaves their howl still whistling in the wind. If you were to stop for a minute, would you feel their presence too, these ghosts that accompany us and covet our mortal flesh? Are they there, behind your shoulder or caught in a reflection, and are they a force for good or otherwise?

I think of how quickly the fortress collapsed after the fire took hold, just moments after I escaped and left my parents to burn. I know you're probably going to judge me for this, but my mother told me to leave her so she could hold Paris down. Eris didn't want my father to inflict his violence on any more girls, so the only way to ensure that was for him to burn alongside her. You probably think that I had some other choice, but in the heat of the moment, there was no time to think. You don't think I replay that moment over and over again?

I shake the snow globe again, and I watch the glitter flurry in a silent explosion. It looks like some kind of souvenir, and I wonder if the figures are supposed to be characters from a movie. Their eyes are bulging, and their hands are outstretched, so it looks like they are drowning in the liquid that surrounds them. I see the panic and confusion, their faces pale and swollen, and their eyes bulge with what looks like asphyxiation. I want to help them, but I don't know how, and I don't have any time to figure it out because I hear the guy at the door to the bedroom, so I shove the globe in the pocket of my jeans that are on the floor beside the bed.

"Fuck," the man shouts as he bursts into the room. "I don't know what you did to me last night, but I'm paying for it now."

Now I see his buzz-cut head and his hardened stare, I remember why I was drawn to him at the club. That curled lip and refusal to smile, those dark frown lines and a thick moustache to hide his features. It all seemed to threaten chaos and violence, and I needed to get lost in that, so I could, for another night, escape Rotherwell. It was all very well fleeing the place in person, but the memories still trailed me.

He rubs his naked stomach with one hand as he scratches deep inside his boxer shorts with the other. As his muscles ripple with each movement, the snake tattoo that is wrapped around his left forearm looks like it is coming alive.

"You finally awake, then," he says with a grunt and slips into bed with me. Too quickly, his hands are around my throat, and he squeezes as he tries to pin me down with the weight of his body.

"You good to go again," he says as an instruction rather than a question. I think of the snow globe and how it's just out of reach, and how it could easily transform from a souvenir to a weapon, and I think of how easy it can be to switch from victim to perpetrator and back again, as the power balance shifts, as the mood alters with the remnants of whatever was left in my bloodstream, and I think of that blood inside of me, riddled with all manner of violence and trauma and genetic quirks. You see, he might have squeezed my throat, but I also squeezed his. He might have fucked me, but I fucked him too. There was a skin-biting, intense greed that writhed beneath the skin of both of us because we are, after all, human.

So I let him go again. I can do that, you see, by draining myself of all feeling, all memory that might remain in the ventricles of my brain, I just ride each thrust as I would the throbbing of my heartbeat. I mean, you aren't painfully aware of each minute movement of the other things in your body, the passage of food through your bowels, or the flexing of your heart or lungs. So why sweat this kind of stuff?

Afterwards, I tell him that I need to go.

"Why?" he asks, but my mind is still blank, after emptying it to let him take me as he needed to, so I have no excuse at the ready. He looks at me, waiting for a reply, but I have none, so I just keep getting dressed and try to distract him by changing the subject.

"What's that smell?" I ask him as I search for my clothes. He shrugs and ignores my question, instead saying, "Stay."

"I really have to go. But seriously, what is that smell?"

"Why do you keep asking me that?"

"Because there's a smell."

I know this isn't going to go well, so I quicken my pace as I gather my clothes and put on each item.

"You're starting to sound like a snob, you know."

His tone goes up and down in a sing-song way, and I suspect that someone once told him that he was boring, and it stung, so he made a conscious effort to vary his voice every time he spoke. Only, it sounds forced; it makes him sound like he is putting on some kind of weird comedy act, and then I think of what he might be like if he dressed up as a clown, with the huge red plastic shoes, and the garish rainbow-colored wig, and a bright red nose that honks when you squeeze it. So I start to laugh at him.

"What's so funny?" he asks, only he's still using the up and down sing-song tone, of course he is, I mean that's just the way he speaks, he isn't going to change it for me, but now I think of the clown, I can't stop laughing.

"Are you laughing at me?" he shouts, only this time I notice that his fists are clenched, and he is straining forward on the bed, looking like he is ready to pounce.

"It's like you're looking down on me, and my place, or, like you think you're better than me, or *summit*," he continues.
Now I remember that I've heard this accent before, when I ordered something in a café round the corner from my university, and someone in a high-visibility vest and a menacing grimace told me to "pipe down." When I tried to ignore him, he raised his voice to drown mine out, saying something about "loud-mouthed yanks, coming here and thinking they are better than everyone else." I don't think I am better than anyone; I think I have maggots for genes that will crawl around inside you if I were ever to have sex with you unprotected. My father was a rapist pedophile, and my mother was a recluse who kept the body of my dead sister in the attic before the whole fucking house burned down.

"I'm not looking down on you or your place. I am simply asking what that smell is. It could be something in your trash can, or maybe something is rotting in one of the adjoining apartments. Hell, someone might be putrefying right above us as we speak. I was merely curious, but now I'm not anymore, so I'll see you again someday."

I have my underwear, t-shirt and one sock on as I try to push past him, but he pushes me back on the bed. With his hands clamped to my shoulders, he has me pinned to a mattress that smells of mothballs. This kind of dominance was what I was looking for last night, when I chose him of all the gyrating mounds of flesh in tank tops, crop tops or vests that were sweating around me, but now, paired with the disgusting smells, it just feels suffocating.

"Has someone died? Is that what it is? Or did they just shat themselves and forgot to clean themselves up?"
I'm trying to make light of it, so we can end on a good note, but the guy has some serious chip on his shoulder because he pushes me around as he starts to scream at me.

"Now you're bein' rude and I don't like rude people, especially jumped up fucking little queers like you."

"Takes one to know one, I guess," I snap back, instantly regretting it as he lifts a fist to punch me, but for some reason, he stops himself.

"Who the fuck do you think you are?"

"I'm no one. I'm just fucking tired, and I want to go home."

I try again to push him off me, but still he has me pinned to the bed. I reach to the ground and my hands make contact with my jeans, and I think of swinging them at his temple so the snow globe cracks his skull open, and I can almost see the blood spraying about us as he looks down on me with confusion. He probably isn't a bad person, not someone who deserves to die so soon, but I don't know what else to do because his grip has slipped from my shoulders to my throat, and he is squeezing so hard that I can see stars. I don't have much to live for, but there is something defiant in me that refuses to let him decide when and how, so I swing the jeans at his head, a little half-heartedly, because I didn't really want to kill him.

"What the fuck?" he screams as he lets go of me and grabs at his head.

I scrabble across the bed, stumbling to the door, and I snatch at the handle, thankful that it isn't locked.

As soon as I am out into the communal hallway, the pungent smell intensifies, and I start to cough.

"I'm sorry," I hear him call from behind me. "Just stay for a little longer."

I hear his footsteps getting closer, but already I am down the stairs and out into the diesel-scented street. Finally, I allow myself to glance back and I can see that he hasn't followed me.

I search for the nearest underground station, but my slow uncertain pace is becoming the source of frustration for the pedestrians who pass by. One elbows me, and another gives me a shoulder-shove as faces are shuffled so quickly that they blur into one mass of fury.

Emerging from the blur are the features I have known my whole life, the bulbous, misshapen face of my mother. There is the same auburn hair of glowing embers, there is the aquiline nose, and there are the eyes of shiny emeralds. Eris, the mythical creature of discord and strife. She presses her way back from the dead to remind me that I carry the same potential for fury and vengeance, and didn't she name me, after all, Ares, her battle-lustful son?

She wants me to remember the vengeance that used to stir in my blood and hers, and how we both harbored fantasies of revenge for petty incursions by people that might not have even registered our existence. We both assumed that this fury kept us safe, that it warned people off from trying to invade and conquer us. But, like a Trojan horse, the true threat had already slipped inside, no matter how many latches and bolts and locks my mother kept on her family home. The fool locked us in with the dangers, making a prison out of that fortress of a family home and keeping the rot and the haunting within.

Eris is casting a spell over me. In the reflection of the passing buses and cabs, she is showing how easy it could be for my own features to distort into her bulbous, misshapen face. I know how easily this could happen if I spend too long on my own, locking myself in the tiny room they allocated to me at the university halls of residence. How easy it could be to cancel plans and hypnotize myself with pointless TikTok posts, becoming fearful of the world outside when the most threatening dangers lurk within.

But I am stronger than she could ever be. I have evolved, so I built my own fortress, only this is one I carry around inside of me. It keeps me safe from feeling anything, leaving me cold and detached because to care about my parents, my sister, anyone, only leaves me vulnerable. Every stranger I fuck around with I ghost before they get a sense of who I am, before those sinews of connection can grow around me, like vines and tree roots to penetrate me from within.

The spice of incense burns the air, and it breaks the spell Eris was casting over me. I pass a shop that sells mystical packets of hope and spells in the form of brightly colored rocks. I'm sure that if I went inside, they would claim these rocks carry healing powers, but I don't know if they'd be any match for the rot and poison that contaminates my blood.

Finally, I see the familiar red circle and blue line of an underground station. A clap of thunder explodes above my head without the warning from any flash of lightning, and a faint patter of drizzle erupts into a torrential downpour. I start to run, jumping into the road to dodge the furious pedestrians. The traffic, you see, crawls at a slower pace than anyone on the sidewalk. I don't know whether this has always been the way for vehicles in London, but it makes me wonder how anyone gets anything done. I see each motorist sitting behind their steering wheel as they stare at the congested road ahead of them, and they seem content to sit in this stagnation. Is this what happened to the once *Great* Britain? They got caught in an endless traffic jam and decided to just sit and wait.

Inside the ticket office, a cloud of damp and other people's breath envelopes me. I recognize this station after a night spent with another guy; a banker or investment advisor or something. I didn't care what kind of career he had chosen. I just liked the way he lifted me onto his kitchen counter that night. I remember he told me in the morning about Balham, this tube stop, and how it was flooded during the second world war when a German bomb landed on the street above the station. I think of the ghosts all swimming around down there like goldfish, still trying to find their way out so they can reach an eternal resting place. And I think of the darkness, that solidity that holds you in place no matter how hard you try to fight it, or how much you wanted it, as my sister did when she threaded the noose around her neck. I can imagine it terrified her to slip like that from the bough of the tree, regretting it too late to turn back and make another go of life.

I don't know what your beliefs are, but I figure that when something catastrophic happens like that, the souls can remain trapped until something similar happens again, and they are jolted on to the next place. It could even be a chance for things to be improved, for lessons to be learned about the nature of humankind. The ghosts might have a hand in all that, trying to show a different way to be, where everyone can make it out alive instead of trampling on each other in a fight for freedom.

I think of the ghosts still trapped within the rubble of the fortress in Rotherwell, still calling me back across the Atlantic so I can join them again. Every night, in my dreams, the fortress is rebuilt to once again become an imposing structure of the finest stone and brick that could be purchased more than a century ago. I can see it now, sitting high up on the hill with its two turrets in place to frame the entrance as it peers down its chimney nose at the houses of newer, smaller construction.

I hear an air-raid siren. It could be a sound trapped from the world war bombing of this station, an echo still reverberating through time. I've read about such things, reminding us how little we know and how arrogant we are to try to constrain all that we discover. Time, space, any species we can skin, eat, or make glue out of.

I realize the air-raid siren has been coming from someone's cell phone, one of those annoying ring tones you can pay to download. World war chic, or something like that. There's a marketing gimmick to accompany every atrocity, like a party bag you can collect after witnessing carnage, an assortment of the body parts of the victim you saw crushed to death at an exclusive event. The kind of event you can only attend if you pay using bitcoin, and invitations are handed out on the down low to people in the know.

My stomach drops with the swift drift and sinking of an escalator that plunges me further underground, deep into the fuggy underbelly of a station that is a tomb. I feel their presence, these ghosts from the Second World War. I imagine their faces, frozen in horror when they realized their fate, sealed tightly by mounds of earth and chunks of the platform walls piling on top to hold them tightly as the water rushed in.

Even though the glare of the overhead lights still shines brightly, I feel the darkness approach, making the light seem more like a memory, and in that darkness, all manner of things can materialize. There are people who I know to be dead standing ahead of me, so the escalator takes me closer to them with every moment. My father, rageful that I would leave him to burn like that, after everything he did for me. My mother, still suspicious, still uncertain whether I was innocent of the violence inflicted on my sister. I tell myself this is the after-effects of the drugs from last night, the stuff I snorted from the naked body of that buzz-cut guy. But it isn't just last night, is it? This angularity of my mind, bending round corners of space and time and reality could be an accumulation of all those chemicals that have been burning through my bloodstream in the five months since I arrived in London.

But it's of little comfort to know that it could be the drugs that are rotting my mind, that it isn't reality that I see as the escalator takes me closer to those rotting corpses that are piled up ahead of me. I see flesh hanging from their bones, and I smell them, the same stench I was complaining about at the buzz-cut guy's apartment, so maybe the smell is inside of me and I am the rot, the taint, the shame to carry.

I reach the bottom of the escalator, and I step through these corpses, and I know they are no more real than the nightmares that haunt me each night, leaving the same sweat plastered across my face as I feel now. I wipe the sweat before it trickles into my eyes.

On the platform I stand with the other passengers, and I try to pretend this is usual for me, part of my daily routine, and that I'm not really floating through a waking nightmare. Is this what happens to the people you hear about, that get carted off in an ambulance and locked away in a secure unit of a hospital, strapped to a chair or bed and force-fed and medicated against their will? Were they also walking through the translucent corpses of their family members and seeing what no one else can see? Ignorance really is bliss, so I try to distract myself by nodding in reply when someone hisses *"Fucking Transport for London."* When I turn, I see that it is a tall, dark-haired guy with headphones on. He fills a snugly fitted suit with rounded biceps and pecs, and our eyes meet.

"What?" he says with a smirk.

I can smell something scented, an aftershave, perhaps, or even a moisturizer, and there is a saltiness about his scent that stirs something in me. I come to, and I feel my veins flooding with life again. I'm aware I haven't even washed the last guy from inside my body, but already there is a writhing beneath my skin that makes me crave for more.

I smile because that's what is expected of me, and he smiles in reply.

"Where are you heading?" I ask him.

He scans my body and then restores eye contact with me.

"Old Street. You?"

I tell him I'm heading to Euston, and he asks if I want to grab a drink. I'm still not sure what time of day it is, but that doesn't really matter because my only commitment is the occasional lecture that I can easily make up by convincing one of the other students to give me their notes.

"Sure. Where were you thinking?"

"I meant at the weekend. I've got a busy day ahead of me," he says with a laugh, his eyes gesturing down at his suit, and then I realize there are many people on this platform who are smartly dressed, so I've been caught up in a midweek morning commute.

I notice a solitary bead of perspiration shuddering at the tip of the man's nose, and I think of the droplet of condensation running down the windowpane at the buzz-cut guy's apartment. There is also the constant rain, unrelenting since I've arrived in this country, and I'm afraid there might be some kind of connection between all of this, a foreshadowing of a punishment that I am yet to receive. You don't just get to watch your family home burn down and escape untarnished.

But then the drugs could just as easily be tangling my brain, as much as the grief and shock of it all.

Grief?

I'm not sure I'm entitled to that, not when I had a part to play in their deaths. After all this time, two years in a couple of months, I still hear the squeal and hiss of the burning flesh. And I still don't know if that was the sound of combustion or a squeal for help that I turned my back on as I saved myself.

It hasn't escaped me how I seem to be carrying on where my mother left off, so that now it is my turn to become haunted and tangled like a knot. Or will I become an incendiary device, blowing apart all I have known and fusing it into something new? I am the son of Eris *and* Paris, after all.

I think of the incendiary devices that have been taken onto these trains, and the damage it caused inside a confined space. The insides on the outside, blasted onto the roof of the train, and missing limbs so people were left to sit, stunned while their life ebbed out from beneath them. In this country, they used to say that the Irish were the terrorists, and then the Muslims, and more recently it's been the *environmental extremists*, although some ask for the proof, and then the answers run dry. There are never trials or convictions as the terrorists have been decimated along with their targets, so it is all down to the media to tell a story that they assume we will believe. And you know how stories go; it all depends on the bias of the narrator.

I used to try to talk about these things with Max, mainly when I was high. I used to ask about the source of all this trauma and violence; whether it was a chemical imbalance or a curse, or even a haunting by some malevolence that we don't yet understand. I knew he didn't get it, didn't even want to understand, and he'd usually just slap me on the ass and try to fuck me again. And the messed-up thing about that was that I enjoyed it. I didn't care that we couldn't see eye to eye on most things, and that he never really wanted to hear my perspective. I'd found somewhere to hide for a while, a place with him where I could belong, even if that portrayed me as some worthless fuck buddy.

It's only with this distance, all the way across the Atlantic from him, that I can see him as the wrecking ball to my stability, a form of insanity that I can no longer afford. Since the fire, I don't trust myself, let alone someone like him, so I'm hoping it will be safer to start again in a new city. The trouble is, from the last message Max sent me, he's made it clear that he's gaining on me.

"I know you're in London. You really think I wouldn't find you there?" he'd sent me. He expects a reply, and the longer I leave it, the greater the fury and his need for revenge.

The only way I know how to handle this is to distract myself with another shiny object, so I reach over to the nose of the snugly fitted suit and wipe the perspiration from the tip of his nose. I lick my finger and smile at him as he smiles back at me, but this is a misjudgment because I hear someone hiss *"Batty boy"* from behind me. There is a sucking of teeth and someone else says *"Faggot,"* and I imagine the passengers becoming a mob and surging forward to push me onto the tracks as the train approaches. But I've heard these insults too many times before, and it only ignites a greater desire to fuck around in front of them. I look at the guy in the suit and imagine plunging my tongue down his throat and unzipping him right here in front of them all, and I might have done it had I not heard rumbling from the darkness of the tunnel.

I feel the rushing wind, so I turn to look for the lights of a train as the air becomes a dusty grey of iron oxide and maghemite. I think of the damage these contaminants are going to inflict on my body, disrupting my nervous system and activating tumors of multiple proportions. Perhaps these contaminants can explain the news reports I keep seeing about people pushing other passengers under the wheels of these trains. One news report claimed that the perpetrator had been possessed by a malevolent spirit that was trapped underground. The passenger-shover, a good-looking man in his thirties, collapsed during the trial, went grey in his face, and spewed up white spittle as his body locked in some kind of fit. At the hospital, after a day of tests, it was concluded that he had a tumor wrapping its tentacles around vital parts of his brain, and the doctors guessed that this had made him act in such a bizarre way. I held onto that story as a Catholic would their rosary beads, hoping that this could explain the horrors that were inflicted within my own family home.

I wait but still I can't see any train, only a solid darkness that seems to swallow the tunnel whole. The rumbling and the wind could be the ghosts still trapped down here, still running through underground tunnels in search of a way to escape the crashing water. I imagine how they must have looked like pins at a bowling alley when the water finally caught up with them, and I want to know what they saw in the aftermath. A solid, inescapable darkness? A light to guide them? Loved ones who had passed before them?

I feel an arm press into my back, and I want to turn around

to see who is pushing me, but then I feel another rumble and another wind blustering through the platform, and this time I see the pinpricks of the headlights of the train. It rushes in to meet us and shudders to a stop. A monotonous voice, robotic with indifference, is stuck on repeat as it reminds us to mind a gap that is barely wider than a coin slot.

As the doors bounce open, I think of how my gnarled-up body might look if someone had given in to their hatred and pushed me in front of the train. Would the passengers have pretended not to stare, pretended not to take a quick snapshot with their cell phone to store for later? I can imagine them opening that image up, once their kids have gone to bed, when they are bored because they don't want to watch another stupid thing on Netflix, and they zoom into the bloody detail of my torn up body and they imagine what their loved ones would look like in a similar catastrophe. They don't tell anyone about these dark thoughts, they just leave them there, hidden in a secret file that has a password to protect it, so their loved ones can keep living blissfully with the ignorant assumption that they are safe at night and there won't be any trauma to be recreated now or throughout the generations.

Inside the train carriage, we all stand too close to each other, so we seethe with a futile resentment. In the throng, I've lost track of suit guy, but I'm too tired to flirt anymore, so it's a blessing.

As the doors close, sealing us into a cloud of bodily odors and frustrations, I struggle to stay awake as the train's movements start to rock me. I've fallen asleep on the tube before, woken only because of someone's sharp elbow jamming into my skull after I'd started to drool on their shoulder. In that waking moment, before I remembered I was in London and not across the Atlantic in Rotherwell, I'd feared that elbow was the remnants of my father, still able to jab at me from beyond the grave. He wanted vengeance for the part I'd played in his death, for taking Eris' side against him and standing by while she duct-taped his wrists to the bedposts. I never started the fire, but I never extinguished it. So did those flames alchemize him into something much worse, something that can now defeat me? Anything is possible when you realize the depravity that even your loved ones, the very flesh that created you, are capable of.

After a few minutes trundling through a dark tunnel, we come to the next stop where the robotic voice again reminds us to *mind the gap*, and the doors slam open. In a flash, I see him reflected in the glass: Max. I turn to face him, but there is no one behind me. Playing tricks again. Yesterday I thought I saw him in the lecture theatre as the professor droned on about easements. Halfway through her monologue, I noticed someone slip through the doors and take a seat in the back row. Every time I turned to take another look, there he was, a man of similar height and age as Max, but he was too far away for me to make out the features of his face. I half expected to watch him edge his way closer to me so I would eventually feel his hot breath on the back of my neck. At one time, this would've sent me wild with excitement. Until the fire, he was everything to me, even though I knew he could never match the magnitude of my feelings. He was married, after all. For a moment, when June, his wife, found out about us, I thought there might be something more that we could build, that he might even leave her for me. But they just carried on, and I was expected to live in the shadows. I don't know what deal he made with her, but she tolerated my presence no matter how much she knew, and for a while, it worked. But then the fire destroyed so much, and something was unleashed, and now the thought of him coming anywhere near me leaves me feeling repulsed or terrified. Fuck, I don't know what I feel.

"You just miss me," he would probably say, "you're seeing me round every corner like I'm a ghost. It's the surefire sign that you have feelings for someone."

When I turned back to check on him, the man had disappeared from the lecture theatre, so I never knew for sure whether it was Max. I still don't know whether he has even left Rotherwell but, either way, he won't let me stay in this nation of dismal grey drizzle for much longer. He doesn't like to let his possessions slip through his fingers so easily, and he has a particular hatred for things he cannot control or understand.

You see, I saw something amongst the rubble of that fortress that once was my family home. Something that terrified me.

"You know what happens to people who try to ignore me," the next message read. I know about the abandoned warehouses Max keeps for people who disagree with him. But the threat of his violence is nothing compared to the horrors that might be unleashed if I return to Rotherwell.

"After all that I did for you," another one of his messages read.

From the moment my family home burned down, Max pressured me to sell the land to him. He had plans to build a tower of apartments with skyline views of New York, and I knew that he wasn't allowing me to stay in his home just so he had someone to fuck. There were plenty of other people willing to do that with him.

For a long time, I resisted giving him the fortress site. The fire had given me a strength that I'd never experienced before, and somehow, at just twenty-two, I could stand up to this guy who was old enough to be my father. I wondered whether it was Eris who was giving me this strength from beyond the grave. She detested Max West as much as she hated my father, so the last thing she wanted was for him to invade and pillage her land. I also wondered whether it was her rage that kept the embers glowing more than a year after the fire had been extinguished. I never asked whether anyone else saw this eerie glow, but even if I had, they might have denied it, as you pretend not to feel a ghost touching your feet when you are paralyzed by sleep.

"What made you leave?" Max asked in another message. "What spooked you?" He's referring to one of the last nights I was in Rotherwell, when I saw something scuttling about the charred bricks and broken window frames. I didn't know how to put it into words that Max might understand. I just knew that the land was rotten all along, and the longer I held onto it, the greater the risk of carnage.

The very next day, I transferred the land to Max and made plans to leave for London. I tried to convince myself that Eris would have approved of my choice of a degree in law because it might have quenched her taste for justice and vengeance. But I still felt like I'd failed her.

In his messages, Max tells me that I have failed him too. He's claiming that ever since I left, the land has been rippling like undulating skin. It seems furious that I have abandoned it, and so Max's plans for a tower are in jeopardy. But what does he expect from a place that is stained with so much blood and violence? Trauma was trapped in there, unable to escape through just the passage of time, so it was bound to distort into something misshapen and ugly. Something dangerous.

In my nightmares, the rippling of the land creates and recreates scenes of my family home destroyed, rebuilt, and then destroyed again. With it, I feel so many old emotions that they fill me all the way up to the brim so that I fear I might drown. Once again, I hear the creaking of the bedroom door as my father makes his way into my sister's bedroom. In this version, I don't witness the violence he inflicts on my sister, but then the land shifts again, and this time I see it all, I see what I initially missed when it happened the first time, when I was preoccupied with my own war with Eris, as we battled for different territories within that family home. In that moment, as I watch my father crawl all over my sister, I am reminded that there are greater dangers than anything Max could ever threaten.

The worst of the nightmares are when I remember that final night at the scorched rubble of the fortress, when I saw the head of my father. But it wasn't just his head. Breaking through the skull and scalp of the head emerged eight legs to help him scuttle from the underworld he was condemned to. In that underworld, he invaded, raped, and pillaged, but still his greed was not satiated, so he turned to me. As our eyes met, he reminded me of the blood we shared, trying to convince me that I should let him make use of me. As I felt the stirring beneath my skin, the same greed that had made him ache, he showed me how the fortress site and my body could become a portal to the underworld, where my father could live once again and inflict more violence.

Chapter Two

~~~

Max

~~~

He may be a pain in the ass, but he isn't dumb, so he'll take my warning seriously. *He, they, it,* whatever he wants to be called now. I told him to knock it off when he used that weird word about binding or something. Or was it *binary? Non-binary,* that was it. He needed to shut up about it because that kind of talk could make me look bad. People would think I was into all that radical shit like it was one of my kinks or something; someone who isn't all man or woman, but something in between. He's still hung like a dude and dresses like a dude, so I don't know what he's going on about, other than jumping on the latest bandwagon.

"Max?" the pastor asks as she peers over the top of her glasses at me. "Did you have something to add?" She always likes to take this condescending tone with me, making me feel like I'm her workman or busboy. If I didn't need her church's land for this new deal tower deal at Mount Pelion Way, I'd smack the shit out of her. The church owns the land backing onto the site, and we're gonna need it for access, something to do with restrictive covenants or the town demanding we use a different route for access, or some other shit that Dylan could better understand.

"Nope," I reply to the pastor. "Nothing to add."
"You just looked like you were going to…Oh, never mind," she sighed, and shuffled the papers on the desk that filled the church meeting room. I still wasn't sure why she had to call yet another meeting when we already had a deal, and the lawyers could go ahead and draft the paperwork. What pissed me off the most was the way she thought she might squeeze in one last contingency, like an addition to the church or a new fucking gymnasium and shit. I hated these pious church folk, lording it up over everyone else, especially when they try to act like entrepreneurs like me are crooks that they can sneer at. The church has been the biggest crook throughout history. I read shit online, so I know how much they've benefited from tax breaks while they screwed everyone else for donations in return for the promise of *eternal salvation.* The biggest scam of all.

I watch as Pastor Pry takes a breath, ready for another smart comment, no doubt, but she's interrupted by the sound of shouting outside the office window. For a week now, the church has been targeted by protestors who don't like the guest speakers she keeps inviting to her church. According to Dylan, these guests lean too far to the right when it comes to homophobia and transphobia. Pry claims the church is accepting of all people, but Dylan says that Pry's sermons are starting to sound like an infomercial by Moms for Liberty.

"I don't understand why these protestors are targeting me and my church," the pastor says with a sigh. She takes her glasses off and bites onto one of the temple tips. It looks like she is considering this, really struggling to work out what they might have against her, when she knows full well. She has told me, quite clearly, that she views herself as a warrior in this moral war where she is defending "basic natural laws" where "men are men, women are women, and only men and women must lay together." Those were her words when we had shared some bourbon after another deal, and the liquor had gone straight to her head. "Without that," she had continued, "what are we left with but debauchery and chaos?"

I've heard it all before. The same old bullshit, only from different people. When I was at school, it was the other kids and the teachers, and at home it was my fuckup of a dad. *Queers are evil. Queers are a curse that should be stamped out.*

No matter how many years passed, no matter how successful my businesses were, I didn't stop hearing the same bullshit. In the locker room, on the golf course, and at the country club. None of them directed it at me because no one knew anything more than the wife and two children that I told them about. I had to keep things straight-forward so no one would use the other stuff, the guys I'd fuck around with, to screw me over in the business sense. Either that or out-number me in a darkened parking lot. I'd seen that happen a few times, when I'd been drinking with some of my buddies on the police force. I mean, I call them my buddies, but I can't stand the fuckers. I just keep them close so they turn a blind eye to one or two things I'm involved with.

It would usually happen at the end of the night. These police dudes would see a guy in the bar who'd been a little too loud or seemed a bit floaty and like a fairy. You know, limp-wristed and shit. It seemed to trigger those police dudes, and I'd see their faces flushing with an intense fury that made it seem like they were gonna have a fucking heart attack. And they always got that worked up over the fairy who had dark skin. Never the white dude.

Each time they saw one of these fairy dudes, they'd follow him to the parking lot and shoulder-shove him so he dropped his keys, and just as the "faggot" was bending down to pick them up, *thwack* would go their fist on the back of his head. "Stay down," another one of my buddies would order him, "otherwise you're gonna get more fucked up." The fairy would follow their instructions, but they'd still fuck him up.

Those fairies were always a mess afterwards. One of them, I'd heard, was in the hospital for weeks. And the fucked-up thing about it was my buddies thought they were doing society a favor. You know, kind of like a service, like cleaning the place up. No less culpable than the armed forces who blow the brains out of a mother or child who happens to have the wrong skin color or pray to the wrong god. They would call it a matter of national pride because who wants to be vulnerable to any old fucking weirdo who invades you, who creeps in at night and wants to fuck you or your son or take your land by force and make you speak their language. They would say this is a crisis, a matter of national security, so all bets are off, no matter who gets hurt. They would say that you should do it too, and arm yourself, if necessary, because if you don't, you're as bad as someone who doesn't salute the flag, or who stomps on it, or burns it, because that is worse than beating the shit out of someone or burning them alive or throwing them from rooftops or gassing them in concentration camps.

I'm sure my drinking buddies would say that their violence is justified because they have a calling or some kind of shit. A professional duty. And the people they beat up were seen as less than, because of their skin color, even though they had the same darkened shade when they were in the sun for too long, at their beach house with the mistress they're fucking. That's when it gets confusing for them, when they start to look like the people who come from the countries their people like to invade. So they settle this confusion with another beer, as long as it isn't the Coors beer that turns you trans or gay or both. They have so many beers that they get drunk and beat up someone else queer and dark-skinned in a darkened parking lot, and they pretend that they never did it, that they are good and pure, *lily-white pure*, and deserving of entering those gates that the pastor promises will open for them. And, after all this, my drinking buddies still say that it is the fairies that are a danger to children.

These are Dylan's thoughts, not yours.

The pastor is staring at me as she drums her fingers on the desk. I've lost time again because I don't know how long I've been sitting here, staring at the woman. Since the fire, this has been happening more and more, as if someone is trying to pull me back into my skull and down into my body. I watch the pastor's fingers as they continue to drum, and I imagine chewing each one off and spitting them in her face. The thought of it makes me sick, but I want to cackle like a witch, and the urge erupts through my body, so I have to clench my fist tightly to stop the ripples of laughter. I don't know what's got into me since that fire. I mean, my mind seems to wander all over the place. Fuck knows what shit they used to build that monstrosity. Maybe asbestos or something, so when it became the town's bonfire it released toxins or whatever. Dylan says that his mother used to call it her *fortress*. Fucking creepy eyesore, that's what it was. If the fire hadn't leveled it, I would've brought the bulldozers in at some point, with or without Eris inside of it.

"This is really frustrating," the pastor complains as there is another roar from the protestors outside. "The disrespect of the youth today," she adds as she shakes her head. "I really cannot think straight with all that noise." She is staring right at me, insisting that I sort it out. She likes to play the role of the helpless, but she seems pretty competent when she's negotiating business arrangements. Last year, she brokered some kind of deal with Rotherwell town officials so she could get a cut of the proceeds from their tax increase. I still don't know the details, and neither do most people in Rotherwell, but rumors are that this taxation deal is set to give the church an extra million each year. Most of the idiots in this town are too busy earning enough to pay the property tax bill and mortgage repayments on their overpriced homes, let alone to investigate the accounting procedures of their town officials or local church.

"I'll go take a look," I sigh as I jump from my seat.
"That would be good. Perhaps you can do it on your way out. I have a conflict that I'm already late for."
You called me, I want to scream at her. She arranged this meeting and updated the agenda three times, and fucked me around about the location, and promised she would invite the

new director of construction, and her lawyer, and no one else came but me, just so we could have a little chit-chat and I could sort out her mess with the protestors and she could fuck off? I hold in the rage by promising myself that one day I will watch her squirm about as she bleeds. I have just the abandoned warehouse waiting for her, on the outskirts of Newark, where we wouldn't be disturbed. I would choose not to knock her unconscious before I poured the acid on her skin, just so she could hear why she had ended up in this situation, reminding her of how much disrespect she had shown me.

As soon as I leave the office, stepping out into the parking lot, the jeering of the protestors assaults my ears. Someone locks eyes with me as they shout, "Fuck your transphobia," and I'm kind of insulted that she would think of me, who has spent a small fortune on my shirt, trousers and shoes, as a church official.

The protestor who has targeted me has a face mask on for some reason, and her hair is bunched up in pigtails, which looks weird with her baggy cargo pants and oversized jacket.

There are a handful of other protestors, nothing to call the police over, and they all seem too well dressed to cause any serious trouble. They have a few flags, most are the pale pink and blue ones, but one has a rainbow splashed across it. One protestor holds a piece of cardboard that reads *Resist Love is a Human Right Leave Trans Kids Alone,* which is confusing and probably could have been reworked (I guess they meant *Resist! Love is a Human Right! Leave Trans Kids Alone!*).

I was never an activist at school, although it wasn't through want of anger. I remember how all the kids who would protest were better dressed than me, and who were dropped off each morning by parents who drove a big, shiny car. I couldn't imagine what they would be so angry about when none of them seemed as hungry as I was, when my fuckup of a dad would refuse or forget to stock the fridge. Funny how he never forgot to stock the cupboards with booze.

"You disgust me," he would hiss if I was clumsy enough to catch his eye. "Call yourself a man?" A year previously, when I'd just turned fourteen, he'd found pictures of men under my bed, and he kept coming back to it, calling me "deranged" and "filthy". I'd torn off the cardboard inserts in packets of underwear at a clothes store because it fascinated me and I didn't want to stop staring at it late at night. It sure took my mind off the sound of drunken snoring that was coming from a passed-out father down the stairs, and the endless worry that the snoring might thicken into congealed phlegm that would choke him during his sleep. I wouldn't have missed the old fuck, but he would've left me alone in that house without any idea about how to pay the bills. His drinking and rages had made my mom move out a few years before that, something I never forgave her for.

When he found the cardboard cutouts of men in underwear, his hands fumbled at the buckle of his belt, his rage making his fingers shake. Despite this, he managed to get the belt out of the hooks on his trousers, and instead of running from him, I just stared, horrified that his trousers might drop and reveal stained underwear.

"Bend over," he ordered. I refused, so he raced over to me and grabbed at my wrist. "You're making this worse for yerself, you little shit." He yanked me so I was doubled over the arm of the sofa, and I felt him pulling at my jeans.

I replay that moment often, when someone cuts me off on the highway, or they take my parking space in town. I think of how cold his fingers were as they clawed at my boxer shorts, and he yanked them down, and how I could've easily jumped up and knocked him out. As I remember the first lash of his belt, knowing he was positioning it so the buckle would bite chunks out of my skin, I think of how I could've snatched that belt from the shaky hands of a self-indulgent alcoholic, and wrapped it around his neck. I smell the leather as I picture tightening it and watching him cough and drools as his veins pulsate in his neck and his body twitches for the last time.

The fact that I never fought back painted me (in his eyes and mine) as one of the weak kids, and this was confirmed later, when other boys in my class took to hurting wild animals. They seemed to get pleasure from capturing and punching or kicking or stabbing chipmunks and mice, even the occasional pet of a neighbor, and yet I refused to join in. From those early days, they jeered at me, calling me "pussy" and "faggot," and when my father heard them as he stumbled about in the front yard, he echoed it when I came indoors.

Since then, I've been fighting this perception and proving to anyone who cared that I can hurt others if I have to. Even Dylan. I'm sure that's why he, *they, whatever*, ran so fast to the airport. I was stupid to tell him so much about my business practices and how I dealt with competitors. I'd never been careless before, but the fire fucked with my head and loosened me up a bit. I mean, I felt drunk even though I've never touched a drop, never wanting to become sloppy like my father or let any ounce of control slip through my fingers. We'd just fucked, and Dylan was doing that hair stroking thing that I like, and I just didn't stop talking. I felt his body tighten when I said about the abandoned warehouses, and I wondered if he was bracing himself for me to take him there. I never did. I only ever took him to the place he grew up, for fuck's sake, a harmless stretch of land right next door to my home. But you'd think I strung him up there and ripped the skin from his body.

You should see the way the fortress site shifts about, the dirt breaking open like fresh wounds. I don't know if there is some mine shaft that no one knew about, or maybe he did and he just didn't want to tell me. I figure Dylan would try to convince me that the place is haunted by certain wacko members of his family. *Their* family. Dylan used to tell me about the creepy shit that would go on inside that house, and if you heard some of it, you'd think that the family tree should've been chopped down and incinerated for all its deformities. I mean, just look at what his mother was like, that fucked up witch who terrorized the street, and his father, a creep who leered at every fucking girl who passed by. Even their daughter hanged herself from one of the trees in the backyard.

I guess that's why Dylan finally transferred the land to me. We did it for a token dollar, and when we stood in my lawyer's office, I flipped the kid a couple of fifty-cent pieces. I watched them fly through the air, one after the other, as they caught the light from a nearby desk lamp. Dylan just let them drop to the ground and after he signed the paperwork, he refused to talk to me for the rest of the day. That hollowed out the fucking victory, which made me mad at him. I mean, I'd been waiting for this day ever since that fortress burned down. It was the only reason I'd let him live in the spare room of my house, the only reason I'd carried on fucking around with him instead of moving on to someone else. I'd been patient with him, and so had June, and I thought he'd be happy to see the back of that site. He barely let himself look its way whenever we would return to my home.

Later that night, I crept into his room once June was asleep. The moonlight was rippling over the muscles of his arms and it turned me on, so I tried to fuck, but he just pushed me off him. He'd never been able to push my body weight off him, but since the fire, there was a strength that was growing in him. He told me that he needed to get away, but I never believed him, because no one I knew did anything without my permission, let alone go against my wishes.

The following day, I sent the diggers to the fortress site. I called some of my guys who were up for a bit of cash-in-hand work, the kind who wouldn't get their ass bent out of shape over town codes and permits. I watched from my bedroom window as neighbors emerged, looking irate because my men chose before seven in the morning on a Sunday to start their work, and they looked up at me with anger, no doubt already hearing about my plans for the site. I just waved down at them and smiled, thinking of how I could get my hands on their land, too. I saw one neighbor try to confront one of my workers, but none of them stopped drilling to listen. They were eager to finish and get paid, and who can blame them? The cash I was paying them would feed their kids, for fuck's sake, so why would they care about an overweight white dude who is jabbing a finger in their face?

The first I knew of any issues was a scream. It sounded like a child or a woman in pain, and the sound was erupting from the rubble. I wasn't the only one who heard it because the workmen stopped their drilling and stared at the pile of bricks and broken window frames. At that point, I didn't care what it could be. I just didn't like to see laborers standing around doing nothing. The driver of the digger climbed out and walked over to the rubble. I saw him peering in and scratching his head, and that really fucked me off. He wasn't paid to think about anything, he just had to drive a fucking digger and clear this site in record time.

I slammed my way down the stairs and out of my house, racing onto the adjoining site. I stumbled a little on the bits of rubble and shouted, "What the fuck are you doing?" The driver of the digger, a stocky guy with a tough and leathery face, knew enough not to answer back, so he climbed back into his digger and fired up the engine.

I caught the eye of Gabriel, the foreman, and gave him one of my looks. He's someone I've been working with for years, so he knows that if nothing gets built, he won't get paid.

I stood and watched as he snapped at the heels of his men, cuffing a few of the younger ones behind the ear when they were slow to jump back into action.

With a throaty roar, a cloud of fumes was sent into the air, and as my throat started to burn, I felt the earth tremble beneath my feet. I figured it might be the movement of the digger in front of me, or the truck on the street that was starting to back into the driveway, ready to be loaded up with the crap from the site. I wanted to feel comforted by the chaos of the workmen, knowing we were finally making a start on this tower, but the ground trembled with more force.

"Earthquake!" shouted one of the men, who had an armful of traffic cones ready to block off the road in front of the site. "No no no," Gabriel shouted, "no earthquakes in New Jersey." Then the ground flipped me, and the workers, and we all fell over. Even the digger was turned on its side, the engine still whirring as the driver screamed and tried to climb out. It looked like the topsoil became a tablecloth that was lightly flicked to straighten it out, and I half-expected to see enormous hands reaching down from the sky and plucking us like delicacies for a giant's feast.

I climbed to my feet and over the roar of the digger's engine, I shouted at them to "Get back to work!" They glanced at each other. One even shook his head in disbelief, but they all got up and collected their equipment from the ground. The driver of the digger managed to climb out, and he flicked the engine off. I guess he was looking to me to find a way to get the digger back up, but that didn't concern me. I just wanted them to stay focused and not grab onto the first excuse to down tools and abandon the site.

"Tie some rope to the truck and pull it back up," I shouted, before I turned my back on them and headed back to my house.

Inside, reassured that I could still hear power tools and trucks idling, I found June sitting at the breakfast bar. She was using her cell phone to listen to some kind of self-help bullshit on a podcast while she peeled a tangerine like she was performing brain surgery. I pressed 'stop' on her cell phone, and she looked horrified.

"What the fuck? They were getting to the best bit," she moaned.

"Breathing exercises and mindfulness. That's probably what they were getting to because it's the same answer from every one of your podcasts. Same old bullshit."

"It might be bullshit for you, but I like it," she snapped, pushing past me and heading towards the stairs. "I'm gonna take a shower."

"It's midday. What have you been doing all morning?"

"Why do I have to account to you for my schedule?"

"I guess you don't, I'm just…Did you feel that?"

"What?"

"A moment ago, when I was outside. The ground was shaking. Felt like an earthquake, maybe?"

June shook her head.

"You been drinking again?" I ask her, and she pauses halfway up the stairs. "I mean, I guess you wouldn't notice anything if you were barely conscious on Long Island Iced Tea for breakfast."

"Fuck off, Max."

"You didn't answer the question."

Her father had died over a year ago, and still she was self-medicating with a toxic combination of alcohol and antidepressants. I only cared about how it was affecting our kids. My son, Smithson, was actively avoiding her, and every time June would open a bottle of liquor, Katherine would get into a screaming match with her.

"I won't let you fuck up their childhood with alcohol the way my dad fucked up mine," I tell her.

"Your dad was a fuckup," she snaps back at me. "I am not."

"Are you sure? I mean, seeing it through the eyes of the kids, are you sure that's not what you're becoming to them?"

"Mind your own fucking business. You have enough of them, businesses, so go control those. You have no grounds to tell me what to do, not when you're fucking around with a kid whose Katherine's age. Would you like them to know about Dylan?"

I clench my fist, but I control myself. I'll lose the kids forever if I let her goad me into doing something violent. Fuck, I can do whatever I want to those business opponents, but this bitch is untouchable.

I should say something to her, to try to threaten her enough so she keeps quiet about Dylan, but we are interrupted by more screaming from outside.

"Guess you have to go," she says with a beaming smile. She lifts a glass of something and adds, "Cheers, my love," which she knows will drive me nuts.

I storm out of the house, ready to unleash my fury on one of the workers or one of the neighbors. I don't care which, but the foreman is shaking his head and his hands, silently begging me not to explode. He has seen me at my worst, when other developments haven't gone well, and workers or town officials suddenly experience unfortunate circumstances.

"What the fuck is it now?" I shout.

"Please," Gabriel says to me in a voice so quiet I can barely hear him. He has always stayed on the right side of me because he got the job done, despite the helpless shrugs he would occasionally offer, and a vicious divorce that had left him weary of the world.

"The land, it shifted again," he continued. "It keeps moving, every time we drill, every time we try to dig. I swear, boss, no joke."

Again, the digger is on its side, the engine still whirring, and behind it, I can see that the land has opened up some more. Something is moving the rubble and the dirt, stirring it like an invisible finger.

"Did you stabilize the digger?" I ask him. Gabriel gives me a look that reminds me he has been in this business longer than I have. But he knows enough not to leave my questions unanswered.

"Yes, boss. I did."

"Well, I can't feel any movement now," I say, "so get on with it."

Gabriel gives me one last pointed stare before he turns to the truck driver and orders him to bring the rope over again. I watch as they tether it around the digger, keeping the other end attached to the truck, before the reverse warning bleeps, and I see the digger move slowly out of the crevice that has opened up.

Soon, all the power tools are cranking back into life and emitting clouds of the diesel that I love so much. I take a deep breath, certain it gives me a high, and I remember how it would smell like this when my dad would drive me home from the liquor store, his grip unsteady as he swerved about the road. Each time I remember my dad, something stirs beneath my skin, a rage, perhaps, that he's been dead for four months, so I can't unleash any kind of revenge on him anymore. Ever since that fire, he became my outlet for that rage, especially towards the end, when he was too unsteady on his feet to fight back. "Not so much of a monster now, are you?" I'd scream at him, justifying this violence over and over again as I'd remember that belt. Each time I'd return home from visiting him with that violence, in his pathetic little shithole of a shack, I would see the smoldering rubble of the fortress site and it seemed to renew my anger, making me want to go back to my dad and beat him some more.

I know this makes me sound like a wack job, but I can feel it even now. With every breath I take of that diesel-scented air, the thing beneath my skin writhes about and makes me crave for someone else to beat. I feel like the land is telling me that I deserve this after all my hard work seizing land and opportunities up and down the East Coast. I built, tore down, and rebuilt so much, making a profit on the back of gullible people. The land knows of this greed, and it tells me that it's okay, that I deserve all my riches because of those times my drunken father beat me with that belt.

I can see it now, how small I was and how he towered over me. The more I breathe in that memory, the more the land stirs beneath my feet. The workmen feel it too. They glance at each other and slow their movements as the vibrations increase.

Then the land shifts with a violence jolt, and the rubble jumps from its resting place. I hear the breaking of glass and timber frames, and I watch as trees collapse along with bushes as the earth's skin folds in on itself. Again, the digger has been flipped on its side.

I can imagine someone else like Dylan or my daughter Katherine saying some kind of environmental bullshit like the earth is in pain, that it is trying to reject these diggers and power tools. But they don't feel what I do, how the land and I are in sync. Dylan and Katherine are just repeating the same old bullshit they've heard online, suffering from the same social contagion that makes them get so irate about this trans shit.

"*Joder esto*," the driver screams as he climbs out of the digger. His temple has a nasty gash in it, but the sight of the blood makes something in me stir.

"Get back in the digger," I growl.
The driver shakes his head in reply. As if that wasn't enough, he actually throws his fucking gloves onto the ground just inches from my feet. I have fantasies of informing ICE about the whereabouts of every one of his ugly family members, and I would very much like to be there to hear their screams as they are rounded up and thrown into camps or back over the border.

"That ground is fucked, boss," Gabriel calls to me from the other side of the digger. "Not stable. No way. Dangerous. Moving too much for us to stand on, but a digger?" He then shakes his head. "No way."

"It's nothing," I hiss through gritted teeth. "Just a bit of movement. Now get on with your job." But already Gabriel is shaking his head and pointing towards the rubble. I turn and see the piles of charred bricks, broken window frames, and the remains of what looks like a door.

"What? It's a collapsed house. What do you want to find? Green pastures and fucking meadows?"
"Look," the foreman says, so I look, and I swear to god that he could've been playing a trick on me. I've heard of this happening, where competitors infiltrate your crew and they say and do all sorts of bullshit to make you feel like you're crazy. Then they'll refuse to work, and just when you are really going crazy, they swoop in and take the land from you, building their own tower with fucking skyline views of New York. I wouldn't put it past Sean Haggardy and his merry band of crooks to try this sort of trick. That fucking inbred who moved from Dublin only a year ago. He's already taken two deals from me and still survived to tell the tale. I don't want to think that I'm slipping. At fifty-one years old, I've got plenty of years left ahead of me to destroy a whole line of Haggardys.

"You better not be doing those all-night benders again," I tell Gabriel. "I thought those days were over for you, now you have your new missus. Isn't she keeping you on the straight and narrow?"

He's shaking his head. He knows what I'm trying to do.

"You realize who you're fucking with, right? Do what you like with your own life, but let it fuck with my business, and I'll destroy you."

"Hands," Gabriel says with a gasp as he points behind me. "There are hands."
"So there's a body," I reply. "Get on with your fucking job."

I don't know why the foreman's making such a big deal of this. The home burned down, and they might not have got everyone out. Shit like that happens. Vagrants sleep in attic voids for years without homeowners discovering, and it only takes one fire for them to never be found. What good is gonna come of informing anyone about this now? It's only going to cause more delays while they try to identify who this useless fuck is and track down relatives who probably wanted to see the back of them, anyway.

When I turn to where Gabriel is pointing, I see the hands, but they aren't lifeless body parts. With broken nails and flesh hanging from each finger, they are moving and clawing their way out through the dirt and rubble, and they are reaching for us. I can smell them too, a stench of putrefying flesh that coats the back of my throat and makes me want to gag. And then I hear a voice, sweet and gentle and it makes me think of my daughter and, fuck, I hate admitting this, but it makes me want to cry. It calls for me, urging me to come closer. I might have done it if I hadn't heard something else in the distance, so far away that it almost felt like a memory, and that was the sound of my workmen downing tools and climbing into the truck. The engine erupts into life, emitting one last noxious cloud, and then it speeds away, down Mount Pelion Way and then out of sight.

Still the rubble smolders, thickening the air around me as scorched clouds gather like phantoms from the ashes. The fire was put out two years ago this November, and yet still there are glowing embers. Makes me wonder what radioactive shit that bitch witch was storing in her fortress, what plans she had to poison the people she hated so much on this street. Sure, it's fucked up what might be down there, but the prospect of failure is even more fucked up. I can still feel the slash-marks on my buttocks, as fresh as those early years when my deadbeat father had ultimate power over me. No matter how many times I beat him as an adult, I still could not shake that little boy's helplessness, like it was coming back as a ghost to haunt me. Don't let anyone tell you that the pain of a beating is the worst part. It's the humiliation of letting someone dominate you, and then other people finding that out, no matter how hard you tried to cover it up. The teacher at school would meet eyes with me when I winced as I tried to sit down without vomiting. He never said anything, probably didn't want to create more work for himself where he'd be hauled into meetings with the principal and social workers and have to fill out all sorts of paperwork and shit.

As soon as I came home from school, Dad would start screaming at me. "You been hanging around the men's underwear section at the store again? Little faggot. No wonder your mom ran out on you. Didn't wanna be around a dirty queer like you."

The stupid old fuck never beat it out of me. I may have married a woman, but I never stopped fucking around with guys, and part of me didn't want to just to spite him. Spite also drove me harder and harder with business, refusing to sit back in case I ended up like him, in a shithole and counting every dime. But Katherine has started to ask me whether I will ever retire. "You need a break," she says as she catches me watching the sunrise as I start my day of calls. "You're gonna burn yourself out." I want to snap back that she has benefited from all this hard work, with the shore house and the apartment in Florida, and now somewhere at Martha's Vineyard, but I know she means well, so I bite my tongue.

"Trans rights," someone shouts from somewhere.

"What the fuck?" I say. I look around and I realize I'm still in the parking lot of the church, still faced with a handful of protestors. That fucking building site has let out some kind of toxin that's fucking with my ability to concentrate. I would go see a doctor if they weren't all crooks who were ready to swipe your credit card before you've even sat down.

"Would you give it a rest?" I hiss at the crowd. They've probably got fired up over some post on TikTok, some half-truth or conspiracy that they know little about. The one who's been shouting "Fuck transphobia" looks a little like Dylan, with the same jet-black hair and sharp-edged cheek bones. Same as Dan, too, the one I fucked around with before Dylan. I must have a type. But this guy, the one who's so worked up about transphobia, seems weaker than Dylan or Dan, and his head slants to the side as if he is losing the will to stand upright. They all do this, the kids his age, they start out passionate about something and then it fizzles out into nothing, and I know this because my daughter is their age and every morning she starts with a new cause to fight for, but by the end of the day she has forgotten all about it.

Staring at the Dylan lookalike, I realize I've seen him on the hookup app. He'd described himself as *Masc Bottom for Masc Top,* and I'd been tempted but my wife had been home, and this kid couldn't host, so I'd ended up with *Hung Bottom Can Host. Hosting* turned out to be a one-bedroom apartment in the next town over, in a large apartment block that had been created out of an old cookie factory. The last time I'd been in this area was about ten years ago, when I had to take my daughter to a birthday party at some laser tag place across the road. At that time, the factory was standing abandoned, and after years of disputes, the apartments were finally added to the structure. Recently I've heard that the developer and council official, who made millions from the deal, claimed ignorance about the asbestos that is tickling the lungs of the young families as they slowly go loopy with all the lead in their drinking water. No one cares, or at least no one has the time or money to do anything about it. I know this much because I used to make money on similar fast-paced low-regulation redevelopments that ended up death traps or cesspits worthy of condemnation. I gave it up as soon as I made my millions, choosing instead to focus on new builds while I lied to myself that I had developed a conscience and chose not to scam poverty-stricken families into early graves.

"Churches house Nazis," I hear a girl in the group call out, and I want to reply "Probably". "Stop the hate," the girl adds, but there's an upward intonation, so it sounds more like a question than a rallying cry.

"Dad!" someone shouts, and then I see my daughter waving from the other side of the parking lot.

"I'm so sorry I'm late, guys," she says as she addresses the group. "I got caught up in something and nothing, but I'm here now."

I walk straight through the sweaty kids, making their group split in two as most of them jump out of the way, except for a remaining brave (or slow) kid who gets forcefully shoved aside by my elbow.

"Fuck, Katherine, do you have to?" I sigh. "I thought you had lacrosse."

"Cancelled," she says with a smile, "which is what I hope the church gets soon."

"Ha, very good. Have you been rehearsing that all week?"

"All month, Dad! Didn't you always tell me that practice makes perfect?"

The other members of the protest look appalled that one of their own might be consorting with the enemy. I try to figure out which one of these unhygienic-looking half-brains is the leader who is ready to challenge me about my involvement with the church. None of them seem up to the job, but then I realize there's one person who's over-qualified.

"Katherine," I say with a sigh.

Leadership is exactly what I've been going on about for all these years, to Katherine as much as her brother Smithson. Seize those opportunities, secure a good college, smile and cajole your way to the top, and then buy take over those businesses for passive income. Queer and trans activism isn't exactly what I planned for her.

"Please say you didn't organize this."

"Why? Because lying to you would make you happier?"

"Oh, for Christ's sake, you've got more important things to be doing with your time than this." When I wave my hand towards the group, a crusty-looking kid with three nose piercings winces as if I'm gonna beat them. If Katherine hadn't been here, I probably would've done it by now.

"Just come home, okay?" I try to reach for her shoulder, but she shrinks from my grasp and starts to sing. Her damned voice is beautiful, so I find it hard to lay down any kind of law on this, even if I did want to defend the church.

"You say that gays will harm our kids when actually it's you," she sings to the pastor and anyone else who might be listening from inside the church. "You say that gays will harm our kids when actually it's you…"

She continues to sing the tune of *The Battle Hymn of the Republic,* but with lyrics that attack the church, and it's fucking brilliant.

I'm ready to walk away and leave her to it when I see the pastor emerging from the church. I know she'll expect me to condemn them and tell them to shut up about it all, criticizing their vulgarity and bright colors, calling them undignified and immoral. I wonder if the pastor has ever even fucked, or, judging from her poor dress sense, she could be a closet case.

"I see you're handling it," the pastor says as she joins me in the parking lot.

"I've told them," I say, trying not to sound too bothered about defending myself.

"But they're not really listening," she replies, "not even your daughter." Her thin lips spread into a smile that reveals discoloration in her teeth from years of drinking coffee to stay awake long enough to deliver the sermons she recycles year in and year out. I want to hear the crack of each tooth as I hammer them. I will pull the jute rope tightly around her wrists, and I'll probably need to tether her ankles too, because she looks like a kicker. "We've got a live one here," Sammy will laugh, as he always says about the ones who try to fight back. I don't have the heart to tell Sammy to knock it off as I've heard the same shit for fifteen years of his help with the bodies. Why would I want to hurt his feelings when all he's ever shown me is devotion? Since that wack job killed his mother when he was fifteen, and I got rid of the wack job, I swear he thinks of me as the Messiah or shit, so anything I need doing, he does it without any questions asked.

"You want me to call the Chief?" the pastor asks, as she tries to dick-swing with me. Maybe she does have a dick, and she's got some kind of *"internalized transphobia."* Wasn't that the phrase Dylan used to use?

"The Chief wanted to know if there were any issues he could help with. He's been an absolute charm."

Only last week, the pastor called the chief of police to pepper spray the protestors who were fucked off that the pastor had allowed a conversion therapist to use her church service to advocate *"detransitioning"* and sell her book and online courses.

"So what?" I'd said to Katherine when she'd told me about this. "So let her talk about that shit if she wants to. Maybe you don't agree with it, but some people might."

Katherine showed me the therapist's website where a middle-aged woman in a peach-colored neck scarf was smiling too widely, so her gums were showing.

"This bitch," Katherine continued, "was the therapist of a sixteen-year-old who threw herself onto the railway tracks here in Rotherwell and was sliced in two. It only happened a month ago, after a year or two of the kid begging to see a different therapist, and telling her parents how suicidal this therapist's approach was making her feel. She was trans and the therapist and the kid's parents were trying to force her to *detransition,* which isn't even a medically recognized practice. In fact, it's really harmful. This therapist was allowed to keep her license even though she's on record as referring to trans and queer people as *vermin,* as the *filth that is spread by social contagion.* And now she's selling her book and online courses, with the church giving her center stage? It's a fucking joke."

"Come on, Isla," my daughter says to the pastor. "Where's your heart? Was it sold when you saw how much those right-wing extremists were willing to pay for it?"
I can see how much it pains Pastor Pry not to bite back or even tear at her face. She keeps looking at me, and then at my daughter, trying to form the words but getting lost in her rage.

"Shame on you," Katherine adds as the other protestors join her in a chant of "Shame on you!" over and over again.

I watch my daughter's defiance, such strength from someone so young when I was a mess at her age, still cowering around my fucked-up dad. And that smile is so beautiful, framed in the same long blond hair that I remember of my mother. I want to join in with my daughter's chants, but I know that I will instantly lose the church's cooperation with the tower development. Already, Katherine has jeopardized too much by simply being here, so I need to show the pastor whose side I am on.

"Come on," I say to my daughter as I guide her by the elbow, "I'm getting you home," and I steer her towards my car with more force than she probably expected.
"Are you kidding?" she squeals as she tries to struggle free. I think of her as a toddler and how she would demand that we

stay out at the playground beyond sunset, so I would end up throwing her over my shoulder as she kicked and screamed, and I bundled her into the back of the car. I remember the shocked expression on the faces of passing dog walkers, because, for all they knew, I was Katherine's abductor. But still they said and did nothing to help her, just as my teacher chose not to help me, so I've learned to take advantage of this self-centered attitude of the people who live up and down the East Coast. As long as I don't intrude on their territory, they are willing to stand by and turn a blind eye to my violence.

"Daddy," Katherine squeals again, "you're hurting me."
I probably am, but only because she's fighting me and making me squeeze her wrists a little too tightly. But I don't loosen my grip as I open the door of my car and throw her in. As I slam the door, I hear her become a toddler again, letting out screams of a tantrum as she pounds her fists on the back of my seat. I never took off the child locks, and now I know why.

"Let's reconvene the meeting tomorrow, yeah?" I say to the pastor. I don't wait for her to reply before I'm in the car and speeding away from the church. My daughter, sprawled out on the back seat, won't stop sobbing.

"What the fuck, Dad?"
"I'm sorry," I say with a sigh. "I didn't know what else to do."
Too quickly, I see the turning for Mount Pelion Way. I need to talk to her more so she doesn't see me as such a brute, but if we get home too soon, her mother will chip in with some barbed comment, and two women rarely break alliances against a man. So I push the accelerator and sail past the turning for our street.

"You have so much schoolwork to do."
"Yeah, and you're keeping me from it."
Finally, she sits upright, sniffing back her tears and wiping her nose with the back of her hand.
"If I hadn't done this, you'd still be shouting abuse at the pastor."
"She deserves it."
"Maybe that's true, maybe not. The point is, try not to get distracted over every little fight. You weren't put on this planet

to become a warrior for social justice, with dreadlocks and poor personal hygiene."

I thought I heard her snort the reluctant beginnings of laughter. "You know I love you, and I want the best for you. I don't want you to throw it all away and end up fighting for everything, as I did."

"But you've done enough fighting for the whole family, and to last us a lifetime. That's a privilege, so I want to use that privilege for good."

"Do you have to? Can't you just keep your head down and study like the good kid you used to be? I dunno what happened, but somewhere you picked up this social warrior thing, and it's kinda getting tired."

"You know who hates Pastor Pry more than me?" Katherine asks me.

Yes, I do, but I'm not about to mention his, *their*, name in front of my daughter.

"Dylan," she adds.

Fuck.

"So what of it? You can't make your own mind up about people?"

"I can. I just happen to agree with a lot of what they say."

"You make him sound like he's dead."

"They. Why do you constantly insist on misgendering them?"

"Does it matter?"

"Yes. To them, it does, so it should matter to you."

"Well, they're not here anymore," I reply.

"I know, I've noticed. And you're still making them sound like they're dead. So answer me: Are they?"

I don't know how much she knows, and I don't really want to find out. I mean, if I had to choose, if you shoved the fucking barrel of a shotgun down my throat and made me pick one, I guess I'd prefer she knew me as an adulterer and queer or bi, or whatever you want to call it. Better that than a creep who takes people to abandoned warehouses and strings them up. That shit would never be forgiven, not even if I said that I had done it, disposed of all those competitors, to feed and house her. She wouldn't accept that because she's smart and kind. I can imagine the look of terror on her face if she ever found out. I know that look because I've seen it on the face of the people I've taken there, the ones who never made it out alive. That look, that terror. I've just about survived seeing it in others. I could never see it in my daughter's face. It makes me think about the last thing this kid said to her dad just before he killed her. It was some sicko in Colorado, who had just killed his pregnant wife and the younger kid, and as he turned to the older one, she asked, "Are you going to do that to me now?". I can't get that out of my mind to think how fragile sanity is, and how vulnerable my daughter is to even my own violence.

I keep driving further away from Rotherwell. We are climbing into the mountains now, towards a reservation where you can lose yourself or other people if you need to.

"Dad?" she calls to me, her voice so quiet and gentle. "Where's Dylan?"

"I don't know. That's the god's honest truth."

"I hope they're okay," she adds.

"I do too."

We reach the reservation in silence, and when I flick off the engine, I stare out at the towns beneath me. An eagle soars over the treetops, and then swoops down at the roadkill that could've been a victim of our drive up here. It is still struggling, still holding onto life, some kind of squirrel, I think, but the eagle swoops down and snatches at it. I watch as it lands on a nearby tree with its prey, and it starts to peck at the torso of the dying animal.

"Can you promise me that Dylan is okay?" Katherine asks. "Jesus, I thought we'd just done this," I hiss, caught off guard for a moment. "I don't know what you want me to say. They fucked off somewhere and I don't know where *they* are. To be honest, it isn't a great way to thank me after all I've done for them. I let Dylan stay with us, and even before the fire, I was giving them work opportunities. You remember when Dylan was fighting with their parents after their sister died? I was the one they turned to for support. So the least *they* could do is check in and say *Thanks for all that, I'm fine.*"

"I miss them," she says with a sigh, "and I'm sorry if you

do too, because missing someone hurts, doesn't it?"

"Look, if you're gonna go on about that kid, we may as well go back home, and you can do your schoolwork. I thought we were gonna have a nice walk together and catch up…"

"We are catching up. You just don't want to talk about what I want to."

"Whatever," I say as I flick the engine on. I back up quickly, without really checking for anyone behind me, and speed out of the bumpy parking lot.

I don't have to look behind me to know that Katherine has her arms tightly folded as she pouts. It's the same expression she's adopted since she could first walk.

"I can understand you want to protest about some things," I finally say, after another long silence. "Your fighting spirit is something I really admire about you." I figure I can turn things around between the two of us if I just focus on any subject but Dylan. "You're a little like your old dad in that respect. I just don't want you to get into trouble."

"What trouble?" she asks me.

"I mean, the pastor is litigious, the stupid old bitch."

Finally, I hear my daughter laugh.

"I've seen her go after people," I continue, "and it's all done behind closed doors, so she can pretend she's all saintly in front of her congregation."

"Really?"

"Yeah. And she wouldn't think twice about calling the police and pressing charges. I just think that if you really want to help all those causes, you need to keep your nose clean while you do it. You can't do much from prison."

"I wasn't doing anything horribly bad."

"You try telling the pastor that. She had her finger on the button, ready to call the cops. And, for some reason, they'll do anything to please her, so she'd probably twist it into a felony. She's probably sucking off the old chief in between sermons."

I hear more of the reluctant laughter coming from my daughter, and I start to relax a little. My hands loosen on the steering wheel, and I sit back in my seat, letting the trees and houses whip by my window.

The laughter continues, only it sounds dry, not like the fresh youthful laugh of my daughter. It has deepened, as if she has aged decades, and the laugh is loud and strong, hitting my ears so hard that they begin to hurt.

"Katherine? Are you okay?" I ask as I glance in the wing mirror, only to find someone haggard and disheveled. Her hair is matted with grease, and her skin looks pock-marked with dried up crusts of bloody skin-picking.

I'm watching you.

"What did you say?"

I swerve, only just missing an oncoming SUV, and I feel that writhing rage under my skin. Something makes me push down hard on the accelerator, making me want to escape. I could keep driving, faster and faster, and I could slam into the car in front of me. I imagine hearing the dying gasps of breath as parts of their body fall like chunks of meat being sliced from a rotisserie. Already I can smell the blood and gasoline and urine of human life and machinery, spliced together like a hastily made noxious pie.

Do it, the voice snaps from behind me. It isn't the voice of my young daughter, but the crooked cackle of a witch, and when I look again in the rearview mirror, I see the haggard face of Eris Gall.

Do it, you fool, the voice hisses in my ear so close that I flinch. I smell stale breath and blood and putrefying flesh.

Do it, old man. You've seen it before, haven't you? That body cartwheeled through the sky as those intestines flew like a tickertape parade. You still feel the impact, don't you? When his body exploded just moments after he was laughing.

I use all the strength I can to pull my foot off the accelerator. I notice a small patch of dampness in my crotch, but I don't care because I can finally ease the car back from the one in front, creating a safer distance between the two. I see the passenger in the back, a hunched blond woman with AirPods in her ears, and she glances back at me with a mixture of relief and fury.

You live to fight another day.

A fire was never going to eradicate everything she conjured

up. Her daughter hanged herself on one of the trees in her own backyard, and she blamed everyone who lived at Mount Pelion Way. She even tried to blame my son, cornering him in the woods as she transformed into the witch everyone suspected her to be. She's lucky I never killed her for that, the way I found him shaking afterwards. He never told me exactly what she did, but I've never seen an eighteen-year-old boy cry like that.

After the fire, Dylan told me the truth about what happened to their sister, and why she killed herself. Turns out, their own father was fucking around with her at night, and Paris got Ania pregnant. What kind of fucked up sicko does that kind of thing? How Eris and Dylan must have raged when they found out. Dylan was hesitant when they told me what they did with that rage, but I understood. But burning in a fire was too good for the old pedo. I would've made Paris suffer for a while, in one of my abandoned warehouses; maybe spent a week or two stripping parts of his skin away so he could feel the salt I would scatter on his wounds, and then I'd let the rats feast on the rest.

I stare into the rearview mirror, and I see on the back seat my daughter again, a terrified look on her face, but she is intact, as beautiful as ever. I shift my focus to my own reflection in that mirror, and I see that Eris has now possessed my own body instead of my daughter's. We stare at each other, sharing the rage as it nestles deep inside us. A rage that won't leave us unless something is done.

Chapter Three

~~~

Dylan

~~~

I keep myself locked up in a tiny room at the back of my university's halls of residence. I can hear the distant rush and squealing brakes of traffic on Euston Road, and I see from the flimsy sash window the legacy left by decades of traffic that has funneled through this city; a dirty grey of exhaust fumes to match the constant overcast sky. To isolate myself in a city of dismal grey leaves me aching with loneliness, and I don't want to end up like my mother, a recluse trapped in a fortress of her own creation, but I'm just trying to keep everyone safe. I avoid most of the other students, cutting them off mid-sentence with an excuse about a prior appointment, but I can't let anyone get too close.

The final night I visited the fortress site, the place where my family home once stood, I was awoken by the sound of crackling wood. I looked out of the window of Max's spare bedroom, and I saw that the smoldering rubble had ignited. I ran down the stairs and out the front door to discover what was happening at the site where my home once stood. By the time I reached the rubble, the fire had died back down to glowing embers. That's if there had been a fire in the first place. Someone or something might be playing tricks on me, or my mind was becoming warped by whatever was being carried by that smoke, so when I turned back towards Max's house, and my eye caught sight of something moving amongst the rubble, I dismissed it at first. But it followed me, so I stopped and faced it, and that's when I saw through the smoke-hazed air something crawling across the rubble. Something with a human head and four legs sprouting out from either side. The legs had broken out through the skin of the head, and there was blood trickling from the eight wounds, and I saw a long tongue flickering at the blood every now and again.

I took another step and the thing, an arachnid of sorts, scuttled towards me. And then I recognized the face on the head, its mouth distorting in a combination of pleasure and pain.

"Jesus, wept, Dylan," my father groaned and squealed as his long tongue flickered again at the blood. "What have you done? What have you done to me, and our home? What have you done, Dylan?"

His voice was deep one moment and then distorted into a high-pitched squeal, like that of a child or a pig at the slaughter. He'd taken me to a slaughterhouse once, in Upstate New York. He said we had to go there to collect some meat that he'd heard about, some deal on pork chops, but a hairline of doubt trickled through the back of my mind, and as I watched him smile and pound his fists together as they slashed at the throat of a pig writhing about on a metal hook, I thought I saw excitement. This was long before I ever suspected that he could be anything more than a loving father. I mean, I was a young kid, no more than nine or ten. So, at that time, I'd piled all my hatred onto Eris, so I had nothing left for him. I had to believe that there was someone safe who was looking after me, even if my mother couldn't offer me that. But as we stood there, and I heard the gurgles of the pig as its throat filled with blood, I saw him nodding and saying, "Yes, that's right, cut it deep."

When I tried to back away from the rubble of the fortress, my father, this thing with eight legs, scuttled closer, and too quickly he was upon me, the smell of putrefying flesh so close that it made me gag. I felt its legs crawling up my body to my face, its long tongue flickering near my mouth.

The legs split at the tips to create pincers that made clicking sounds, and two of the pincer-tipped legs pinched hold of my eyelids, peeling them back so I could watch as he inserted his other six legs into every orifice of every person I could imagine. People I cared about, like my sister and mother, but also people who I barely knew, who I'd met fleetingly, but he could gain access to through my eyes and mind. No one was spared as the images flickered like an old-fashioned movie reel, the picture grainy and seemingly stained with something. They started to flash faster, horror sped up to intensify the pain of it all, and I longed for it to stop. But he wasn't finished. He made me watch as he tunneled through their nerve endings, making them scream as he pushed in further and reached the vital organs that made them twitch. You would think this would kill them, and they would hope for death, but somehow, they remained alive, their eyes flickering as he rummaged about their innards, and his long tongue flickered at the bodily fluids that oozed and splattered about.

He wants me to see more. I think he's trying to make excuses because he wants me to believe that the world is filled with parents who fail to protect their children from horrors that can be inflicted, even within the apparent safety of a family home. He wants me to see that there are other parents who have been the ones to inflict that violence, because they could, like an empire invading a new territory, because there is no one big or strong enough to defend them. He keeps my eyelids peeled back as he shows me parents ripping apart their own children and laughing about it as the blood soaks into the sheets, and children in strollers but missing a head, or other children tucked up in bed with holes where their arms used to be and plastic toy soldiers shoved into the bloody stumps. And why stop at the children when there are others who are helpless, needy, vulnerable, like the ones who are starved in hospitals or prisons or facilities for the old, and they are beaten as they are tethered to a chair, no matter how helpless they are, how much they piss themselves. Surely they deserved it for not following orders, or they were cruel and abusive when they were parents themselves.

"You see," he says to me, his voice thickened with a coating of blood. "There is always a reason, always a trauma hidden somewhere within the folds of your skin that you can pluck out and use as a *get out of jail* card, so you can continue to hurt others as you loop round that trauma cycle like it is a merry-go-round."

Somehow, he knew of my plans to leave for London, so he also showed me the atrocities that have been inflicted here; it was never just about malevolence in one family home on one particular street in one particular town in New Jersey. "Don't comfort yourself that you can sit and watch someone else's carnage and you will somehow remain safe from it," he told me.

"Just look at their London underground," he said to me, "blown apart by spite and vengeance packed tightly in with the explosives hidden inside a backpack. Do you know what happens to a body when a bomb rips through it? See the shockwaves tear through the skin and break bones. Parts of you turn inside out, so you can see the veins and nerve-endings and pus that were only meant to stay on the inside. Internal organs burst like liquid-filled balloons, and the mess is shocking and ridiculous, comical if it wasn't so devastating. You know all this, because you've already looked it up, haven't you? Don't think I didn't know what you were doing late at night, in your bedroom all alone. You were scrolling through the dark web that others see you scroll through, no matter how many times you erase your internet history or switch to cognito mode, they see all the pages of your filthy curiosity, because they are curious too. Only, they have the power to condemn you for it, to imprison you, because they don't like you, they've never liked you and your faggoty ways, and neither have I. What the fuck was wrong with you, ignoring all those pretty girls who loved to chat with you, when you didn't try to fuck even one of them. You disgust me. You are the filth that should be eradicated, should be washed away in a storm, like rats flushed from a sewer. You deserve to be condemned and beaten and thrown into a prison full of other faggots so they can fuck you raw, because that's how you like it, isn't it, that's what you want really, and how you'd love it if they could somehow knot together the bedsheets as they do in the movies, and tether you to a drain pipe while they fuck you some more, and maybe it will be filmed by some prison guard, or the CCTV footage might be sold to the highest bidder so there can be more pages added to the dark web, more categories of fetishes and filth that can be watched, and they can be imprisoned and fucked too."

My father shows me these horrors as a reminder of how much violence he can unleash on anyone I start to care about. He destroyed my sister and mother, so he can go after anyone else that grows a connection with me. He will thrive under the conditions of that warmth and kindness, using it to prise open a portal from the underworld, and he will use me to wreak havoc and violence. I know this because every moment I spent with Max after the fire seemed to give that arachnid greater strength. I would see it at night, this monster that was once my father, scuttling about with greater fervor each time I shared an intimate moment with Max. The stronger the attachment I felt to Max, the more power that arachnid seemed to possess. So I had to get away from Max and Rotherwell. The only trouble is, I don't know if I've left a trail of breadcrumbs for my monster of a father to follow me here. That's why it's safer to isolate myself from others, to stand guard without emotion, like a stone-cold terracotta warrior. I've been given another chance to keep everyone safe, when the first time round, Eris would say that I failed to fulfil this role for my sister.

But the loneliness is starting to turn on me. In the darkness of this tiny room, I see things; shapes, faces, scuttling legs that taunt me. If I am not to slip into an oblivion, where I cannot identify reality, I need a monotone blip on the heart monitor to remind me that I still exist. So I snort the line and pop the pill, and I haunt the tube stops of London, spending only just long enough with each hookup to feed my hunger, this greed that writhes beneath my skin. And then I am gone, slipping back into the night with the rest of the ghosts.

Last night's hookup took place in a late-night London park that is known for cruising. I'd seen the name of the place scrawled on the wall of the bathroom at the student union café, and so when the bars closed too soon, and I'd been too drunk or high for anyone to invite me home, I found the park and hopped over the iron railings.

I glanced at every guy who passed me, making a quick calculation about the contours of their face, their height, and the size of their muscles. One lingered for a little bit longer than the others, slowing his pace and then looping back, so he stepped right in front of me and blocked my way.

When he offered me a line of something he was carrying in a baggy, I accepted without asking what it was, and it was only after I'd snorted it from a nearby bench that I realized he hadn't taken any himself.

I didn't care, especially when I felt the charge of something spreading through my veins, and I allowed my head to flop back as he kissed my neck. To quickly lose my inhibitions felt terrifying as much as it was a turn-on, and he must have noticed, because he was soon maneuvering me into the bushes where we started to fuck. For all I knew, this stranger could've drugged me and ended up shoving a plastic bag down my throat. I'd seen news reports of this happening only last week to a kid in his late teens. It took a month for them to find his body in an empty apartment in south London, and that was only after the neighbors had complained about the smell.

I can imagine Max would be disgusted to see me doing so many drugs and fucking strangers in dark city parks. He would've said that I was getting sloppy and slutty, but he probably would've still fucked me anyway. We never did it in a London park, or any kind of park, but he liked to take risks, especially when he thought his wife might come home. I mean, she'd already found out about us a while back, but I think he harbored fantasies of a threesome. Something I would never entertain, and I doubt June would've either.

I hate that everything comes back to Max. So much of what we shared was dominated by his temper tantrums and then intense makeup sex. He consumed me, and he was my first. If he had anything to do with it, he would've been my last. I sometimes have nightmares that he has me locked up somewhere, in an empty warehouse or in his attic at home; somewhere hidden from view, like his sexuality, and eternally preserved solely for his enjoyment.

I don't remember much of the sex in the park that night, except that the guy seemed to be in a hurry, so he was rough when he unzipped my jeans, and he smelled of cigars and tasted of beer. He insisted we save each other's number in our cell phones, and I was too fucked up to input the wrong number. It turns out, his name was Robert, and before he left me in that park, he suggested we meet for dinner sometime. I burst out laughing, and he didn't seem to like this because he slapped his hand over my mouth. My first instinct was to bite his hand, but he was a lot taller than me, and I was too tired to fight.

When I reached the halls of residence, I still felt drunk or drugged up, maybe both, so I struggled to get the keys out of my pocket. Still swaying in my stupor, I gazed at the Georgian buildings that curved round Cartwright Gardens, the street where my halls are situated. I lucked out with this place because it overlooks a quiet park and tennis courts, an oasis tucked safely away from the fumes and chaos of Euston Road.

Cartwright Gardens used to be called Burton Crescent but a hundred years ago, it was renamed to break the association with some unsolved murders of women who were beaten to death for a handful of cash. How easy it seems to wash away the blood and put up a new name plaque and pretend the violence never occurred. But the ghosts linger to remind you, and I sometimes see them, these women with faces beaten out of shape, trying to hide from yet another predatory man. I wonder if they have heard the scuttling of those eight legs, knowing there is no escape, now they are trapped in an eternal loop of the afterlife.

I can imagine Max wants to change the name of Mount Pelion Way, and, knowing him, it will become something obnoxious and self-serving, like West Villas or Maxwell Way.

I finally got my keys out, only to drop them on the steps that led up to the front door. As I reached out my hand, someone else grabbed at them.

"What the fuck?"

It was Robert.

"What are you doing here?" I asked him.

"I followed you."

"Well, that's kinda creepy," I replied.

"Maybe. Or you could say that it shows you I'm interested."

"Cool. Awesome. Well, good night."

I heard his footsteps behind me as I climbed the stairs, and then I saw his reflection in the glass of the front door as I walked in.

"You really are going to follow me all the way to my room?"

"Yup," he replied.

"And then what?"

"Then we're gonna fuck some more."

I probably should've told him I was tired, or suggest another night, but his aggression stirred something in me. Something that reminded me of the way Max would just throw me onto the bed or the kitchen table and we'd start fucking before I'd caught my breath.

I wanted to keep people safe, but if they forced their way in, surely I couldn't be blamed. Not when they ignited that greed that writhed about beneath my skin and made me want to choke them. So I did.

After we got back to my room, and he slammed me against the wall, tearing each other's clothes off, I grabbed at his throat and squeezed. I think he liked it at first, but then he looked worried. Maybe he expected me to stop, and then he couldn't speak because his voice was chalky and soft. I could've torn and clawed at him, I could've bitten flesh from bone, and as we started to fuck, he didn't seem so into it anymore. I saw saliva drooling from the side of his mouth as his skin went grey, and instead of gyrating or thrusting, he went limp.

Ever since that fire, the thing that writhes beneath my skin burns with a greater intensity. It is a greed, a hunger that won't be satiated, no matter how many times I try. I wonder whether something escaped from my home when the fire took hold, some kind of toxin that had been sealed into the land, or the materials used to build my family home. Whatever it was, it made the ravens and blue jays take flight. They abandoned the skies above Mount Pelion Way, and they still have not returned. Soon after, the other wildlife followed suit, leaving the fortress site baron and parched and haunted. Some say they feel cold when they go near the site, and others want to cry. When I go near, this writhing feeling burns with a greater intensity. Perhaps you've felt it too, or something similar. That greed, that impatience, that need for more, no matter the cost.

I watched as Robert dropped to the floor, and I was afraid that I'd killed him.

Fuck.

Then he snorted and choked on phlegm, his face going bright red as he sat up against the wall.

"Not so rough," he pleaded. "I'm not really into choking and rough play."

"Okay."

"Can we try things a little bit more vanilla?"

"Sure," I replied, "whatever gets you going."

So we tried again, only a little more gently, and I felt this thing beneath my skin, the greed that burns through me, and I thought of Max and how we are no better or worse than each other. I hate to admit it, but I started to miss him, so I pretended that I was fucking around with him instead of this guy who was starting to ruin the moment by asking me permission before he made his every move. He was a big ass dude, well over six feet, but he didn't seem interested in overpowering me. In fact, he wanted me to do it to him.

I shouldn't have let him stay the night, but I passed out. By the time I came to, it was morning, and he was stroking my hair with an annoying amount of attentiveness.

I asked him how he trailed me from the park without me even noticing.

"You were pretty fucked," he said. "I'm not sure you would've realized that anyone was following you."

"True, you have a point there."

"But I do have experience."

"What, as a professional stalker? Or is it a PI? Oh wait, you're a hitman."

"None of the above. I'm a police officer."

I thought of the drugs that were stashed under my bed and I wondered how much jail time this country handed out for possession of Class A substances. He had been the one to give me the coke earlier on, but maybe that was part of his honey trap.

"You have a good body," he said, probably to change the subject. He's probably used to doing this. I can't imagine many people want to dwell on the thought of fucking a cop.

"Thanks," I replied.

"You work out?"

"Not really. You?"

"Sure. Most weeks. I mean, you've gotta stay fit in my line of work," he said.

He was cute, in a beefy, blond and curly-haired cherub kind of way, but he spoke each word with a dull monotone. I felt myself drifting, bored with the kind of petty exchange that Max would never waste his time with.

And yet.

And yet here was Max's voice coming from this police officer's mouth, a ventriloquist's act, perhaps, to distract me from an impending attack.

"Is something up?" he asked me.

"No. Why?"

"Only, you seem a little…And who's Max?"

"Why?"

"You keep calling me that. Especially when we were, well, in the heat of the moment."

"Oh, come on, my little bobby on the beat," I wanted to say to him, "you can say *fucking*. If you can nestle your face into my every orifice, you can speak of it; those Victorian sensibilities can't run that deep." I'd like to say all of this, but I don't have the energy, so instead I just tell him that Max is someone I used to know.

"Like the Gotye song," he said.

"What?"

"Gotye, that singer who did *Somebody That I Used To Know*. I love that song." He then started to sing, and I wished he would just leave. He was trying to grow some kind of connection to me, I could feel the nerve endings starting to wrap around my wrists like vines around a corpse, and it took all my energy not to scream at him to get the fuck out of my place.

"So, is this Max fella an ex or something?" he persisted.

"Sure. I guess you could call him that."

It occurred to me that this could be a trap, that Robert might have been sent here by Max, to package me up and bring me back to Rotherwell.

"So you don't know an American guy called Max West?"

I felt like a dick to ask because if he was one of Max's henchmen; he wasn't going to admit to it.

Robert shook his head in reply, but he could've been lying. He also said he was single, but he could've been lying about that too, with a boyfriend or husband, girlfriend or wife waiting for him at home. I thought of that person refusing to kiss him when he finally did return home, knowing that he would smell of the body of some random guy. Everyone I met was starting to seem like a liar, and the more they explained themselves, the more I disbelieved them. I could always tell when Max was lying because he would spread his hands out as a preacher would, beseeching me to follow his every word as if it were the gospel truth. I guess I did worship him at one time, which makes me feel pathetic and weak now. I gave him that land, didn't ask for anything in return, and I was just grateful that I had somebody left to give things to.

"Are you really a cop?" I asked Robert, trying to turn my thoughts to anything but Max.

"Why would I lie about something like that?"

I rolled my eyes as I imagined he viewed his job as some kind of spiritual mission for justice, or worse, that it elevated him to the same status as the royal family who take a chunk of the pittance of the salary they throw to him like scraps to a peasant. I bet he flexes his muscles at night, as he stands in his uniform in front of a full-length mirror in some tiny apartment somewhere in London. He probably jerks off while he does this, getting high on the illusion of importance as he tries not to smell the damp and the strangely scented aroma from laundry that is hung up on radiators. Why do the British refuse to install dryers in their homes? It just adds to that crushing sense of *making do* that defines these simpering, but ever so polite, oddities. They make do with the shitty weather and the cramped confines of their tiny homes and the flooding and the roadworks that slow vehicles to a stop. And they make do with the illusion that they are not still subjugated by imperial warriors in a run-down palace.

"What's it like being a police officer in this country?" I asked Robert.

Max always hated the police. He referred to them as stupid and racist and homophobic, but I don't think he really cared about any of those things. He just didn't like being told what to do. He thought he was the ultimate authority, above criminal as much as civil law, and he would laugh at the idea of taxation. "That's for the stupid," he'd say as he waved his hand in the air with a dismissive flourish. "If you're paying any tax to those crooks, then you've failed the system."

"What do you want to know?" Robert replied as he sat upright in bed. He seemed about twenty years younger than Max, in his early thirties, with softer-looking skin, but he was less toned, so as he leaned to one side in the bed, a small belly sagged under the weight of gravity. This would've made Max do extra sit-ups each morning until he toned up again.

"It isn't what it used to be," Robert said with a sigh. "What with all that diversity nonsense and people's rights? You can't do anything these days without ending up on TikTok. And there's a lot of paperwork and procedural stuff."
"Sounds very British, at least from what I've witnessed so far.

You guys like your bureaucracy and rules and regulations. But at least I can cross a road here without getting run down."

"Sure. We're a pretty safe nation."

"Safe and boring?"

He looked confused, and I wondered whether he had ever experienced boredom.

"Just safe. The country is safe, and mostly thanks to us coppers. The people in this country should be grateful that we ensure safety. Isn't that enough?" Robert said all this with wide eyes that made him look younger, as if he'd just learnt this in school and he couldn't wait to rush home and share it with someone.

What was I supposed to do with this? Nestle into the protection of a police officer and make-believe that I'd never seen the horror crawl out of the smoldering rubble in Rotherwell? Ignorance is bliss, right? Isn't that what they say? This fairytale, this pretense of protection; a guy who plays dress up in a uniform that he probably irons every night, but leaves him defenseless in the face of the atrocities that my father wants to show me.

As I lay in bed with that police officer, his flaccid cock resting on my thigh, I searched for a sign of something more to this guy. I still don't know what I was searching for. Maybe the same greed writhing beneath his own skin, or some kind of sign that he had more strength to offer than I feared he lacked. But there was nothing. I can't imagine how he might react if I told him about my sister hanging from the apple tree, and the vengeance that burned through my mother's veins as she crushed the aconite with plans of poisoning the people on our street. And all the things I did with my seething vengeance, as Eris was shaping me into Ares, her battle-lustful warrior. What would simple Robert, with his cleanly cut nails and hands smelling of soap, and his vanilla taste in sex, make of all this filth and contaminants? I've heard that the police in this country don't even have a gun, and they're expected to defend themselves against all manner of horrors by wielding what looks like a rubberized dildo.

"Why don't you carry a gun?" I asked him, but I don't think

I spoke loudly enough, or maybe I didn't speak at all and it was all in my head, because he spoke over me with his own soapy words about budget cuts in "the force" and something and nothing. That grey dishwater tone of obscurity allowed me to drift away in the moment, knowing he would probably not even notice that I had gone. I needed this liminal state, where I no longer existed, where no one required anything of me because he didn't matter, and I didn't matter, and we were both lost to each other.

"Are you listening?" he had asked me after a while. He'd been prodding me with his elbow, and I'd been vaguely aware of it, but then he'd shaken me by the shoulders, and I'd come to with a jolt.

I pictured myself as his housewife, where I sat with my hands neatly folded on my lap as I listened to his endless stories. I would smile and nod at the right moments and be there to convince him that he was big and strong and deserving of that promotion that seemed so elusive, when they just wanted to give it to someone female or black or queer or all three. I'd say the words for him that he used to shout at his mummy, "It's not fair!" although I wouldn't do the foot-stamping or throwing myself on the ground in tears. I'd turn a blind eye to the hush money he would accept from the drug dealers in Canning Town, even when the school kids would die of overdoses. *It's none of my concern*, I'd say, as I'd step back into the paisley wallpaper and pretend that I didn't feel anything when he fucked me from behind with extra vigor and he still didn't come, barely even got it up anymore, and always smelled of shit.

I could do all that because I would stare into the oblivion and never feel anything again if he needed me to, if he wanted me right here, but not really, not the true me, because that would make him go soft again while he tried to get inside me. So I would keep quiet as he gripped me by the throat and he squeezed tighter, which would seem to get him going, and I would try not to think about where he might have learnt this new technique, which whore was teaching this old dog so many new tricks, but at least it kept him hard enough to come in tidal waves of relief that radiated through the both of us, so hard that he started to cry because he was still holding me by the throat, and he hadn't realized during those waves of joy that he'd squeezed a little too hard, so hard I thought I might blank out, and then I realized that I had already blanked out, and, in fact, I was already dead, a fucking corpse that is cold and rotten inside, with my innards slipping out of me, and things feasting on me, but I was still there for dear Robert, my dear old Peeler, my big strong boy. Who's a big, strong boy? Who's a clever boy?

I wanted to tell Robert that I found out why the British called cops *Peelers*, but I didn't think he would like it. It might have made this *big, strong boy* turn nasty, and I had no energy left to fight anyone. It turns out, the police on both sides of the Atlantic started out in similar ways; they were racist hired hands of the rich who were paid to beat up the poor. No better or worse than the henchmen Max employs to dispose of his business competitors.

Just when I tried to tell the cop to leave, we were startled by the sudden rainfall that hammered against my window. It came from nowhere, darkening the morning sky to change the colors on my walls from pale orange to blood red. The flimsy sash windows rattled in their frames, and I longed for them to smash, just so I could watch the explosion of glass fall like confetti.

"Fuck," Robert gasped, "you're not gonna make me go out in this."

"I'm sure it will pass at any moment."

"We'll see."

"I was told about the rain in this country, but I didn't expect this."

"This isn't normal," Robert replied. "I figure God has had enough of us, and if we don't find an ark soon, we're fucked. We could pair up, though, you know, like the animals did with Noah. And I can be a bit of an animal if you want me to," he said with a smile as he pulled me closer to kiss me. It felt wet and cold, so I pulled away.

"I've got lectures soon," I lied. He didn't have to know that there were never any during the weekend. "You should go," I lied. I slipped out from under his arm, out of the bed, and started to dress, hoping he would do the same.

"Jeesh, I forgot you were still a student," he said as he sat up in bed. "Could never hack all that reading. I always ended up falling asleep. What are you studying?"

"Law."

I heard the storm fade as quickly as it had begun, so I nodded towards the window and said, "Now's your chance. I can give you an umbrella, if you like."

"Everything's rush, rush, rush with you. Fuck fast, fuck hard, get dressed again, get out. You need to calm down a little."

He jumped out of bed, and his foot landed on something hard, making him stumble.

"Mother fucker," he cried. "What the hell is that?"

I saw that he had stepped on the snow globe from the buzz-cut guy's apartment.

"Just a souvenir," I replied, unwilling to offer any more. I wasn't about to tell him that this stolen item served as one of the five points to a pentacle of protection that I created around my bed. Sleeping is the most dangerous time for anyone, when you are the most defenseless, so I wasn't leaving anything to chance. There is always the fear that the arachnid with my father's face could appear, and as Paris always detested the truth about my sexuality, I figured an item from a recent hookup might be a good shield against the threat of his presence. Could it be that a part of me was looking for a knight in shining armor, hoping that one of these hookups might care enough to protect me from him?

But my father is not the only danger. Even before the fire destroyed my family home, my dreams were haunted by other terrors. The hooded creatures, the ones who still linger even now, trying to show me things that I don't want to see. When I slip from consciousness, they sit on my headboard and wait for me to realize something, and I'm afraid they are trying to tell a different story than the one I am narrating to myself, and in that story, I am portrayed as the perpetrator after all.

These hooded creatures are the same ones that used to haunt

my mother, which is even more terrifying because this makes it more likely that they exist. Wasn't a mother always supposed to say that it was okay, that it was not real? Shouldn't she have reassured me that those things that go bump in the night were not the hooded creatures dragging a disembodied head down the stairs inside one of their sacks? Shouldn't she have told me that I don't really feel their sticky little fingers prising my eyelids open to watch Paris return? That he isn't ready to slip in through the gaps around the door, or even rise up through the floorboards, and possess my body so he can inflict his violence on more of this world.

The more times Max held me down and forced himself inside of me, the more I wanted to do it in return. Especially after the fire. I took out all my rage on him, and it seemed to excite him. They say that human interaction is based on reciprocity, a *quid pro quo*, as Eris would say, so I guess it made sense that I would grow to do to him whatever he had done to me. Max liked it in the end, told me to do it to him again, but in the beginning, we had each used force on each other, and that terrified me. What good are sigils of protection when the threat is already inside, ready to inflict violence like any Trojan warrior?

Robert was finally dressed and looking around my room. He spotted another item on the floor, the second point to the pentacle, and he pointed to it, asking what it was.

"My mom's locket," I reply, my throat tightening a little under the pressure of scrutiny.

I figured he might have encountered pentacles of protection in crime scenes, drawn carefully around a body laid out as a sacrifice, and the police are just another branch of the ill-informed, too afraid of their own childish notions not to make snap judgments about blame and causation, so I wasn't about to tell him the truth.

"I must have dropped it earlier, when I was having a bit of a moment. I've been missing her since I left the States."

He lapped that up, snaking his arms around my shoulders to play at the dutiful police officer comforting a grieving kid.

"I get it," he said. "I would be crushed without my mum.

I'm sorry."

I didn't tell him that inside the locket were strands of my sister's auburn hair, taken by my mother as soon as Ania died. When the fire took hold, when she knew there was to be no escape, she pressed the locket into my hand, hoping that she could at least preserve something of her daughter in a future that Eris would not survive. But ever since that arachnid scuttled from the rubble of the fortress, I'd been afraid that the scent of his daughter's hair might lead Paris to me. Another trail of breadcrumbs to bring his violence across the Atlantic.

Robert didn't see the other items that formed the points of the pentacle, so I didn't have to explain to him that the silver bracelet was Ania's, something she never asked for but secretly desired. She loved the panda bear pendants, especially the way they would make a jingling sound, and she'd say that it sounded like fairies were approaching. Every time we passed that jewelry shop, she would say hello to the panda bears, and hope that they were okay at night after the sunset. She finally got the bracelet on her sixteenth birthday, so she only got to wear it for two months before she was frozen in time as forever sixteen, and she became nothing more than a victim of my father's violence.

Robert also didn't get to hear about the photograph of Katherine and I, the fourth point of the pentacle. It was taken just a matter of days before I left the States, when Katherine told me about her plans to protest at Pastor Pry's church. I'd always hated Isla, especially when my sister died and she preyed upon my family, trying to suck us into her bullshit with talk of salvation when really she was after more donations. I promised I would join Katherine at the protest, but she gave me that look that showed me she suspected bullshit. She even wrote on the back of the photo "Remember that you are loved" when she handed it to me. She could always tell when something was up. I mean, she'd been trailing me around her home ever since the fire, trying to make me laugh and offering to take me to the creamery. I wish I hadn't stonewalled her, but how could I explain what was going on? Fucking her father was the least of the mess that I was trying to hide from her.

The last point of the pentacle was an item I kept at the far corner of my room, deep beneath my bed, where no one, including Robert, would find it. Sometimes I've pretended that it wasn't there, especially when I've been fucking guys on the bed above it. But then I get scared that if it isn't there, then the sigil would be incomplete, and I would be helpless to any of the horrors that might haunt me.

I found it in the charred rubble just a day after the fire, and I kept it beneath the bed in Max's spare room in Rotherwell. I'm surprised it made it in my suitcase through customs, so it either has a mythical power to remain undetectable to a scanner, or airport security is worse than it has ever been.

The way it was sitting at the gap where the back door used to be. It made me think that someone had placed it there, a message of hope, I chose to believe, rather than a threat.

Sometimes I take it out from beneath my bed and look at it. When I do, the writhing beneath my skin becomes so strong that it's almost unbearable. I have the item wrapped in a napkin that has her initials embroidered on it, her old initials of *E.G.* I can't explain how a napkin could've survived a fire, any more than I can explain why my mother's jawbone was lingering in the darkness like that, like a family secret just waiting to be discovered.

When Robert finally left, I retrieved the jawbone from its place beneath my bed. I needed time with it to try to work out what I could do about Max. But I was interrupted almost immediately by a hammering at the door.

Robert.

"Did you forget something?" I asked as I swung the door open, only too late to consider that it might have been Max. But it wasn't him or the police officer. It was a skinny dude who I recognized from these halls. We'd passed in the corridor a couple of times and nodded out of politeness, but I'd never even said "Hello."

"Oh," I said, letting out a long sigh of relief.

"Sorry. Bad time?" he asked as he pointed to my boxer shorts.

"Kind of, but… Don't worry about it. What's up?"

"Ruby and I wanted to personally invite you to a party."

I didn't know who Ruby was any more than I knew this dude. I'd also never had a group of friends invite me to a party and feel pressured to attend, but I'd seen enough on TV to know that it was a headfuck of expectations. All that bending yourself out of shape to meet the demands of others where you can't put a foot in front of the other without stepping on a landmine because you say or do the wrong thing and someone gets pissed and someone else steps in to defend them, and they all say you are as bad as they suspected, and you want to scream that you never wanted to be included in their friend group in the first place.

He had caught me off guard, so instead of being polite, I just responded with a "Why?"

"What do you mean *Why*?"

"I mean, I don't know why you and Ruby are inviting me."

"Does there have to be a reason? But if you really want one, I guess we figured we hadn't seen you at any of the student union functions, so, you know, come along!"

I nodded with a non-committal "Cool."

"Great. It's this Friday, in High Street Ken, so you can take the Victoria line and change at Victoria Station."

"Perfect," I said.

We just stood there for a moment, two idiots smiling and staring at each other, until I said, "So, I'll see you…later?".

"Oh, right, so you're kind of busy?"

His big, brown eyes stared at me as his long eyelashes blinked, and for a moment he almost looked upset, so I said, "Sorry?"

"Oh, no, don't be sorry, of course. You're busy. It's tough settling into a new country. I mean, I hear a bit of a twang of some accent. Am I right?"

"Yeah. I'm from New Jersey."

"Awww, New Joisy," he said, attempting some kind of accent. "That's so cool, man. I've always wanted to go to the US of A but I dunno, since that tangerine prez, I'm not so sure us brown people are welcome there. Am I wrong? What's it like?"

"Well, I've chosen to be here rather than over there, so maybe that answers your question."

"Aha, I see. Well, I probably won't ever get round to visiting because I'm gonna spend the rest of my life paying off these student loans."

I faltered.

"Oh shit. Don't tell me you're another one with rich parents. What is it about this damned university and all the rich kids?"

He was still smiling, but I guessed he was stinging a little.

After a moment, he slapped me on the shoulder and said, "Hey, relax, it's all cool. And, in case you're wondering, the top facts on me are that I'm from Aberystwyth, although I'm originally from Swansea, which I prefer because it was more diverse, which is really saying something about the lack of diversity in Aber. But anyway, my parents moved to Aber a couple of years ago and they love it there, and so does Vafia, my sis. But I think she just likes it because that's where she's going to university. And I'm yabbering away without giving you the chance to say anything about yourself. You probably don't even know where Aberystwyth is."

"No, sorry," I lied. I wasn't about to invite questions about my father, so I kept quiet about how Paris' descendants came from the very same town.

"Oh, well, I can be your tour guide there some day. It's a cute little town on the west coast of Wales that swells for nine months of the year with students and tourists, but then gets kinda quiet for the rest of the time."

"That's great, but..."

"And did you know that sailing ships used to leave Aberystwyth for the States? I think it was a few centuries ago, or something like that, I'd need to check that with Mr. Google. But yeah, sailing ships used to load up on cotton and lead and nickel and head off to America. And now here we are, no ocean between us."

"Cute. That's really cute," I said, but really I was thinking about the damage all that lead must have done to the brains that grew on the East Coast. I thought of the descendants whose genes were mutated by those contaminants, creating distortions that are still haunting those families today. But, it seemed, nothing of that type of malignancy had ever crossed this skinny kid's mind because he continued to go on with his wide-eyed stories of wonder.

"The uni is cool there. That was my reserve choice, in case my grades weren't up to UCL. But my parents were pretty impressed when I got in here because neither of them went to uni. They are originally from Balakot, and they came over here when they were teenagers, so I'm living a lot of firsts on their behalf. And I'm figuring you also don't know anything about Balakot?"

"No, sorry."

"Hey, I probably don't know a lot of places in the US. And most people haven't heard of Balakot, but it's in northern Pakistan, a really remote place but kinda beautiful with the mountains."

"Cool. Listen, I need to go," I said. I was finding it harder and harder to break away from him and I didn't know why, when all the other guys I had met in London felt easily disposable. I think it was those big brown eyes and long eyelashes that felt like a trap, but one that I didn't really want to escape.

"Oh, cool, yeah, sure. Didn't wanna hold you up, I just thought we could, you know… Listen, crazy idea, but if you aren't doing anything else, do you want to study together? I find that I can only concentrate if someone else is taking their studies seriously. Otherwise, I'm scrolling through TikTok and looking up random facts about dead celebrities."

"What are you studying?" I asked him.

"Dude, really? We're on the same course."

"Oh, fuck, sorry."

"Now I'm heartbroken. I mean, you're kinda saying I'm not memorable, which really cuts deep." He was holding his chest like I had shot him with a bow and arrow.

"Nah, man, I'm kidding," he said. "It's all good when there are masses of new faces. And half of them are brown like me. Who would've thought they'd let us into UCL, where all the Oxford rejects go to learn?"

"Is that true?"

"Yup. Most of the kids I saw in the heats at Somerville College ended up here. But don't get too comfortable. Come June, if you don't pass every component of the course, they'll kick you out."

"Seriously?"

"Yup."

"Look," he said, "you probably don't even know my name, do you? Don't worry, I'll save you the embarrassment and I won't test you. I'm Viqaas. You're Dylan, right?"

"Yes. How did you know?"

"I eavesdropped on your conversation at reception when you moved in. You sounded pretty pissed when you found out there were no ensuite showers in the rooms."

"Oh, man, did I sound like a complete douche?"

"Not really," he replied. "I mean, everyone complains about it when they move in. This place is clever with their marketing."

"Those communal showers are pretty skanky."

"Oh yeah, I'm with you on that one," he said as he nodded his head. "The number of times I've found people passed out in there or vomiting after they've drunk too much."

"We've all been there."

"Nah, man, not my scene," he said. "I don't touch the stuff."

"Jeesh, that's gonna make for a difficult university life. I mean, you're what, eighteen? Nineteen?"

"Eighteen."

"And you've just moved out of your family home for the first time, so you have all the freedom in the world."

"Yup."

"So, what do you do for fun? Read the Bible and pray every night with a nice glass of sparkling water?" I said mockingly.

"Almost right, although switch the Bible for the Quran."

"You what?"

"I'm Muslim. No Bibles for me, and no alcohol. It's kinda forbidden. *Haram*. You know?"

"Oh, okay. Gotcha." I didn't know what else to say, so I replied, "And I'm queer and non-binary."

He burst out laughing, clapping one hand over his mouth as the other clutched his belly.

"Aw, shit, I've never heard that comeback. You make it sound like being queer and non-binary is your religion."

"Yeah. I dunno why I said it like that."

"You Americans are nuts. Half of your people think Muslims want to behead every white dude, especially the queer ones, and the other half don't even know what a Muslim is. Come on, nuff of this nonsense and let's go study. You don't wanna be part of that scary statistic come June."

"I really…"

"But I do insist that you first put on some jeans or tracky bottoms."

"I would like to, really I would, but I already have plans," I lie. "But another day, yeah?

"Totally. I'm gonna hold you to it."

I can imagine he would continue talking late into the night, just standing there on my doorstep, but my cell phone had been vibrating for the last few minutes.

"You should get that," he said.

"Oh, I dunno. They'll probably ring back."

"Nah, it's cool. I've gotta go and tell Ruby that you said yes to her party."

"I did?"

"Oh yeah, you're not wriggling out of that one, too."

"Later, Dyls," he called, and he was already waving back at me as he walked down the corridor.

Shutting the door and locking it, I found my phone on the floor. I knew I shouldn't have looked at the messages. It was easier just to pretend that it wasn't happening, but as I suspected, it was from Max.

"I'm giving you one last chance," his message read. "Tell me where you are or you're gonna make this worse for yourself. You know what will happen if I have to come and find you."

That night, I dreamed of my father again. In that dream, his eight legs scuttled over to a bedroom where I knew that he would find a little girl. I didn't want him to go there, so I screamed out as hard as I could, but, of course, I couldn't make any sound. It was a dream, after all.

I thought I'd hear eight legs scuttling across the hallway,

but instead I heard each floorboard creak. Someone else was approaching, and as I felt the warmth of their body next to mine, I knew they were waiting for me to do something to save my sister.

In this dream, Ania is still a baby, so at first, I thought Paris wouldn't be interested in her. He might have been checking things out, making preparations for years ahead, when she was fuller and bigger and stronger. But he still crawled into her room, and into her cot as she slept. He could barely fit with his spindly, spidery legs. One knocked her cheek, and she stirred, and this made him curious, so he leaned in closer, crawling all over her and deciding what to do next.

I tried to race forward, to throw him out of her room, but I could not move. I was screaming without sound and thrashing without movement, so the energy built up inside of me, that writhing, burning feeling with nowhere for it to go. It filled me with a rage that I wanted to unleash on someone, anyone, so I could rip at flesh, so I could stop this once, just once, instead of witnessing it over and over as trauma so often repeats.

I woke before I saw what happened. I never really knew what happened.

I have dreams like this all the time. With each frame, more and more layers of my sister's trauma are revealed. And as the scene is set again, as regularly as the daily breakfast and dinner table, so I am cast in a new role where I fail more and more each time. Slowly, Paris is winning from beyond the grave, and he is stripping me of any power I thought I had, any certainty of my innocence.

I hear my mother's voice from an age much younger than I can see. "*It's only a dream*," she tells me, and she repeats this, over and over again. I guess I took this the wrong way because I assumed that whatever haunted that dream could not exist in real life. *It's only a dream*, so it is all fantastical, and I am safe here, away from that creaking bedroom door.

Just because it's a dream doesn't mean it's not a memory.

Chapter four

~~~

Mother Earth

~~~

The fortress site sat unattended and unexplored. It was scaring everyone away, and even the wildlife abandoned it. Mother Earth knew of the empty skies where birds used to call, so it longed for the natural rhythms to be restored. But no one looked upon this place and thought of it as anything natural. It was an abhorrence, an eyesore worthy of destruction and replacement, and Mother Earth saw how these ant-like men drew up plans to tear it apart again, and she was disgusted. They thought that they were building something new and bigger and better than before, but they were just perpetuating the same old trauma they have inflicted on Mother Earth for centuries. Whatever they build will grow old and become stained by the exhaust fumes and the rampant invasive species that are brought here to wipe out anything else. The land will flood because of the choked-up waterways where people dump their trash, whole refrigerators and plastic bags left there to choke the young wildlife that roams there. Have you seen how the plastic binding wraps around legs and throats, cutting them like a razor blade? The air is choked up too, with the trucks and SUVs that idle, and the factories that pump toxic fumes when they produce stuff that decorates tables at parties that no one wants to attend, and everyone despises because the hosts are show-offs, and they throw the little sparkling plastic table decorations in the trash as soon as they leave. All that toxicity makes the air unsafe to breathe, so they demand that it is cordoned off somehow, that the contaminated sites are segregated, where only the poor people should live and work and produce more sparkling plastic table decorations.

Mother Earth knows more than these ant-like people. She knows that you can't just segregate it off, no matter how clear the demarcations and how zealously they guard the boundaries. She knows that they are all in it together, as much as she is embroiled in it too. Each time she watches the collapse of one building, city or empire, she knows the new one is doomed before it has been built in its place; decline and fall, boom and bust, Mother Earth is caught up in it, too. *We hurt the ones closest to us.* As much as a community might torment a recluse, as a father might sully his own daughter, as a young girl might break her own neck, these ant-like people inflict their violence on Mother Earth, their nearest and dearest, and it is a vicious trauma cycle that will keep looping round unless she does something drastic. Mother Earth sits and waits for the right time to seek her vengeance, some kind of recompense for all we have taken in our relentless pursuit of progress. *Quid pro quo.* That helpless teacher was just the beginning.

And yet people still blame the land. They say the fortress site is rotten, evil even, and it should be avoided. Just look at how unsightly it is, how wildly the tufts of grass have grown as the ivy wraps around the broken window frames and bricks. Even the trees stoop with a bending back. When it looks bad, they say, it is bad, and that badness could be contagious, so keep away. Unruly and dangerous, like an uprising that needs to be quashed. All empires do this, especially when they start to fail. They blame their subjects for how they look, and they force them to work harder, condemning them as unclean and unsafe. But the fortress site wasn't to blame for any of this. The people did this. With their trucks and fumes and chemical sprays to create paint-green lawns. They were distorting this land, choking the waterways as much as the air around it, because they viewed it as theirs, as something to subjugate and strip and pillage.

Things still grow from that land. The trees and the apples and the aconite, for example. But all of it is toxic or spoiled or pungent, like the stench of rotten flesh. Some are drawn to that smell as you might be drawn to the unwashed smell of your mother, and stories about the place have been reproduced throughout social media, luring the ghouls in to take a closer look. This is a place to dare each other to visit: *Go on*, they say, *eat those shiny apples, I dare you!* But rarely do the stories get shared about what happens to those people after they've eaten the fruit. Most of the posts about the after-effects are flagged and removed, and the users banned for persistent posting of stories about blood and bodily fluids. But if you look hard enough, deep in the dark web, you'll find the accounts of those who have survived long enough to share their stories. Ice-cold whispers from the edge of death, about apples that are eaten and painful convulsions. How they clawed at their belly and tore at their skin, trying to escape their own body, and how terrifying it was to see skin rippling as something stirred beneath it. Something was alive inside those organs, something that had its own greed and needed to gnaw its way out to seek out more.

Mother Earth wants more of these accounts to leak out, no matter how many times they are reported and removed. She wants more people to know about the writhing of something beneath the skin, rippling it as the land can shift about beneath your feet, as hands can claw their way to the surface to drag you into an underworld of pain and suffering because you have created so much pain and suffering here. *As above, down below.*

We make up tales of ghosts and ghouls with and without heads, and hooks for hands and fangs for teeth. We tell of possessions and witchcraft and houses that are haunted, even ones that whisper to us when we try to sleep. We set up pentacles of protection to ward off the dangers from all of this, and yet here is Mother Earth, already unleashing all manner of horrors, and we barely notice, or we claim we can know it and tame it like a domesticated beast. Don't you know that there is no more terrifying and gruesome a horror story than a tale about Mother Nature?

Recently, Ralph, who still mourns the loss of his sister, discovered that Max West had bought the fortress site and had plans to build a tower right on top of soil that is still soaked in his sister's blood. He imagines the steel cables plunging through the soil that is now Ellie's flesh, tearing her apart again and waking her from a slumber. She will get no peace, not in this world or the next.

He wants to know why this keeps happening to his family, and why some prosper so much from the violence inflicted on others. He searches online for hours late into the night. He stares so hard at the screen that his vision goes blurry, and when he hears movement outside his bedroom door, he longs for it to be his sister again, just so she can stroke his hair and reassure him that everything is going to be okay. But of course, it's not his sister, and of course it's not going to be okay. Nothing is ever going to be okay.

He tries to stare at the computer screen again, but a voice is distracting him. A siren call for violence. At first, he thought it might be his husband, but of course, Ralph's husband never called for violence, and he isn't even here anymore. Ralph's husband gave up on their marriage a while back, moving in with his mom in Maine, even though she still makes cruel comments about "fags." But he couldn't stay and watch as Ralph twisted with grief, hunched for hours over a computer screen as he gathered so many facts about one man. And all for what? What was Ralph planning to do to Max once he finished all this research? He didn't want to stick around to find out, so he kissed his husband one last time and left.

What are you going to do about it? Ralph thinks he remembers his husband saying to him, the last time he was in this apartment. *What can you possibly do with all that information? What use is it if you don't act on it, if you don't make plans to use all that pent-up energy that's writhing beneath your skin?* Ralph thinks this is the memory of his husband's voice, but his tone was never laced with so much vengeance. His husband never spoke of the violence that he can now see, such atrocities to be committed where people are slashed and burned and strangled or drowned.

Just look, the voice tells him, *at how much carnage a mere sixteen-year-old could inflict only last week, when he took an assault rifle from his father's closet*. He knew of the news story because it made the national headlines, for half a day, at least, until they got distracted by the fraud trial of an ex-President.

The kids had been cutting up construction paper and decorating it with glitter glue when he burst into their elementary school. They were making posters for Memorial Day when he blew holes the size of apples in those tiny faces and bodies. Some were found holding hands, some in pretty summer dresses, and one was clutching a snuggle panda bear that she must have smuggled into school that morning. All this is shocking, but is it any more shocking than the father who smothered his four-year-old twin boys because they were making too much noise as they played? The father had been beaten as a kid, so he was twitchy about sudden loud noises, and they say that damage within the skull can make you jumpy and angry and violent. Does it make it any better or any worse than the person shooting their way through an elementary school? And what about the guy who was knocked around by his husband? For years, he tried to keep up with the incessant demands, and yet he would always fail, and he would get hit, and it became embarrassing when his friends knew that he was lying about walking into a door to blacken his eye. One day, he'd had enough of his husband's violence, so he took a hammer to him. Was that justified? Or was it inexcusable because the husband was defenseless in his sleep? We create rules of conduct, but they don't seem to fit the ever-changing landscape, like a war-paint that cracks with every move in offense or defense. We create structures to house things that grow unruly, that should never have been confined, and then we call it unnatural when all it is doing is responding to its natural inclinations.

Ralph wants to ask this voice, this siren, what it means when it urges him to take action. Does it mean that he should shoot up a school or beat someone's kids to death or attack someone with a hammer as they dream of a long life never to be fulfilled? Is this kind of violence it wants to see, where people pay with their lives and Ralph ends up hated for a day until people are distracted by another headline? Ralph's sister would never approve of all of that, but then this voice urges him again, and says that his sister needed protecting, *she needed a warrior who would be stronger than her, so why are you, Ralph, wasting time deliberating over what she would have done? Don't you see how her innards spilled out after they were torn open? Can't you see, Ralph? Doesn't it make you seethe with the pain and fury that is endless grief? There has to be some kind of outlet for this, a bloodletting so you can breathe again. You might not get caught, and your husband might never know, so if you do this, you can move on with your life and even ask your handsome, loving husband to return to you once more.*

The voice, the siren, tells Ralph to take a closer look at his sister's mutilated body, and as he does this, he sees things that he could not possibly have seen without the help of this entity that speaks to him so kindly, that seems to understand his plight as intimately as if it had experienced such grief itself. The voice, the siren, shows Ralph how the principal rolled her eyes when Ellie was escorted from the school, and how hard Ellie fought not to cry as she clutched her box of construction paper, scissors, and glitter glue.

"Stop," Ralph gasps. He also tries not to cry and so it stays within him, that energy set to burst, that writhing need for vengeance.

"Stop it." Spittle flies at the computer screen, covering his sister's face, and he gets a tissue to wipe it clean. There is a brief moment of calm as he tends to her image, keeping at bay the reality of her death for just a moment while he allows himself to believe that he is wiping tears from her eyes.

The voice, the siren, calls again, so close to Ralph's ear that it tickles him, sending lightning bolts down his spine.

Remember how rotten this woman is, the voice says as it points to the principal, *as rotten as this one*, and it points to an image of Max West. *You won't get much from the principal because she was sliced to death in a road traffic accident last month. But Max still lives. He still breathes the air that froze in your sister's lungs. He still tastes the food that she could not afford, and he fucks and fucks others over, and he loves it. He's rotten to the core and anything he begets, anything he builds, will spread that rot to multiply like spores of mold in every lung. He is a contaminant that needs to be eradicated because there is nothing more dangerous than greed. So, answer this, Ralph, what are you going to do about it?*

Chapter Five

~~~

Max

~~~

I let out an angry roar of pain and pleasure, and then it's over. Nothing to beat my chest about, no muscle-flex, but something I had to prove to myself; that I could still convince a guy to come back to my hotel room. Yet again, it took longer to find someone, and it was already getting harder during my forties, but now I am in my fifties, the cumulation of it feels like it deserves a warrior's cry of victory.

I knew it would come to this. I mean, I used to sneer at the older guys in the queer bars, the ones who would wear a baseball cap just to cover their bald patch. I remember going home with a couple of them when I was really young, and I'll never forget how red-faced they became at the point of climax. Once or twice, I thought I'd killed them because they'd just slump to one side, unresponsive for a moment as I searched for my clothes. They probably looked like the way I do now, all hot and bothered as this dude trembles beneath me, all covered in my sweat.

At fifty-two, I look twenty years younger than my dad ever looked at this age, and I'm richer, and my wife stuck around. I've won, but the victory feels empty without the fucker around to rub his nose in it.

How much power I felt when I was in my twenties, and before that, in my teens. Fuck, I could make guys buy me anything with just the idea that they might get me to suck me off. The first guy I ever did anything with, a neighbor of my dad's, bought me a new bike after we'd fucked. I think he was in his late forties. I used to watch him chat to my dad in the driveway and come across so friendly, and it fascinated me that someone could be this two-faced. So pleasant-mannered with my dad, boring even, while all along he was fucking his neighbor's eighteen-year-old son.

When I met Dylan in a similar way, when he was also around eighteen or so, I never thought that I was giving him power over me. He probably didn't realize it either; he never showed me that he felt anything more than, fuck, what's the word Dylan used? *Subservience*, that's right. He never seemed to want anything more than subservience to me, on his knees, on his back, on his front, however, and whenever I wanted him to be. But since the fire, something has changed, and he no longer seems content for me to dominate him. He once told me about trauma, how much it fucks with people's heads. I mean, he didn't say it like that. It was more along the lines of *unlocking parts of us that were crying out for freedom*. So maybe that's what happened to him after the fire; the true Dylan had been unleashed. And without a leash, he was bound to run away from me.

It's been too long. I waited two weeks for Dylan to come back to Rotherwell, so now I've had to fly here to London and step it up a little. Dylan should know that it doesn't end well when people disobey me.

You know what they say about the British, and their poor work ethic? How they want to take tea breaks and lunch breaks, and three-week holidays? It's all true. "Clocking off for the night" and "That's too far out of my direction" was all I heard from these deadbeat cab drivers as I tried to make my way back to the hotel with this dude I'd pulled at the bar. It should've been the busiest time for these cabbies, just when the bars were closing, so I don't know what the fuck was wrong with them. These socialist shit holes, all handing out endless stacks of cash, so no one has to do an honest day of work.

The guy I'd pulled, Jason or Joe, whatever the fuck his name was, suggested we walk a bit further, so I agreed. As soon as we turned the corner, I recognized some of the buildings I'd helped to redevelop a few years before. For a while, I was part of a joint venture where we were trying to take advantage of the excessive premium that is London's land value.

I stared at the glass and steel, and I felt sad for the people I'd kicked out of their tiny apartments, tearing them out of their beds in the middle of the night with duct tape over their mouths. These were immigrant families and seamstresses and other kinds of people who had no voice, no contacts who might have fought for them. It was a simple cleanup exercise and in one night, the whole mold-ridden apartment block was emptied, just a week before we demolished it to make way for the new glass and steel development. It'll probably last another five years or so before another joint venture makes their millions redeveloping it, probably to look like the original building we knocked down.

I don't know why I felt sad when I thought of those people who were evicted. I mean, I'd done it countless times before. Maybe it was because everyone lived on top of each other, so when we'd wrestled them to the ground in such a cramped space, it had felt personal. Every fucking detail of that night stayed in my mind, even the bright colors of one mother's rug that I slammed her face down onto. She seemed more upset that her scarf had been dislodged, revealing a head of glossy black hair, and she spat on my boots before I duct-taped her mouth.

As Jason or Joe continued to walk me through the London streets, I felt the rush of a double-decker bus swish past. It pulled into the stop just ahead of us, and the amber glow of the lights, and the soft-looking fabric-coated seats, made it seem comforting. It made me think of the home I'd left behind, where Katherine would be buzzing round the kitchen because she recently got into cooking. Smithson and June love this because they would rather someone else feed them, and everyone knows that isn't going to be me.

When I've been home with her, I've made a conscious effort to stop staring at my laptop and instead watch as my daughter unloads items from cupboards and the refrigerator. It was fascinating to see how hard she concentrated as she made mental calculations about ingredients and portion sizes. But there's always a gravitational pull back to the endless emails and spreadsheets that are layered upon each other, always a potential threat looming that needs to be neutralized.

Katherine asked if she could join me in London because she hadn't visited it since she was in middle school. I wondered if she wanted to check on me, to see if I lied to her about Dylan. I'm afraid of how quickly her mind works, what a fine line she will have to tread between a life she already enjoys, where she can afford to use that amazing brain to be kind, and another life, where she uses it to rule others.

Back at the hotel, after an hour of fucking around, I just want the guy to leave. I'm not in the mood for casual conversation, but he isn't taking the hint. I'm naked while I'm pacing about the hotel room, but this seems to turn Jason or Joe on again, so he strokes his own naked body and suggests we both jump into the shower. When I say no, he points at my legs and asks, "What happened there?" He's referring to the burn-marks that scar my thighs. They have whitened into scars, reminders that my fucked-up father wasn't the only one to overpower me. Most days, I forget about them, and it feels better that way, to pretend that it never happened. But after I've fucked or had a shower, for that split second before I put on clothes or a towel, I can see the glint of light bouncing off the freshly formed skin.

"Nothing," I snap. "You should go."

I haven't slept since I landed. I hate those fucking red eye flights.

"I didn't mean anything," Jason or Joe says as he pouts with the big lips that made me single him out in the bar last night. The same lips that I took a bite out of when I started to climax.

"If you don't want to talk about it, then don't," he continues, but this time he uses a tone with me that I don't welcome. I walk right up to him, stirring as I smell the mixture of his cologne, stale alcohol and bodily fluids emanating from him, and I seize him by the throat.

"Stop," he gasps, barely making any sound. I use my thumb to stroke his Adam's apple, and he seems to like that, but he is also scared, his eyes searching me and the room. He might be looking for a weapon; a bedside lamp or an iron. I'd like to see him try.

"You're definitely a gym bunny," he croons. It's his attempt to calm me down, but it only fires up a new rage inside of me. "So far, I've been nice to you…"

"Get off me," he gasps, clawing at my hand. I let him prise my fingers off him, and he stumbles backwards, grabbing at his clothes from the floor.

"…but I don't have to continue like that." Something dark clouds my eyes, and my voice deepens to a demonic growl. "I could snap your throat in two."

Do it, the voice hisses, so close to my ear that it makes me jump.

The man's face distorts as I chase him. I fall to my hands and knees so I can climb about the room on all fours. I snap at him like a crocodile, and I manage to get close enough to catch a bit of his calf between my teeth.

Tear him apart as others have torn me.

I could bite down, but something stops me, and he stumbles backwards and away from me.

I really want to fuck with him, so I yowl "I thought you wanted to play," but he has already got the door open and shrieks as he runs down the corridor.

Go after him.

I'm panting as I crouch there, still fully naked.

He's getting away.

I think of Eris, and how terrified my son must have been to find her gaining on him in the woods. I don't want to do her dirty work, so I slam the door and pace about my hotel room.

Pussy.

The voice sounds different now, deeper so that it makes me think it is a man's voice rather than one belonging to Eris.

You let her get away too. Never knew what to do with women, did you, you faggot-ass bitch?

"Don't call me that," I shout, as if my father is still staggering over to take a swipe at the back of my head. Sometimes he would miss, when he'd been drinking for too long that day, and this only made his rage intensify.

Faggot-ass bitch. Pussy. I can call you whatever I like.

It was what he would say to me when I'd come home with my face smashed in by the boys in my grade. I don't know why they always picked on me. Maybe they caught me looking at one of them in a way that I shouldn't have, or maybe it was because I'd cried the first time, when they'd pinned me to the ground and shoved dirt in my mouth. But I quickly learned, and each beating after that, I taught myself how to go numb, rolling with the rhythm of their fists as we were caught in some bloody dance. Sometimes that would annoy the kids even more, because I wasn't giving them the reaction they were looking for, but I guess they didn't know that I also had practice at home when my old man would lay into me.

Destroy or be destroyed.

That was the only advice he gave me, and he was so wasted when he told me he didn't stop to think that I might use it against him. You see, most nights he passed out drunk, which was a relief because then I could finally unwind. Sometimes it would come as early as half six or seven o'clock, and those were the most peaceful times of my childhood. I would just sit there, watching him take ragged, phlegm-filled gasps, and I longed for a silence to descend, when I could watch his lips lighten to ice blue.

It never came. Still, he woke, in an even worse mood than before, and still I counted down the hours until he would pass out again, and each day I shaped and reshaped in my mind the words he had shared with me: *Destroy or be destroyed.*

Finally, I jumped to my feet one night when he passed out, and I grabbed his shotgun from the safe he left unlocked. It was already fully loaded, and for a moment I considered shooting the boys in my grade, or even shooting myself. Once, the school counselor told me that if I got angry, I should write a letter to the person without sending it. She said it would help. I didn't know how, but she seemed to know what she was talking about. I kind of had a crush on her, that counselor, in a non-sexual way. I guess it was more a feeling of hope that she might rescue me from my dad, maybe even replace the mom who'd fucked off and chosen her own life over mine. But after the summer break, I returned to school to find out the counselor had moved on to another place, and because of budget cuts, they weren't going to replace her.

I did write the letter, though, but instead of writing one to the boys who tormented me, I wrote one to the person I hated the most, my father. I can't remember what I said in it, but I pinned it to his chest using thumb tacks from the pin board in the kitchen. He'd drunk so much that he didn't move a muscle when I pushed the pins in. He also didn't stir when I leveled the shotgun at him, and then pressed the barrel in between his lips. My rage intensified. I'd suffered so much, and he wasn't feeling a thing, so I shoved the barrel in harder and chipped his front tooth. That sure made him wake up, and I think he cut his lip on the broken tooth, because I saw the blood trickle from the corner of his mouth.

I pulled the trigger, but there was no deafening explosion, no splattering of brains and blood from behind my father's head. There was just the sound of a smooth click and a sigh from the two of us.

"The damn safety's on, you dipshit," he wheezed as he struggled to get off the sofa. He tried to chase me round the house, but he was still too drunk.

The following day, he must have thought about how close he came to having his brains blown out the back of his head, because he rarely touched me after that.

Destroy or be destroyed.

I can feel the scars burning through the skin of my thighs and it brings me back into the hotel room. The burning makes me crave for more of Jason or Joe, even though I've just chased him away.

Go after him, I hear from inside my skull. *Don't let him get away.*

I can taste blood. His, mine, who knows, but I lick it all the same and something stirs in me, making me want more. More blood, more fucking, all of it. This greed, this writhing urge beneath my skin. I can't be sure if it started after the fire or when I sent the diggers in, but it's definitely getting stronger.

You're pathetic.

This voice that speaks to me, through me. It isn't that witch Eris any more than it's my fuckup of a dad. It's something far more powerful, an ancient force that has existed for longer than my father or Eris or even her descendants who seized the land they used to build Dylan's family home.

I don't know how I know any of this, but I do know that it leaves me with a sickening loathing, telling me that it has waited for a long time for revenge.

Tear it all up, devour it.

I might've disrupted something when I sent in the diggers. I dunno, broke a seal or something, and set it free after it had laid dormant, trapped inside the soil by the concrete foundations of Dylan's home. Sounds credible, but I'd rather say that it had nothing to do with me, and it was Dylan's fault for playing a part in that fire that destroyed his home.

Either way, this force has followed me here to England. I remember feeling its strength grow as the plane climbed into the sky, drunk, perhaps, on all that combustible fuel.

To think that border control was more concerned about an old lady importing dried fruit. You can spend millions fortifying a *scepter'd isle,* but you can't do much to stop the spread of contaminants, the kind of biological warfare that people only find out about when it's too late. What was that horse Dylan would always go on about, the one that the soldiers used to sneak in and attack? *The Trojan horse*, that's right. Is that what I was? A carrier of some destructive force to rot and haunt this country from within.

You probably think of me as a terrorist, but I had no choice. Those images of Katherine that this ancient force wanted me to see. I couldn't bear it. They, it, whatever the fuck, showed me how they might bring Katherine to one of my warehouses if I didn't go after Dylan. They let me see how she might squirm in agony if they hanged her from a hook, and they promised to slice her from ear to ear so I could watch her face flap about as she struggled for freedom.

Quid pro quo.

I kept hearing this from the fortress site, and always late at night, but whenever I asked June about it, she would claim that she hadn't heard anything.

To distract myself from the voices, I would stroke the small of her back in the way she liked me to, and as I kissed her neck, I would snake my hand further down her body. For most of our marriage, this had led to something more, but recently she had been pushing my hand away.

The last night I tried it, and she rejected me, the night I later discovered Dylan had gone, I jumped from the bed and started to pace about the room. June would say that I had a sense that something was up with the kid, even before I knew Dylan had disappeared. Some kind of psychic ability, I guess, but I think that's bullshit. My restlessness was because of the smoldering fortress site. As I paced back and forth in my bedroom, I passed the window that looked out onto the ruins, and every time I saw the glowing rubble, the burning beneath my skin would intensify.

Rumors have started to circulate about the development. One of my funders has been calling to tear a strip off me for not giving him the heads up sooner. Unstable land, sightings of bodies, it isn't exactly what he signed up for. Of course, I was going to deny it all. Reputations are sliced and diced every moment up and down the East Coast, and I wasn't about to become the focus of the next smear campaign. As soon as someone makes a success of things, everyone circles, just waiting for them to fall, so I had plenty of jealous people who would be only too happy to take advantage of this shit show.

I went into damage-limitation, choosing instead to ruin the reputation of the foreman I'd hired. Even before the call, I'd been spreading the drug bullshit around, and I made sure I first called his girlfriend to break it to her.

"Fucking drugs," I'd told the funder on the phone the other night, using the same words I'd used with the foreman's girlfriend. "Could've killed someone." That's the kiss of death for a foreman in the construction industry. No one wants a jackhammer going through their gut because someone was too drugged up to prevent it from happening.

"He's been getting the stuff from the streets," I said as I tried to make myself sound as sad as possible. "And he even sold some to kids at the local high school," I added, because no one likes it more than to think of themselves as a guardian of the young.

"That low-life fuck," the funder hissed.

"I didn't want to blast his private life wide open until I'd found a way to handle it. But now things have gotten too much, it really has to stop. Trust me, it pained me to let him go, but I have a good team to replace his men, so, starting Wednesday morning, we're gonna turn this thing around and have that tower up in record time."

"Well, you better, because it isn't just reputations or finance on the line. You know?"

"Yeah, you fuck," I wanted to say to him. "I know what you're saying. I say the same shit to countless other goons, only I act on my promises. So let's just see who gets to the weapon first, and if I'm quicker, then I'll turn you into mulch and spread you around the landscaping of the fucking tower. Roses bloom beautifully out of bullshit artists like you."

Instead, because I need his funding, I replied, "Absolutely. Understood. You can trust that I'm gonna get this done."

Those fucking funders, they're always such tough talkers until they see me standing over them with a razor blade or dentist drill. Kinda funny, really, listening to them beg for their lives, and then telling me they don't wanna leave their kids without a parent. They always throw that in at the end, that family bullshit, as if they give a shit about their kids any other day of the week.

"You know," June said as she sat up in bed. "When I can't sleep, I like to write out all my worries on a piece of paper and drop it into a box on the far side of the house. In the morning, often the stuff that was written there doesn't even seem worth my worry anymore."

She always did this. She had little else to do, so she created a role for herself as the self-proclaimed expert on all of life's challenges. I heard her with the neighbors, throwing around affirmations like it was confetti. I used to hate bedtimes with her because she seemed to save up the cheesiest lines for then, when I had no escape.

"You have inner strength, Max," she would say, and I think she really believed that she was helping me.

"You know the way forward. It's sitting there, right in front of you," she would add, and I'd look down at the floor, pretending to search for it.

"No, you fool!" And she would burst out laughing like I was a fucking idiot. "Not literally in front of you."

"Well, where the fuck is it? Under the floorboards?" I was humoring her, but the routine was getting old, and I was starting to wonder what the blood and violence of an attempted divorce might look like. Katherine would never let me get away with that one.

"You'll feel it," she'd say with a smile as I stared at her once gleaming white teeth that had dulled to a sickly yellow. "Inside, it will hit you when you least expect it." She would point to her chest, and then take a deep breath in and let it go, letting spittle fly onto the sheets that covered her. She never noticed when she spat with her words.

Despite all the years of interactions that ran along a similar pattern, she never noticed that I was pretending not to get it, and until she finally found Dylan and I that time, she never noticed how I was fucking all those other guys, and she never noticed how I pretended to still find her hot. With those broad shoulders and thick eyebrows, how the fuck was I supposed to feel any kind of passion? No, she became my wife because of circumstance, not any Romeo and Juliet story; her father was well connected in Cape Cod, and I needed to make inroads in the real estate there; it was the last part of Massachusetts that I just couldn't crack. The trouble was, I never came from money and the landowners there could smell it on me, that desperation to fit in. Luckily, June's father had also come from shit, so he brought me into the sweater-on-shoulders brigade, and one by one, I made my mark. I gritted my teeth, played pickleball with them, and kept a list of the ones who had fucked me over. As soon as I got my hands on their land, I bundled them into a truck and took them on a journey to one of my warehouses on the outskirts of Newark.

I remember watching them sway as we listened to the planes landing at the nearby airport. How far away they must have felt from the safety of their country club where they hosted christenings and birthdays and anniversaries and they kissed their family members who were dressed in smart suits or pretty dresses, and they'd huddle together for group photographs as they smiled through their hatred for one another.

You might think of this as senseless violence, and of course it would come across that way if you've never seen what I have, if you've never heard how viciously they attack one-another, as crazed birds might peck each other over scraps in a cage. I've seen them sniggering at a nephew who has Down Syndrome and rolling their eyes and avoiding a niece who is autistic. And they can't help themselves with their comments about an overweight aunt, even though they spend each gathering vomiting the meal or washing down an Ozempic pill with another appletini.

Last year, one of their nephews shot himself because of their relentless sneering and name-calling when he wasn't yet out of earshot. "Here comes the faggot," he would hear them laugh, "better keep an eye on your sons around that little pedo."

I know you'll try to say that I'm a hypocrite because of all the violence I've been responsible for. But every person I took to my warehouses used their power to hurt vulnerable people. I never laid a finger on the vulnerable. So you could say that it was a form of social justice to dispose of those unsavory characters. I mean, who was going to miss a silver-haired banker from Chatham after he had spent years beating his Venezuelan cleaner so badly that her own mother didn't recognize her at the hospital? The banker shat himself when I hung him on the hook. I told him he disgusted me, and I made Sammy get him down so he could clean up his own mess. Sammy had already stripped him earlier, so I watched as the banker's little prick wobbled about while he wiped up the floor. I thought of the young girl this banker had been caught with, barely fifteen, her parents allowing the two of them to go to a ski resort together because they wanted her to pursue a career in banking. She never wanted to go, but her parents pushed her, reminding her to be nice to the man. Things got out of hand, and the banker wasn't very nice to her, forcing himself so hard that she had to go to hospital and she'll never be able to have kids.

Now do you see what I saw as I watched the banker's flaccid little cock jump around with every scrub of the warehouse floor? Do you see why the need for vengeance burned beneath my skin, so that laws or ethics or values were irrelevant, laughable even? There was a need to dispose of that banker, and wouldn't you have done the same? Wouldn't you have taunted him, saying that he could escape if he wanted to as you nodded towards the open warehouse door? He cried when I did that. He actually bawled his eyes out and thanked me when he saw that freedom was just a matter of feet away. He struggled to his feet, hands dusty and smeared with his own feces, and staggered towards the open door. I waited until his face lit up with the daylight before I slammed it shut on his outstretched hand. I must have caught a finger or two because he shrieked like an animal, collapsing onto the ground as blood trickled from his clenched fist.

I slid the bolts across, sealing him in with us, and turned to face him. Would you believe that he looked indignant? In moments of shock, we all forget where we are, resorting to the only way we know, the very first mold that was set for us at a young age. For the Chatham banker, he became once again the spoiled, indulged and indignant brat.

"How dare you," he screamed, like I was a busboy who'd spilled water on the tablecloth. "That isn't fair!" he screamed. That entitled little shit actually said this. *Fair*.

"*Fair*? You talk about fair?" My voice took on a monstrous roar that even made Sammy wince, and he'd heard and seen a lot from me.

"Was it fair what you did to that child?" I swipe a backhand at him, forgetting I had a spare hook in my hand, so I'm surprised by the chunk of flesh that flies from his shoulder. He twitched on the ground and I stood over him, smelling his shit on me, and this only intensifies my rage.

"Is it fair how you tore her open?" I bellowed, taking another swipe at him. This time, the hook lodged in his skull and his left eye shot to one side. His eyes slipped out of line with each other, so he looked like a joke in a cartoon or a mistake.

With another swipe, one eyeball exploded, and I thought of the undercooked eggs that June once served to me when we were first dating. When I tried to show her how to do it right, she took offence and refused to cook anything else for me.

I don't know if I can admit to many people what I next did to the banker from Chatham. Sometimes this violence horrifies me, but then I remember the girl who will never be the same again after he seized whatever he wanted.

Just because he could.

We all have a hunger for vengeance, that thing called justice, and as soon as you admit that to yourself, the floodgates are open, and then, who can say who is the abuser and who is the abused? We all tend to our cravings; no one can pretend that they don't. We are greedy for vengeance, for food, for fucking; it all writhes beneath our skin. But for us to see justice prevail, someone has to suffer. For you to eat, someone must starve, to fuck someone gets fucked, right, and our resulting waste from it all has to pollute someone or somewhere.

I still smell the banker's blood on my hands. Of course I do. Even here in this London hotel room, I smell them all, those people I took to the warehouses and who never made it home to their families. And I still feel their breath beating on my face in that final moment of intimacy, so I shower to try to get rid of them.

The water comes out in a pitiful dribble; the typical half-hearted effort of this limp-dicked country. From the shower, I can see the streets surrounding the hotel. Despite my involvement with plenty of developments, I'm always surprised to find the glass and steel of high-rises, especially here in a place that wants you to believe that there are only cute little thatched cottages and country lanes. Kind of like the guys here who indulge you in unnecessary apologies and polite requests. *For King and country,* or something like that. They kept that same damned civil tone even when they were losing thousands on their developments, and all because some spotty pipsqueak of a lawyer forgot to get an over-sail license. Either that, or we were told we couldn't build there because of a conservation area or a listed building, or some dimwit at the local council went on another fucking lunch break and yet again refused to consider our planning application. They were drowning in regulations and codes and policy guidance and case law and statute, not to mention the restrictions imposed by the unions and the general cultural expectation that in the morning no one worked before half nine or beyond the hour's lunch break, and in the afternoon, no one worked beyond five minutes to four. I tried to pay off as many people as I could, but I always found out there was another layer of authority over the person I just paid, and then the ultimate authority was the fucking Royals. No matter how many Teslas or hot tubs the Brits buy themselves, they'll always remain peasants who live off the scraps that are thrown by this family of inbreds.

Dylan and Katherine always talked about privilege. I would hear them in the kitchen together, raging about the *haves* when there are so many *have-nots*. They acknowledged their own privilege, expressed shame over it, and they wanted others to feel that shame too. I don't feel anything remotely like shame, but I wish Katherine could know that I understand, and I wish that she could see that I was once a warrior, too. Wasn't that how the warehouses came about, when I first loaded them up with members of the sweater-on-shoulders brigade, to fight some kind of social injustice? I wish I could tell Katherine this, so she could see that we have more in common than she might believe. I want to become that old war veteran who shows his medals and pictures of when he was once hot, as if he is trying to show that he was once a human being too.

Of course, I could never tell Katherine any of this, so when she rages about the super-yachts that are bought by the supermarket billionaires, I just sit in silence. That's what happens when you don't talk to anyone, at least when you don't talk about the things that matter to you. I've seen it in old people who have no one left from the life they once knew; they give up and wait for death, slowly disappearing into their shell as they numb themselves out. And then they drift so far from themselves that nothing matters any more.

How pitiful their attempts were to try to break free; those members of the sweater-on-shoulders brigade. They barely even fought back. Each time I would start the procedure, laying out the implements like an over-paid surgeon, Sammy would lift each one down and stand back, just watching as I began the torture. The door was always open at first, so we could listen to the aggressive rush of traffic in the distance, and still they wouldn't try to make a bid for freedom.

Even when the first blade went it and they would vomit or piss themselves, they still didn't run. That's the trouble with the ones who were brought up as ultra-rich; they never had to develop any kind of survival skills. Even until the end, they probably thought someone was going to rescue them.

See how Katherine cries.

I flinch, clench my fist, and slam it into the tiled shower wall. It's cheap, flimsy shit, so the hole is bigger than I expected.

If you bring Dylan. back to Rotherwell, we won't hurt her.

"Don't fuck with me," I shout to nothing, or that ancient force, or...

I'm everything and everywhere. I'm with Katherine now and I see her in that warehouse. You hung her from a hook just like the others. You pierced the flabby flesh on her back, the parts she hates and makes her want to get up early and play tennis to burn it off, but she's too lazy, too indulged because you never wanted her to struggle the way you did.

"Fuck you."

Oh, come on, that isn't very nice. We can be civil, can't we? We can be polite and mannerly as we watch Katherine smiling, without any survival skills of her own, so open-hearted that you can actually see her beating heart beneath the ribcage you cracked apart, after you split open the skin of her chest. Your very own daughter. That must've taken strength to do it with your own hands and nails. How big and strong you are, finally showing your old man that you aren't afraid, that you don't still flinch when someone lifts their hand to wipe sweat from their face, humiliating yourself in front of your own workmen because it is baked in from such an early age. What is it, imprinting? Like a waddling duckling, searching for a mother who hated you so much, she had to leave you behind to be beaten with a belt, your buttocks ripped raw by a father who didn't care if his own neighbor was fucking you til you went numb.

"Why don't you sleep in the spare room" June had suggested that night in Rotherwell, clearly irritated that my pacing about the bedroom was keeping her up.

"Sure," I replied, knowing that the spare room was next to Dylan's, and she was practically giving me permission to go and fuck him.

As I crept across the hallway, I felt the urge, that writhing beneath my skin, and I couldn't resist. I knew it was risky with June there because she'd made me promise not to do anything with him when she was in the house. But we could always lock the bedroom door from the inside and keep the noise down. He, they, liked it when I would tie a gag around their mouth.

I pushed the door open, whispering, "Are you awake?" before I noticed that the bed was empty. The first thought was that they were out fucking around with someone else. I felt like a jilted teenager, slamming on the light to take a better look at the empty bedroom. And then I realized their closet was open and none of their clothes were there.

"You little fuck," I hissed.

With every moment of Dylan's absence, the ancient force from the fortress site grew stronger. The siren song of *Quid pro quo* warped into a screech, a piercing wail that promised violence and vengeance. And the first target was to be my daughter.

Time is running out, old man. Dylan will take everything from you. Quid pro quo.

I try to ignore the voice by focusing on my body. It feels good to massage the soap, even if the water is weak. I notice light bouncing off the shiny white scar tissue that is scattered across my thighs, and at first I think it's moonlight, but I realize it's just the bright floodlights of a rooftop party on a nearby building. There are some cute-looking guys dancing at the party, and I rub myself under the shower water as I watch them dance. From this distance, I can believe that one of them is Dylan, simply because he is tall and dark-haired and slim.

He wants to take everything from you. You're getting too old to keep up, aren't you, Max? Bring Dylan back.

My hand pumps faster as the tension builds inside of me.

Destroy or be destroyed.

As I reach climax, I imagine the men dancing their way closer to the edge of the rooftop building. Their bodies still gyrate in time as they topple over the edge, and they are sliced in two as they crash through the glass roof of the entrance lobby below.

Still, I am not there, so I push myself to picture Dylan's face on each of them; the version of Dylan before the fire on one of them and the version of Dylan after the fire on the other victim. Then I can finally climax, my whole body rocking with waves of it beneath the shower water as I imagine his eyes closing for one last time as my eyes close in unison.

That night, I sleep with the lights on but still I'm found by things that belong in the darkness. They wear hoods so I can't see their faces, but they still terrify me with their slow, deliberate movements. Usually they just stand before me, swaying in unison, but something has made them restless.

They have dirty, bare feet that climb across my headboard as they make their way to my head. I can't move, just as they like it, and as one of them strokes my hair, another uses their sticky fingers to peel my eyelids back.

Bad things happen to bad people.

They all stink of rotting flesh and apples and bark, and they urge me to watch as they show me more of the horrors they can inflict on my daughter. I want to ask them if they were the ones who took my mother, that this could make things better if I knew she never intended to stay away for so long, that they were holding her against their will. But I can't find the words to ask them. Maybe they snipped my tongue with a razor blade and stitched my lips together for a quieter night.

They remind me that there is work to be done, and I shouldn't get distracted. They've been watching me with the guy from the bar, and in the shower, and they shake their heads with disappointment. They let me know, somehow, without making any sound, that I am wasting time and energy.

They point towards my phone, and I know what I need to do.

"Time's up, Dylan, I'm in London," I say in a message. "If you keep jerking me around, I'm gonna cut your fucking head off. Tell me where you are."

I also call him, but the little shit doesn't answer, as I expected.

The hooded creatures nod and they leave me in peace for now, but they promise with their silence that they will be back before long.

Eat or get eaten.

Chapter Six

~~~

Dylan

~~~

Phones have always been a portal to violence. When I was in school, there was a kid who would constantly call and threaten to kill me as soon as I left my house. He'd put on this sickly sweet act at first, asking how I was doing, and saying that I was cool and kind of funny. But then a switch would flip in him, and he'd say "No, seriously, Dylan, you're a fucking douchebag, a loser, a fucking faggot, and as soon as you leave your house, morning, noon, or night, I'm gonna cut your balls off and stuff them in your mouth. Pussy ass faggot. I see how you stare at the other boys in the shower, your tiny dick getting hard at the thought of it."

His name was…

You know what's fucked? I can't even remember. He terrorized me for so many years, made me scared to answer the phone, and now he's just some nameless person who I can't even Google to make sure that he's living more of a miserable life than I am.

I remember his face, though. Those pimples all crusted and bloody to show that he couldn't stop picking at them, revealing a restlessness that probably kept him up at night, when he would catch a hint of something else on the TV or online, where kids were smiling or some kind of shit, and then he'd feel sad. You know what that sadness could've done? Made him try to be a better person and stop picking on people as much as he was picking his spots, but he just couldn't do it. And you just know that wasn't the only urge that was driving him insane, twisting him inside, because when he was terrorizing me, he was projecting. When he told me that I was watching boys in the shower, it was really him. All the queer-bashing bullies do that, no matter how much they try to deny it and beat the unsettling thoughts out of someone else.

For all I know, this kid, now twenty-two like me, could be dead by now. But if he is alive, I want him to be miserable in some dead-end job where every day seems the same, and customers are bitches to him, and he snaps back at one, so his job is on the line, and he has no one to vent to about all this, because he's pushed everyone away and they're tired of his bullshit. This doesn't seem like punishment enough, though. This feels petty, especially when I know that I survived his torment, but other kids haven't. Others have been pushed to overdosing or cutting themselves or binge eating or skipping school, so they fuck their life up, and all because of people like him.

These are the moments I long for the hooded creatures to reappear. Or I think of that arachnid at the fortress site, and how it should crawl all over the nightmares and waking fears of the ones who torment people and call them faggot or fat or stupid or ugly. I want those tormentors to watch eight legs scuttle about their ceiling and walls, taking time to bring terror to their minds just long enough for them to wet themselves and say sorry for all the damage they inflicted. But even that doesn't seem enough, because what good is fear if it doesn't threaten real consequences, so I admit it, I do want them to be dragged by that arachnid out of their beds and from their tiny bedrooms, and all the way to the smoldering rubble on Mount Pelion Way. There, I want to see them kicking and thrashing about, and begging not to be dragged into the ruins, and beneath the surface, where the underworld awaits them to dole out their eternal justice.

I'm sure you are disappointed in me. You might have hoped that I would never wish for that arachnid to return, because you and I know whose head sits within the heart of those eight spindly legs. That head with the face still distorted in pain but mixed in there, if you look carefully enough, you will see his hope that he can somehow convince me to join him, become one with him, because he wants me to believe that we are the same. And of course, I would recognize that glimmer of hope when others wouldn't, because I am related to him, his blood, and only close family members can recognize these subtle changes, only kin would notice when he mouths the words to me, "We are the same." It's unavoidable, really, when we share some of the same genetics. If only I could filter my blood so the impurities were left in a sieve, that blackened tar that I taste in me, reminding me of the story so commonly told: That we are born without knowledge that we are in fact separate from our parents, and so, for a while, we just co-exist, content with an illusion of symbiosis. But then something happens, and another thing, and there are ruptures and fragmentations, and we can struggle free, or for some they might be cast aside, but either way, we have space to breathe and distance to see that there are differences, a whole body that is separate from us. But as we age and wither, we return, as they say *dust to dust*, and we see similarities, we even yearn for them, because we've tried so many other ways, and they all just did not fit. So, what to say about this? Am I destined to take the form of an arachnid and scuttle about your nightmares, forcing you to see horrors as I pierce you with my poison?

After I saw the threat from Max, I allowed myself to check all the other messages that I'd been ignoring. I didn't just read the calm and carefully worded ones from Max, but I even scrolled through the deranged ones from an unknown number.

"Pussy ass faggot," the first message began. I recognized the wording from that nameless kid from high school, but it seemed a stretch that he would choose now, after all this time, to get in contact.

"You want to be cut?" another message said, again from an unknown number. "I'm watching you," it continued, "you're gonna look so good with your skin turned inside out. I know where you live. I've seen you walking home at night after fucking guys and getting fucked. I'm sure you love that, don't you, the way they stick it in? Is there shit when they pull it out? Do you like the smell of shit? Do you smear it all over your pale, scrawny body, using it as lubricant so you can get fucked again, and so you can fuck, and spread your diseases all over this country, and further, across the world, because that's what you're doing isn't it, you dirty faggot, you're a one-man pandemic, ending up responsible for killing all those innocent people because you refuse to wear a condom. I've seen you and your kind, all slithering down to the STD clinic behind Tottenham Court Road, in the backstreets where the rats and ants crawl, where the garbage bags are dumped with all the filth that spills out and makes a mess of everywhere, filth and scum like you, Dylan. That's right, I know your name and I know everything about you, you whore, you batty boy, you shit stabbing faggot. I'm sure you have to go to that clinic on a daily basis to get scraped and swabbed, and even when it's positive, proving you to be the disease-ridden whore that you are, still you go straight to the next gay bar and shove your unprotected dick into the next waiting hole, because you are scum and filth and deserve to die. They should flush you away with the rest of the filth and waste of this world. I would happily watch as you were sucked down that tube, for once the sucking not giving you any kind of pleasure but instead the most intense and exquisite pain. I would pay to have front row seats at that spectacle, as you suffer for days amongst the filth and the excrement, and the rats start to feed on you, gnawing your flesh down to the bone."

I don't know why I kept reading these messages. Maybe I believed that the person who was sending them was right, and

I deserved to be flushed down the tube like the rest of this planet's waste. Or maybe I was hoping to scroll through and find a punchline, a *"Gotcha! I was just kidding!"* explanation, so I could feel safer each time I left the university halls.

"And if they can't flush you down that toilet," one of the messages continued, "because your ego is so big, and you'd block up the delicate intricacies of the Victorian plumbing system, then the least they should do is lock you up. That's what you deserve, isn't it? They should lock you in a prison cell while they re-introduce the death penalty, and then put you on death row, and tell everyone what you did, as you spread your disease around London, and then everyone will write to their MP and demand that you are put at the head of the queue, so you can be hanged by your neck at dawn, the very next dawn, so everyone can watch as it's live streamed on *This Morning* so families can gather and they can reassure themselves that they are not like you, that they are good and pure people because they want to see your neck break as you piss and shit yourself."

They used to execute queer people in this country. No one talks about it anymore; it isn't really a relevant thing to most. I mean, it's in the past, isn't it? No need to look in there, deep inside the closet of dusty old history where they quote scriptures at the queers and throw stones at them and declare that anyone who looked like a queer should be hanged or stoned.

I can imagine how the executions might eventually creep back in, and how much people would demand that it was televised. After the execution, I wonder if everyone would feel better about everything that's going on in the world because they'd know who to hate, they'd have an object for the rage they feel about their own dissatisfying life, but they won't talk about that dissatisfaction, they won't complain about the people who are getting rich while they work harder and the food portions get smaller and they are told that they need to tighten their bootstraps and keep a *stiff upper lip* about such austerity measures because we are *all in it together* (except the ones they execute, they don't count). I can imagine how people would be told to stop complaining about the hunger pangs in their stomach and instead mark their calendars for the next execution, so they can feel safe and soothed by the knowledge that they are being looked after and they can suckle at the teat of this great nanny state and fall into a deep sleep of blissful ignorance, knowing that someone somewhere is watching over them and keeping their streets clean.

I've started to hear conversations on the tube where they spout shit like *Hate the sin, love the sinner*. Pastor Pry used to say this, and she is probably doing it right now, reminding her congregation at every service who they should hate for the week. She reminds people who they should keep an eye on and who to steer well clear of because you don't want to encourage any sort of sinful behavior by giving them the benefit of the doubt, your business, or support. As Pastor Pry shakes her collection tin, I imagine she feels reassured that she is guiding her flock in the right direction, and those flocks need a bit of guidance because life is so busy, so no one really has the time to stop and think for themselves, I mean, not really, not to examine anything in great detail.

Katherine was the one to infiltrate the services for a while, before she got more active with her protests and the pastor barred her from the church. She'd report back to me with a wide-eyed "You'll never believe what the old bitch preached this time" as we'd share some ice-cream in front of a movie.

She's been messaging me, too. At first, Katherine sounded concerned as she told me that she was missing me and she understood that I might need time away after everything I had been through with the fire. But recently she has started to sound angry, saying that I could at least let her know that I am okay.

"Did you have to leave me with these crazies?" she said in her last message, referring to the parents she would always complain about. "I don't know why they don't just get a divorce," she added, letting me know they had been embroiled in another blow-up. "But then, what do you care? I guess you're making a new life without me, and that sucks, Dyls."

Sometimes I wake from a night terror where I see my father

escaping the rubble and slipping into Katherine's house next door. I'm frozen in this dream, so all I can do is watch as that arachnid scuttles up the walls of the stairwell, creeping into Katherine's room to seize her in her sleep. She always hated spiders.

After I'd finished checking the messages, I make the mistake of listening to the voicemails. Most of them are from that cop from the park, Robert, and he's asking why I haven't called him back. He suggests that we meet up again, for dinner, coffee, another fuck in the park, anything, anywhere, if I can just call him back.

His follow-up voicemails sound more and more irate, declaring in one that he "doesn't appreciate being treated like shit," and he isn't "someone who deserves to be ignored."

"I'm a nice guy," he adds in his last voicemail, "and patient, but this is starting to annoy me. Who do you think you are, coming over here and treating people this way? Really very rude. You could just send a quick text if you haven't time to call me. Do you think I'm boring? Did we not have fun together that time in the park, and then at your place? You could come to my place this time, and I could make a meal for you. I cook really well. Mum always says I make a good Sunday roast. I can show you how to do it, and maybe you can take the recipe back to America. We could go visit New Jersey together one day. I've always wanted to go. Why won't you call? You could even just text a quick '*Hey*' back. I don't know why this keeps happening, why everyone gets tired of me so quickly. I try, I really try, and I can keep trying if you give me another chance."

In my mind he shrinks and shrivels, becoming a little troll that hides under the covers as he crafts each sentiment, his face lit up by the light on the cell phone to highlight the joy he gets from harassing me.

I keep every one of his voicemails and the anonymous messages, but I'm not really sure why. Evidence, perhaps, of a crime of passion and violence that is yet to be inflicted on me? But who's going to gather that evidence? Who's going to record it all in a log somewhere with dates and times so it's ready for the prosecution? Maybe Robert's mates down the nick, the ones who make transphobic and racist jokes, and eat too much while they sit behind computer screens because they're too scared to walk the streets of London with a rubber dildo instead of a gun. But they won't give a shit about these messages, they'll just laugh at them and take the piss out of Robert for a while, but they're not gonna arrest him, let alone send him to court, because he's one of them, and they can turn a blind eye to whatever he wants to do with his dick, as long as he doesn't try it on with them, you know, not even at the Christmas function, when they're really drunk. Although they have wanked each other when they shared some lines of coke once, when there was a dry spell with the girls. But that doesn't count. None of it counts really, not when you've disposed of the log of messages and voicemails, even after the recipient was found floating in the Thames with a plastic bag shoved down their throat and their innards trailing like pond weed. You have a job to do. I mean, there are deviants to lock up, perverts who fuck in parks and throw their dirty condoms on the ground so the kids find them the next day when they retrieve their ball from the bushes. And there are the dudes with dicks that wear dresses and try to force their way into women's bathrooms, probably to fuck the women because the dress is an act, a cover for what they really want to do, because that's what men are built for, to fuck women, and we have proof of that because of the very first man and woman to fuck, who was Adam and Eve.

For those police officers, life is very simple, and they really don't know why others have to make things so complicated and fuck things up with gender bending and the whole rainbow of sexuality. Robert also likes to keep life simple, where sex is vanilla, and people say "Please" and "Thank you." Most of all, he wants a life where people reply to messages and voicemails.

I throw the cell phone into the corner of the room. I want to smash it. I want everyone to lose contact with me so I can never be found again. I could run from this room and from this city, not returning to Rotherwell, but going far away from any place where anyone knows me. I want to race head-first into an oblivion where I don't have to think or feel. I don't know if this is being passively suicidal or actively suicidal, but, either way, it's dangerous.

I notice the cell phone knocked the snow globe from one of the points to the pentacle. I don't know what this means. Am I now exposed to the dangers that are closing in? The siren still calls me back to the fortress site but what if this was never Eris or Ania, and it was a trap set for me by my arachnid father who has been trying to lure me back so I can serve as his portal from the underworld? I can't go back there, but Max has almost caught up with me.

Last night, I heard the jawbone rattling beneath my bed. Eris might have been trying to tell me something, and as I tried to decipher the message, the wind picked up and the panda pendants of my sister's bracelet started to stir. I imagined the jawbone and bracelet, and my sister's hair from inside the locket, all combining into one, a sort of chimera or at least the beginnings of one. If these parts had fused, would the result become a source of comfort and guidance or a threat of violence to be unleashed?

Right now, the wind is whistling between the gaps in my window, and I try to listen for clues, but the dead only whisper in riddles, and there's still my own voice to contaminate any potential message. All of this is just a story that depends on the bias of the narrator, and maybe that's why I wanted Katherine's picture to form part of the sigil; it recreated parts of the story as something pure, convincing me that I could be a force for good and not just someone who is dirty and twisted and has maggots for genes.

I crouch onto the ground to reach for the picture of Katherine, but then I hear the voice.

Still fucked her father, though.

I jump up from the floor, and I think I see something in my reflection. It stares back at me from the window, and it has the same dark hair as my father's.

I run out of my small room, leaving behind my cell phone that is still somewhere on the floor, and I race down the corridor in search of anywhere but that room of memories.

Some of the students have their doors propped open, and kids go back and forth between the rooms. I see Viqaas walking down the corridor towards me, laughing with a girl who is towering over him. With so much length to her, she doesn't seem to know what to do with her arms and legs. I wonder if that's why she wears such bright, garish lipstick, to distract from her disproportionate body.

"Dyls, my man," he calls. "Join us."

Ever since I met him, not even a whole week ago, he's been trailing me with endless invitations to hang out. And each time he tries to convince me with that charming smile.

"In a minute we're gonna hang out in Ruby's room," Viqaas continues, "and laugh at the diabolical brilliance that is Eastenders."

"You could've just asked him if he wanted to watch a soap opera. They might not have Eastenders in America," the girl says to him. "Care to join?" she says as she turns to me.

"I can't," I say instinctively, too quickly to think of an excuse.

"Ah, no problem," she says in reply, and then walks on to what I assume to be her room. I hoped that Viqaas would follow her, but he instead he falls into step with me as I make my way out of the halls.

"That was Ruby, by the way," he finally says as we step into the evening drizzle. "She's the one who's having a birthday party this Friday. Remember?"

"Sure," I lie.

"So, you coming?"

I shake my head in reply.

"Really?" he says with a sigh. "You have other plans…tonight *and* Friday?"

"Something like that," I reply, hoping he'll give up and return to Ruby.

"Well," he continues as he sniffs the air around me, "you smell good, whatever you got planned tonight. What is it, Calvin Klein?"

"Oh, the cologne? Sure, I think so. Listen, I should go."

I wish I could tell him straight out that he should keep away from me, that he will be left with something toxic and sticky on his fingers if he gets much closer, that I will burn and scar him and make him wish he had never met me. I wish I could tell him this, so he doesn't look so sad right now, as he struggles to come up with some other way to win me over. He doesn't seem like the kind of guy who is used to people stonewalling him like this.

"But when you're back,' he continues, "swing by my room if you want. I promise, we can watch anything you like. I'm still stealing my sister's Netflix login details."

I keep walking down the steps and away from him, this time choosing not to offer anything in reply. With every step, though, I can't stop thinking about his soft eyes and long eyelashes, and that time, a couple of days ago, when he took off his sweater and got his t-shirt caught up in it, revealing the rippling abs.

I try to keep any more thoughts of Viqaas out of my mind by visualizing the dick picks I'd received earlier on today from *Versatile, Can Host*. This guy I'd selected on the hookup app had insisted that we exchange dick pics after he had asked me in a message "What is this *they/them* bullshit in your profile, because I'm not into any of that tranny shit, so you still have a dick, don't you?"

Usually, I would just stop responding and block the dude, but earlier on he'd mentioned that he had "a very high-profile career in Westminster," and the thing beneath my skin, the greed, seemed to stir at this and urged me to respond to every one of his ridiculous questions: *How often do you douche? How often do you get tested? Are you cut? How often do you shower? For how long do you scrub your hands? Do you clean under your nails? Do you moisturize? Do you use hand sanitizer? What do you place on toilet seats if you have to sit down? How do you handle the risk of splash back when you stand up? Are you shaved down there? Will you, if I ask you to?*

Finally, he told me where to meet him, and he explained that it was an Indian restaurant in Westminster.

"*Indian?*" I replied. I'd been starving myself all day so I could let someone top me. Yet he wanted to eat curry, for fuck's sake.

"It's a great place. You'll love it," he insisted.

I agreed to it, even though I couldn't understand why he would meet me in a public place if he had such a "high-profile career in Westminster." He was also married with kids. I knew he wasn't going to invite me to his family home to meet the kids and play with his dog, but I assumed there would be some second home or even a hotel room to go to. Maybe this was part of the foreplay, to keep things dangerous, and the repressed part of him wanted to be caught and spanked as he'd probably endured in some boarding school. I really hoped this wasn't going to be part of the role play.

After a long tube ride, and a wet walk in the rain, I find the restaurant. He's waiting for me at the top of some elegant stone steps, and I'm disappointed to find that he's shorter and chubbier than I expected. He has grey and dark streaks in his hair that remind me of a racoon, and his lips are tight like the ass of one.

When I join him at the top of the steps, I see tufts of hair sprouting from each ear, and as he smooths an eyebrow with one hand, I try to imagine what he does late at night with those fat and stubby fingers of his. A confusing mixture of repulsion and intrigue stirs within me as a series of images form a dark web porn movie in the attic of my mind.

"Was that Westminster Abbey I just passed?" I gasp as I finally reach him. "The place I've seen on TV, where they have weddings and funerals for royals? It looks amazing." I realize I might be talking too much, and I don't know why.

He doesn't answer me but instead, as he leans to my ear, cigar-smoke and whiskey peppering his breath, he whispers, "Remember not to embarrass me. Westminster is my patch, so be on your best behavior."

He walks me inside and I see the remnants of its former life as a library. Behind the rows of blue leather benches, there are books stacked on shelves that reach to the ceiling. I long to choose a couple of them and curl up in the corner, soothed by the low murmur of polite conversation as I let the books transport me to another world of someone else's concern. I can't remember the last time I did this; it was surely before the fire because since then this thing beneath my skin hasn't let me rest.

"You're a little less muscular than your photo," he sighs. His eyebrows are bushy, and he is so pale that I see the bones of his cheeks pressing through the paper-thin skin. He could be on blood-thinning medication, and I think of how hard it might be for him to climax, and how much he would bleed if I bit off his penis at just the right moment of pleasure.

"And you're hairier than your photo," I reply. "But here we are, so let's try to make the best of what we have."

The whites of his eyes look discolored with something, but in the dim light of the restaurant, I can't tell if it's a sign of jaundice or some other sickness.

"*Quite*," he sighs, and we both stare at the menu.

He orders for me without asking what I would like. Of course he does. He then proceeds to tell me his life history, including his childhood blighted by a boarding school he loathed, while he also insists that it was "character building, nonetheless." Every Brit I've spoken to seems to do this about their adversities. It's probably a hangover, something left in their genetic makeup by forefathers who had no escape from the air raid sirens, and as they heard and saw the bombs screeching through the air, they just had to slip into a parallel world where it wasn't really going to blow them apart, it wasn't even going to hurt. "Just a scratch," their ghosts might have said as they searched the rubble for their missing limbs. "I'm sure we can tidy this up in no time" they might *pip-pip-pip* with cheery British stoicism as they found bits of their children splattered all over the rubble.

The food arrives and my eyes glisten at the sight of the juicy cuts of lamb with potatoes and broccoli drenched in an unidentifiable sauce. Any thoughts of bottoming tonight are drifting away with a hunger that hurts me. The aromas play with my senses, taking me by the hand to times I'd rather forget, in the cafeteria at school, when I would stare at the food so I didn't have to see the faces that laughed or sneered at me because I was sitting alone. Food then became a comfort, a softness that I couldn't find anywhere else, and I became obsessed about when I could next devour something warm that would feel so good for too brief a moment. Those nerve-endings that were stimulated when the food slipped through me; it didn't just guard me against the loneliness; it reminded me that I was alive. It turned against me, though. I didn't notice until the sneering at school transformed from "Weirdo" and "Freak Show" to "Fatso" and "Fatty Faggot." So I took hold of the situation, and instead of beating the fuck out of my tormenters, I turned on myself, forcing my fingers so far down my throat that I tasted blood as I retched.

After the fire, Max told me he did the same, which I found hard to believe.

"You're serious? I mean, you did the same in terms of… I mean, which bit?" I asked him.

"All of it," he replied. "You and I are not that different. You're not the only one to sit alone at school, eating your feelings and shit. And yeah, I made myself vom. Grosses me out to even say it now. But then I got into the gym."

I guess fitness replaced food as his next addiction. I mean, he never missed a 5am workout. He took me once, and it nearly killed me when I was so sleepy that I almost decapitated myself with the weights of a bench press.

"You're just lazy," he told me when I refused to join him the next time. "But that's what separates the winners and losers in life," he said, his face plastered with self-satisfied smugness.

It's the same smugness that is plastered all over this British dude's face right now. He keeps telling me about his life with barely a pause to check whether I'm listening, whether I'm still conscious, and I wonder if he would notice if I just slipped away.

The light is bouncing off the polished wood and it's making me squint, and I think he interprets this as failing to understand him, so he repeats himself, adding unnecessary back-stories as I take more and more mouthfuls of the vinegary wine.

"Look," I finally declare as I hold up one finger. I notice my hand drift to one side, so I must have drunk more than I intended. 'If we're gonna do this, let's get on with it."

"Do what?" he asks, which makes me snigger a little.

"Oh, come on. Let's get out of here and get on with it. I have things to do, plenty of other people to fuck, and it feels like I'm stagnating in here."

His face distorts a little, folding creases where they hadn't been, and making his eyes widen and then shrink into his face. He's making me wonder if he is fizzling with embarrassment, confused, or he's just amused and getting a little turned on by someone finally pushing back at him. Maybe all three.

"Fine," he replies as he gestures to the waiter for the check.

Outside, he guides me by the elbow down the backstreets, past smart-looking old buildings without any of the soot-stains on the brick and stone. The thing beneath my skin stirs when we pass the Houses of Parliament, the Cabinet Office, and the Ministry of Defense. I think of how much greed burns through the people who use these buildings to plan invasions so they can pillage and amass wealth. They dress it up with so much pomp and ceremony, giving the greed official titles and ranks with departments that get funding, and they dress the foot soldiers in uniforms and ask them to salute their leaders. But all of this is no better nor worse than the Galls all those years ago, seizing land that would amass the wealth that I have now inherited. My inescapable legacy that could, if I'm not careful, lead me to hurt so many others.

Eventually we come to a row of houses, and *Versatile, Can Host* walks me up the steps of one of them and unlocks the door. There is a brass knocker in the shape of a lion, and I find it quaint that the British think that this might guard against the dangers that can invade a home and tear apart its inhabitants.

He doesn't hold the door open for me, so I catch it before it slams in my face, and I walk into the hallway. My footsteps echo on the black-and-white tiles, and as he leads me up the winding staircase, I see cobwebs threaded from one light fixture to the next. I'm suddenly afraid of what might be scuttling about the hallway outside the bedrooms, so I mutter something about spiders, and this thing beneath my skin, but he misinterprets it as something sexual, and too quickly he is clawing at the buckle on my jeans. He is rough, as he rips my clothes off and slams me onto the bed, but this feels familiar, so I just drift away for a while, vaguely aware of what he might be doing to me. It's lonely in this liminal state where no one can find me, and I wonder if eventually I won't find my way back from it, and someone will have to call an ambulance or dispose of my body.

He cried when he came. In the heat of the moment, he looked like a suckling pig, red-cheeked and chubby and squealing with fear.

"So, what do I call you?" I ask him.

"I did tell you," he sighs as he lights a cigar. "You just didn't listen. It's *Charles*. You're going to do a lot better in life if you remember that you have one mouth and two ears."

I don't want to be schooled, but I don't have the energy to fight back.

The rain starts to hammer so hard that it rattles the sash windows.

"I should go," I say.

"In this?"

"I mean, if I waited for the rain to stop in this country, I'd be waiting forever."

"Suit yourself. It's been getting worse. This city won't cope with much more. The Thames Barrier isn't fit for purpose, so the city will be under water before long. Hope you know how to swim."

"You say it as if it's an inevitability. Aren't you a politician? I mean, shouldn't you devise solutions for this kind of thing?"

"Solutions? Are you simple? What kind of solutions do you think there are? Do you think we should put the city on stilts? Or maybe just take out the plug on this giant bath."

I hate the way he patronizes me, but it finally gives me the motivation to jump out of bed. I search the floor for my clothes, and as I reach under the bed for my underwear, I brace myself for what might scuttle out from the darkness.

"The biggest companies have already made plans to relocate," he continues as he puffs smoke circles above his sweaty, fat head. "They've moved to places on higher ground. Some even left the UK entirely. Bye bye British economy."

"I haven't heard any announcements about flooding or companies leaving."

"Oh, come on, we don't want mass panic. What's the point in telling them anything? The ones who can afford to move probably already know, through the back channels. If you have the right conversation with the right person, you'll get the right information at the right time. But, of course, you have to be the right kind of person to be privy to that information."

"And the ones who can't afford to move?"

He shrugs and takes another puff of his cigar, the blue haze drifting over to make me cough as he starts to laugh.

"Look at your wide-eyed innocence. This isn't some government conspiracy, you know. Things always turn out this way. If you look hard enough, you'll probably find something in small print online about the Thames Barrier and how it won't prevent flooding in London, and *blah, blah, blahdy bloody blah*. And everyone has just got used to the increased rainfall. That isn't exactly a noteworthy headline. People barely notice, even when they announce that someone was drowned in their basement flat. Everyone is too busy to really care. And besides, what can they do? The Thames Barrier was always a gimmick to shut the people up, and it made certain people very rich. The same can be said for the crisis response services that are now popping up all over the place."

"The *what*?"

"I shouldn't be telling you this, but there are companies out there with access to all the early warning systems we maintain."

"*We* as in the government?" I ask him.

"Yes. These companies paid us a fairly sizeable sum to have access to our information so they are ready to rescue their subscribers, should there be the threat of flooding or a terrorist attack, or even an uprising because the prices at Tesco have gone through the roof. You should see their task force and fleet of helicopters. It's really quite impressive. But these companies can afford it because their subscribers pay an exceptionally high price for the service. I don't think even I could afford it, and sorry, old chap, you aren't eligible because you're a foreigner. British nationals only at the moment, although that might change in time."

I think of what would happen if this ever got out, and how people could loosen the blades of those helicopters so they slice through the necks of every one of those billionaire subscribers; a latter-day guillotine for what they might come to refer to as the Great British Revolution. But then I look out the window at the dismal weather and I remember the apathy that has defined the culture in a city of royal subjects.

"I should go," I say as I get on the rest of my clothes. He kisses me so hard that I can feel him trembling beneath my lips. I smell hand soap and the remnants of his vinegary aftershave, and he makes me feel sad that he can be this old and yet still hunger for more out of life. I let him keep me locked in his gravitational pull and I imagine meeting his force with a greater strength and crushing our mouths together so that I feel teeth and bones buckle under the weight of it all.

Finally, he breaks free, gasping as he says, "Call me." I say that I will, even though we both know that I won't.

Outside, the night air is tinged with the smell of wood smoke. I start to remember a story Charles told me as we walked home from the restaurant. He told me about a neighboring house with noisy kids that prompted him to lodge complaints with the residents' association. I didn't really pay attention at first because he went on and on about the kids that he would see from his bedroom window, and how they spent most days staring at an iPad while they were left, it seemed, without parental supervision. I got bored when I assumed that he was projecting feelings from his lonely days at boarding school, but then he finally got to the point of the story by saying, "You know, the mother killed the nanny."

"I'd seen her a few times, the nanny, I mean," he continued as he lit a cigar beneath one of the streetlamps. "Such a frail-looking girl with glasses too big for her face. And so timid. She always winced whenever the mother was around, and now we know why. I'd sometimes see the nanny crying as she rocked herself, with her hands over her ears, as the mother screamed at her. In the end, by all accounts, the mother chopped her up and tried to barbeque her in the middle of the afternoon. Everyone wondered why the entire street smelled of that sickly sweet aroma of burnt flesh. Can you believe that? At least wait until the cover of darkness, for goodness' sake. I don't know whether they fed bits of the nanny to the kids, between a burger bun and all, but they were caught when one of the kids who lived next door to them climbed on their garden wall and asked if he could come to their barbeque. Imagine his horror when he saw the limbs crackling under the open flames."

I have to wait for the whole tube ride home before I can fill in the gaps to this story. I find my cell phone still on the floor, and I search for the missing pieces. You can always find decent accounts online, on Reddit and the dark web, sufficient detail to get to the truth that is so elusive elsewhere, with their pretense of community guidelines and other such bullshit.

The nanny was beaten with a claw hammer because they found traces of her scalp and hair on it after the police tore through the house. They also found a bone saw with her DNA and duct tape with her blood on it. According to Anon1379, when the neighbor's son climbed the garden wall, the mother tried to drag him down and onto the barbeque, and she only narrowly missed his skull with the claw hammer. It was when he started screaming that others came and eventually rescued him, and when they arrived, they found her scampering about the garden on her hands and feet, blood and other bodily fluids drooling from her snapping teeth.

I keep scrolling through more and more accounts, my eyes getting dry. I think I hear the snapping of that mother's teeth, and I know of that greed that burns beneath the skin and makes people want more. It's a primal need, an ancient force that drives us all, and no matter how many people online jump in with their comments about possessions or curses, I know differently. The mainstream media would never speak of the writhing thing beneath the skin. I'm sure it would be censored by some government official out of fears of some kind of social contagion. But I expected at least some people to admit the truth on the dark web, to confess that they too were feeling it, this writhing, this greed that burns me so intensely since the fire.

I keep scrolling, twisted up with a rage that won't be quelled. It's a burning desire that hurts me as Max hurt me, when he used the glowing embers of a joint to burn holes into my thighs. He probably thought he was keeping me in line, handing out punishments for an unruly kid, as I am sure this mother thought she was doing when she shouted at the nanny. But then it went too far, and she hit her. At first, she didn't mean it. Until then, she probably prided herself on being anti-violence and she might have even marched with Allies Against Domestic Violence with her other mummy friends. But when she slapped the nanny, and it felt justifiable, not only right but righteous, and in one crazed moment, she thought she might be saving the young girl from further suffering if she just put her out of her misery. You'd do the same to a starving dog.

She beat her, throwing anything that would come to hand, including a snow globe, a stool, even the PlayStation her kids had been playing with just earlier that day. Everything was slammed into that stupid young woman's face because she did something irritating or careless, although, to be honest, she can't quite remember what set her off in the first place. But it's never just one thing, is it? It's more a cumulation of things over a period of time. That's what she could have learned if she had ever volunteered for Allies Against Domestic Violence, where I'm sure they teach you about the cumulative effects of triggering behavior, but I guess they meant this as a way to help the victim rather than justify the violence.

She still doesn't know where the claw hammer or the bone saw came from.

When Charles spread my legs apart, when he ordered me to lift my hips more because he wasn't as agile as he used to be, he scolded me for hurting myself. He must have seen the whitened scars, remnants of the burn marks on my inner thighs.

"I didn't do it," I tried to say, but he was already too intent on fucking me.

"I didn't do it," I repeated, over and over again, but he was lost to me as he snarled, and I said that he was hurting me but that didn't make him stop. Max would do the same, sometimes going harder just to shut me up. But that was before the fire, when I was younger, when I didn't know that this wasn't the only way to do it with a guy.

As Charles thrashed about, sweat dribbling from his forehead and into his eyes, he told me to keep my hips up, but his voice became Max's as his hands snaked around my throat and he started to squeeze. I figured that Charles was thinking about how he fucked over his constituents, squeezing every last penny out of them through austerity cuts to make the rich richer, and how it kept his boner up to know that he was forcing people into poverty, just because he could. He wants to show those parents who packed him off to boarding school that he now has power, and he won't ever let anyone make him feel so vulnerable again. His parents have been dead for a decade, so maybe instead he'll show his wife, so she doesn't end up leaving him as she has been threatening of late.

With each thrust, Charles becomes Max becomes Charles and Max again, and I think of how they might meet and melt into each other, skin fused to skin so that any sudden move would cause it to rip as he rips me inside right now, and I wince so he snarls again, getting a renewed sense of vigor with the sight of my pain.

I could've slipped away right there, with that hand around my throat, and I think again of who will end up disposing of my body. If they ever found me, I don't know who would identify me, who would care to make that trip across the Atlantic. There is, at least, Katherine who might do it, and I think of her practicing her tearful gaze out of the airplane window before she live streams her journey on Instagram or TikTok. She would constantly check for how many followers she had gained because of this journey that she was embarking upon for her *dearly beloved friend.* I don't know whether that's what she really considered me to be. I mean, I've not had much practice with friendships, so I can't really identify the features of them any more than I can identify who I am to her father. Does it matter that he would hurt me when he fucked me, any more than it matters that he burned his initials into me? Does that make it more or less of a relationship?

I can hear knocking on my door and a girl's voice calling my name. I want it to be Ania, or Katherine, but it sounds like it might be Ruby because she's asking if I want to study with her. These figures of my present haunt my past, but I've learned to sit and wait, and I can usually exorcise them.

Eventually, the room is returned to silence again so I can sit there, with the cell phone light illuminating my face, so I feel like an internet troll who tells suicidal people to throw a noose around their neck and jump. I could do that myself, with the bedsheets, like a prisoner who has no other options, so I look at the sheets and start to think about what it might feel like, and whether Ania will be horrified or relieved to see me again. But I'm distracted by the alert of a message on my cell phone.

"You're wasting my time," Max says in a message. "Name the place to meet me, or I'll come and find you."

I think of the bullshit that I believed in, that a pentacle could ever protect me, so I pick up the silver bracelet. The panda pendants jingle as I now remember that this was a gift from *him*. Eris didn't like to venture out of the fortress unless she really had to, so Paris went to the jewelry store and picked it out himself. I think of how madness has riddled our family tree and how it can be contagious, passed down through the generations like a family heirloom, so I open the window and throw the bracelet onto the trash cans.

I am just about to shut the window when I see a face in the apartment block across from my bedroom. The figure is standing so close to their window that I see their breath misting up the glass, but with each breath the mist evaporates for a moment, and I start to make out their features. My breath falls into rhythm with theirs, and I lean closer, as they do too, and then the breath fades for good, as if they have stopped breathing, and I can identify the eyes of his solid stare. It is the same lifeless expression that I have been seeing in my nightmares, and it brings with it the same putrefying stench of my dead father.

Without breaking his stare, I see that his window is opening, so there is nothing left to separate us. With every breath, his filth is carried through the air to invade me; tiny black molecules attack, multiplying inside of me before I have a chance to defend myself. That lifeless stare, that gap before a reaction when the horror just hangs in the air between us, as silent as the frozen blackness of space where no hope can prosper, that vast expanse of nothingness that swallowed whole my sister and mother and father. But he was spat out, returned to stare at me now, with that same gaunt expression. My father, Paris Brown, now a creature as hideous in physical form as he has always been inside. I see the legs that have sprouted from him and distorted him into an arachnid. They twitch into life before my eyes, and he crawls up the wall and onto the ceiling. He is ready to pounce.

Chapter Seven

<div align="center">~~~</div>

Mother Earth

<div align="center">~~~</div>

Can you see me, beneath the concrete and electric cables and high rises with and without skyline views of New York? Can you see the folds of green, which you think are all that is to me, but I am also violet and indigo and blue and yellow and orange and red; every color of the rainbow. I am the building blocks of you, you cannot exist without me, and yet you claim possession of me by invading and raping and pillaging me. You are the ones who turned me into a warrior.

All that relentless progress, turning me grey with acrid skies as the leaves shrivel to a dirty brown and the carcasses of my beautiful array of species lay rotting at your feet. And to what end? So you could amass food mountains to sit on so you could look for miles and see all the starving masses, and the lines on the maps that you redraw so you can say it is yours.

Dick-swinging comparisons at the urinal, claiming yours is bigger than theirs.

You're an addict, seizing, snorting, injecting or fucking every last opportunity as you build your empires, devaluing all others so you can feel better about yourself, only you can't devalue me because your life depends on my value. There is no escaping me. I am not some woman who you have broken free of after suckling enough to survive, and you now want to dispose of or claim never existed in the first place, as all climate deniers try to do. I am here, keeping you upright, I am the ground beneath your feet that you assume will not shift, that will not swallow you whole and spit you back out as you try to bury the dead along with the secrets of your nocturnal misdeeds. Of course I am going to punish you as every mother would. You've made a warrior of me, so let's see how this war turns out.

See how the apple trees regrow with vigor. They are taller and stronger than before, and they bear even more fruit. Just yesterday, two boys, who were always getting into trouble at school, decided to skip class yet again, and they found themselves at the fortress site. They'd been warned to stay away, and they'd heard the horror stories, but that only made them more determined to disobey their parents and go and explore. Then there was also the siren call that urged them to approach, and it sounded so sweet and inviting that they couldn't possibly believe that any violence could exist in such a place.

"They tried to scare us away," the taller boy declared, when he sneaked into the backyard and found the trees hanging heavy with fruit. "They wanted this place all to themselves, so they told us some bullshit."

The smaller boy didn't like it when his friend cursed, as he'd grown up to believe that cursing was bad and deserving of a slap around the head if he did it even once. But because he was shorter, he could never say anything, never disagree, so that's why he ended up here in this strange, abandoned site, doing what he was not supposed to do and regretting every moment of it.

The taller boy didn't mind walking on broken glass and rubble if it meant that he could reach the apples hanging in the tree. He also didn't mind climbing onto the bough of one of the trees, but he thought it only fair that his mate took the first bite. He'd read something about miners using a canary to check that the air wasn't toxic, so in case the horror stories really were true, he ordered the smaller boy to eat an apple.

"Why?" the shorter boy asked.

"Cos you're my mate and I picked these just for you," he lied. The smaller boy suspected this was the curse word the taller boy had used, but how was he to argue with someone so big? He'd always been told by his parents that his height didn't matter, that he was going to go far in life and even surpass his annoying friend, who seemed a little slow when it came to math and reading. But so far, life had shown the small boy that his parents didn't know what they were talking about.

"Just eat it," the taller boy demanded as he slid from the tree. "Talk about ungrateful. I risked my life to get you that. I could've fallen on the broken glass or hit my head. The least you can do is say thank you."

"Thank you," the smaller boy grumbled and, without thinking, he took a greedy bite.

After a moment of crunching and a hard swallow, the two boys stared at each other. Then the taller one laughed.

"Your face," he sniggered, "like you were shitting yourself or something. Seen a ghost?"

"Nope," the smaller boy said with a smile. Maybe this was what his parents were trying to promise him about a future of superiority, because he had something that the taller boy did not, and that was the apple inside of him. He remembered his father saying that he should be patient and wait because he was going to go to a much better college than his friend, and he'd probably get a much better paying job, and one day, he might be the boss of that very same tall boy.

I'm sure you can guess that neither boy lived to graduate high school, let alone college, because as soon as the tall boy saw his friend smirk, he snatched at the apple and bit into it himself. In fact, they felt so much greed and vengeance for each other that they couldn't stop devouring more and more of the swollen fruit.

At first, the boys might have thought that they had eaten a bad crop. There was a twinge in their stomach, nothing more than indigestion, they thought, but then the smaller boy could taste blood. He was too scared to put this into words, so he stepped backwards, thinking he might run for help. His dad would know what to do in a situation like this, because he'd always known what to do.

He took another step, but his foot caught on a brick or something because he stumbled, and the pain intensified, spreading through his stomach and up into his chest as he doubled over and tasted more blood. He didn't know what was happening to the other boy because he was too terrified for himself, but if he had looked up, he would already see how the taller boy's t-shirt had ripped and splattered with blood as something was tearing its way out from his stomach.

There was the siren call again, only this time it wasn't so sweet and melodious. Now it was deep and loud, so loud that it tore their ear drums apart, making parts of their skull break open like freshly boiled eggs.

They saw things emerge around the broken window frames and rubble. They saw a girl with a rope around her neck and a woman with blistered skin. They seemed to be running from something and they ran right through the boys, which would've been shocking if they hadn't then seen something else emerging from the rubble. It scuttled about with long, spindly legs, and there was a face at the center of the legs that seemed confused at one moment and then in pain the next.

They could hear movement from behind them, from where the trees had stood, and just as they thought of turning round, they felt more pain searing through their body as they noticed that tree roots were bursting from their insides. They were torn apart, and at the end I wonder if they welcomed death, longing for it as they watched something sprinkle parts of their body as if they were fertilizer for the soil.

Destroy or be destroyed. Eat or get eaten.

The story leaked out from the parents of the boys, who told people they thought were close friends and who promised they would never tell. But of course, those kinds of promises are never kept, because the greed is too much, and it writhes beneath their skin too, making them crave for the attention that those grieving parents were getting. So, the friends told other friends, and the teachers at the school, and the reporters, and, in fact, anyone who would listen.

According to these treacherous friends, the parents knew what happened to those boys, every detail of the horror, because they found in the room of each boy a notebook with all of this written in long, spidery handwriting that crawled up and down the margins and didn't stay within the lines. Each parent swore that this wasn't the handwriting of their son, but who else could have written so much detail about what the boys endured? The words that were formed were chaotic in shape and size, as if fifty different souls had been responsible for recording this account, and the only explanation that could fit within any semblance of reality, was that the boys had experienced some kind of premonition, a nightmarish vision of how they were to die.

Mother Earth is glad these boys perished. If they had lived beyond this age, they would've matured into swollen men who would spend the rest of their lives raping and pillaging their way through the world. Mother Earth could already smell something putrefying on them, even before they were dead. As there was something rotten about them, why not prune the diseased limbs before the whole tree was destroyed?

And what about you? Do you think you are worth saving or part of the rot? And what about Max and Dylan? If any of you were duct taped to a chair and forced to tell the truth, would you say that something had gotten to you to shape you in this way? Some kind of haunting or possession, perhaps, or a genetic quirk or touch of insanity rippling through the generations. Or maybe you would point to some kind of toxin that leached out of the chemicals people have been spraying to make their lawns thick and green and glossy? Would you blame the heavy metals in the air from your factories and exhausts from idling cars, or would it be the lead pipes in the home you paid over the odds for because you wanted to out-do your sister who had recently bought a similar home?

Mother Earth would say that you did it to yourself. She gave you all the support and riches you could possibly wish for, and you contaminated and hoarded and starved each other. Faced with the rising sea levels to drown you, the parched wildfires to burn you, the air that is slowly choking you, and the dwindling food supplies to starve you, she wonders if you are hoping for some kind of redemption. Do you think you are deserving of forgiveness? Only time will tell.

All of this wrath and vengeance echoes around the skull of Ralph Jones. And he still has no outlet for it as he burns with a fury that writhes beneath his skin. He's aware that he keeps looping round the same old thoughts, so he seeks relief in other battles for justice. He's heard there's another protest at the church in Rotherwell, organized by this nice girl called Katherine, so there he can let out his rage about the heartless and the cruel.

Katherine is kind and complimentary, saying that Ralph has the nose, lips and physique of Jeremy Allen White. Ralph disagrees, but he secretly loves the fact because he remembers how hot that actor looked in a commercial where he did pullups on a Manhattan rooftop.

Ralph likes the way Katherine evokes softened feelings in him, something that he hasn't felt for a long time, not since his sister's death, at least. So, he makes it a regular thing to join Katherine as she protests this and that, but it's only when he's midway through a chant about trans rights that he looks at this nice girl called Katherine, and he realizes who she is.

"You guided me to her," he tells Ellie later that night. No one is really there, except his cat, but Ellie always loved Ralph's cat, so he takes this as a sign that she is somewhere nearby and listening to his every word.

"This young girl's name is Katherine," Ralph continues, "and she is a good person, despite who her father is. She told me her dad is in London for business, but he's returning to New Jersey soon, and then we'll see what happens after that."

Ralph is silent about his plans but his thoughts are a torrent of violence that makes his head swirl and as he tries to get up from his chair, he stumbles and knocks his desk. The cat runs away, and he's afraid this is a sign that his sister can tell what he is planning for Max West. Ellie wouldn't approve because she never liked violence, but Ralph hopes that eventually she will understand.

And now all that's left for him to do is wait for Max to return to Rotherwell.

Chapter Eight

~~~

Max

~~~

I'm trying to enjoy my evening meal in one of the restaurants recommended by the hotel, and I see spiders scurrying about in the corner near my table.

"Are you fucking kidding me?" I snap at the waiter. He looks confused.

"That is disgusting." I point to the corner where there is a whole swarm of them scurrying over a lump of meat. "And it stinks," I continue. "Can't you clean it up?"

I've never known spiders to do this. They remind me of ants the way they are acting in unison to heave this lump of meat across the floor.

"I'm terribly sorry, but I'm not sure what you mean," the waiter replies. The poor kid has been forced to wear a bowtie, so it makes him look more stupid than he probably is. Despite this, he looks well built in his snugly fitting shirt, so I try to soften my tone.

"That. *That*," I repeat as I point again at the swarm. "Are you blind?"

The waiter is still confused, and this is really starting to piss me off.

"Would sir like another table?" he asks me.

"At this rate, I'm considering a whole new restaurant. Just clear up the damned mess."

"Sir is welcome to sit elsewhere," the waiter adds.

"Where? I can't see any empty tables."

As with all places in London at this time of the evening, there's barely any room to serve the plates of food, let alone for anyone to be choosy about their table. I figure this is why the Brits are so repressed, because if they don't keep their elbows in and hands down, they'll knock someone out with their first gesticulation.

"I'm sure we could find something suitable," the waiter mutters.

"Why would you just dump some meat on the floor like that?"

The hotel probably recommended this restaurant out of spite, just because I said I didn't want to dine with them. Their sad little corner of the reception, with four empty tables and elevator music, suggested bland or unsafe food, so I opted for this place because of the Michelin stars.

"I'm sorry, sir, I don't understand."

"That! The fucking mess, and the spiders."

"I don't see any spiders," he admits.

"Fuck that. Let me speak to your manager."

"Right away," he says with a bow, probably relieved to get away from me as he disappears into the kitchen.

I look again at the corner and the spiders are still moving it across the floor, only some have dispersed, and in the clearing I can see a face on the meat. I realize it isn't just a lump of meat but somebody's head, and it isn't just anyone's head. Katherine hated spiders, no, fuck that, she *hates* spiders. Present fucking tense.

"Is everything okay?" someone asks me, making me jump.

A severe-looking woman with her hair efficiently tied back peers down her long nose at me. She looks so skinny with stress that I think I see her cheekbones pressing through the pale skin of her cheeks.

By now, the hooded creatures have appeared. They surround the spiders, and they start to sway with the same rhythm as the disgusting swarm. My eyes feel heavy, and my stomach starts to churn with a dread of something dark to swallow me whole.

"You saw that?" I ask her, now more uncertain than I'd been with the waiter. "Please tell me you saw that." I've now turned to face her, and I feel ridiculously childish, a lost soul that is willing to accept the reassurance of any stranger.

I can imagine this restaurant manager has to deal with plenty of strange customers, and I guess she's allocating me into the '*druggie*' pile.

"Does sir feel okay?" she asks me. Her accent is nasally, maybe French or something, and it's fucking annoying. "Would sir like some fresh air?"

"No."

"Very well, then. Marcel said you'd mentioned something about spiders. Perhaps also some spilled meat? I can't see anything of the kind. Can you?"

I turn back to the corner, and of course, nothing is there.

"No," I admit.

"Very well, then. Please rest assured that we take hygiene very seriously and should you have any further concerns, please do not hesitate to let us know."

She was here for damage limitation, not to reassure me or even apologize. The last thing she wanted to do was let some *druggie* ruin her restaurant's reputation.

Poor Katherine. How she hates spiders. Time is running out.

"Fuck you," I meant to hiss in my head, but I think something leaked out because the manager grimaced at me. She opened her mouth, probably to ask me to leave, but my phone started to ring, so I held up my forefinger, instructing her to keep silent. It was always a ballsy move but, most of the time, it worked.

"Yes?" I snap without recognizing the number.

"It's Pastor Pry."

It always fucked me off the way she couldn't refer to herself as plain old Isla.

"Please say that my little bird got it wrong," she continues.

"I don't know. Depends on what your little bird said."

"You're in London?"

"Yup."

"When we were supposed to sign the paperwork. You need our land for access to your tower development, and yet you've decided to have a holiday in London. Do you understand what this means?"

"Not really," I reply. I'm getting tired of her schoolmistress tone. I have visions of her tethered to a cross and a garland of her own entrails wrapped around her head. I'd suggested to Sammy we use her entrails as rosary beads, but he reminded me that she was Protestant, not Catholic. That guy's smarter than he looks and sometimes I wish he'd made more of his brains than following my every command.

"We had a deal," she continues, either oblivious or ignorant to who she's talking to. "And that deal included a timeline."

"There only needs to be a slight delay. I'll be back in a day or two."

"No, I don't think you understand. If you can't meet that timeline, the deal's off."

"Chill. I'll be a day or so, and then we can sign the papers. Right?"

I hang up before she can say any more. I've already made sure Sammy won't let her back out. If she doesn't cooperate, he'll pay her a visit and make sure her hand signs the paperwork, whether or not the rest of her body is in agreement.

The phone is ringing again, only this time it's Sammy.

"You got anything?" I ask him.

"Yup. Your funder is a Douglas Parsons, forty-two, nice little house and two kids in Connecticut. And a husband, no less. Seems everyone's jumping on the queer bandwagon these days."

Sammy let out a phlegm-filled laugh.

"You should quit those cigarettes," I tell him, eager to change the subject.

"Hey, I've been smoking them for years."

"Yeah, and it sounds it. If you don't look after yourself and you drop down dead, who's gonna help me out with everything I need doing?"

"I'm sure you'll find someone."

"Yeah," I said as I stared at the corner where I'd seen the spiders. "I probably would."

"You want me to pay Parsons a visit?" Sammy asks me.

"Do that. But be quiet about it."

"Of course. Before sunrise. Don't worry, I'll step silently around the kids. And I won't mess up his pretty face. Well, I won't this time, at least."

"Just make sure he learns the virtue of patience."

"Sure thing."

He hangs up as he erupts into another fit of coughing.

Katherine never liked Sammy.

"He's creepy," she'd say when she was as young as eight or nine.

"What does creepy even mean?" I'd asked her. At that age, she'd pointed to inconsequential things like his scratchy voice or the fact that he wore the same ACDC t-shirt every time he was over to talk with me. But by the time she became a teenager, she admitted that she didn't trust him. That, and he had the nervous movements of a weasel.

"I just get a bad vibe from him," she whispered as I'd tucked her into bed and kissed her cheek. I loved the way she still wanted me to tuck her in at night, even when she would flick her hair at me during the day and tell me not to walk so close to her if her friends were watching.

"You don't have to whisper," I said with a smile. "He's in Florida, so he won't hear you here in New Jersey."

"I know. I just feel bad saying things like that about anyone. It would hurt his feelings if he heard me."

"I'm sure he'd get over it."

"And it would kind of make me as bad as him. You know, bad

energy and all that. I only ever want to send out positive vibes to the universe, and that way, I'm more likely to get them back."

"Okay, now you're starting to sound like your mom," I said with one last kiss and then flicked off the light.

If she could get it right about Sammy, and from such a young age, what made her so blind to the fucked-up things I'd been doing her whole life? Ever since she was little, she'd been trailing me around the house when I tried to take work calls, and the older she got, the more sophisticated were her questions, and I felt like I was living with the fucking FBI.

Still, when your heart gets in the way, then all sense of judgment is off. Katherine may see Sammy for exactly who he is, but for some reason, she's way off when it comes to Dylan. She loves him, *them*, like a brother, probably more than her own brother. And yet Dylan's inflicted more than their own share of violence.

I can still feel the burn-marks searing into my thighs, making me squirm on the seat in this shithole of a cramped restaurant. I can see the manager leaning on the bar as she gives me another withering look.

I need to piss, so I jump up from my table and make my way to the bathroom.

It's one of those multi-gender, *Hey, I'm good with anything* bathrooms that Katherine and Dylan would appreciate but leaves my generation rolling our eyes. I mean, there are more important things than where to take a piss or what to call yourself. Things like who's selling a piece of land on the East Coast, and how well my shares are performing, which, come to think of it, I need to check on. I slide out my cell phone at the same time as my cock and the relief of the green arrows on my stocks, as well as the long-awaited piss, gives me ripples of pleasure throughout my body.

When I'm finished, I drop my pants to take a look at the pale white scars on my thighs. At the time he inflicted them, he was upside down, so you'd have to stand on your head to realize that he'd seared into my flesh a *D* and a *G*. He'd fucking branded me, and he'd chosen Dylan Gall because he wanted to try to sever any links with his old pedo of a father, Paris Brown. As if he would ever live down that association. He'd told me once that his mom would sometimes call him *Ares*, her *battle-lustful son,* so I guess I'm lucky I didn't end up seared with a fucking spear and shield. Who the hell obsesses about motifs of war and calls their son Ares? That crazy woman spoke too much about wrath and vengeance, acting out nothing but petty jabs. It's no surprise that she ended up burning herself alive in her own fury. Can you believe she was planning to poison us at my son's graduation party? Dylan told me that she had sprinkled aconite into some caramel apples that she brought to the party. I still see the purples and blues of that fucking weed that keeps regrowing every time I get the guys to spray it.

Destroy or be destroyed.

But understanding where Dylan comes from doesn't make him any less dangerous to me or my daughter.

Eat or get eaten. Time is running out.

I brought him into my home. Even before the fire, I was letting him stay when June was at the shore house. I was careless. All the guys before him hadn't got anywhere near my family, but maybe there was something different about Dylan compared with the rest of them. Or maybe I was just getting older and tired of performing a role that no longer fit me.

It worked for a while. As soon as I would see her car disappearing down the street, Dylan would sneak in to join me in bed or in the shower, and the danger of it only added to the excitement.

It worked until one day, when June returned home earlier than expected. She caught us in the shower, mid-fuck, and for a surreal moment we just carried on until she threw her handbag at us.

Dylan scampered off to hide somewhere, and June followed me into the bedroom, slamming the door behind her.

"When were you going to tell me?" she hissed. "I mean, were you going to wait until I contracted an STD before you admitted anything? Fuck. I could already have something passed from you."

"Oh, that's nice and bigoted of you. Would you say that if I'd been fucking around with a woman?"

She stares at me for a moment, eyes wild. "Yes, you idiot. I would. I don't care if he has a dick or not, I care that you've been exchanging bodily fluids with someone, and then doing the same with me without giving me a chance to consent. At least wear a fucking condom."

"How do you know we don't?"

"With me, goddamnit. Oh Christ, this is going in circles, and it isn't even the point. You always do this, you always twist things, so I get confused, and then you get away with it."

"I can't help it if you can't follow a conversation. Maybe if you went to work, it might crank your brain into life."

She's shaking her head, and I'm sure she wants to hit me or spit at me.

"You're a misogynist. A fucking woman-hating narcissist or sociopath, or both. Fuck, I don't know if you can even be both, but I'm sure you'd find a way round that, too."

She might have been right because I was just about to turn things on her, blaming her for coming home too early from a tip to the shore house, or blaming her for walking into the bathroom when someone was having a shower. I was going to throw the concept of privacy at her and see how it stuck.

I wish she'd said something in that moment, anything but curling her lip in disgust and standing there with her arms folded. Looking back, I realize she might have just needed an apology, maybe; I don't really know. Either way, she just screamed, "Fuck you," and stormed out of the bedroom.

I expected her to pack a bag that evening, but instead she stayed, and a weird silence lingered for days. Katherine kept asking what was up between the two of us, and all I could reply was, "Ask your mother." Even Smithson asked, "So, are you guys getting a divorce?" and I just shrugged my shoulders.

She stayed, though. After a week of silence, she found me in the driveway, loading the car for a meeting with Pastor Pry, and she told me that we needed to set some parameters.

"Such as?"

"Never in my bed. Not even once."

"Okay."

"Never when I'm in the same house, and never when the kids are around."

"I can agree to that."

"How very noble of you," she said through tightened lips. "And if anything happens to you, he gets nothing."

"Ooh, ouch, you're already planning for my death," I said with a laugh as I clutched my stomach as if she'd just stabbed me. I knew I was pushing my luck by making light of it.

"Fuck you for your stupid jokes and fuck you for doing this to our family. But still, I've seen what broken homes look like, and I'm not going to let you do that to this one. I know your daughter will never believe anything against you, so she'll blame me and turn against me…"

"I'd never let that happen," I lie.

"Whatever. Just agree to the terms and we'll be done with it."

"Okay."

"And get a fucking blood test. The full HIV, STD, whatever you need to show me that you aren't carrying anything and haven't passed anything to me."

"Absolutely," I say as I flash my gleaming white teeth at her, "and can I have the same tests carried out on you?"

She opened her mouth to snap something back, but then she stopped. With the vivid morning sunlight highlighting the wrinkles under her eyes, she looked tired, and I instantly regretted saying this.

"You don't have to," I added.

She just shrugs and says, "whatever you want, Max, as always, whatever you want you'll get. Only trouble is, you miss the vital point. I've never given you any reason to doubt me, and trust is more important than any clever business move."

With that, she reached out, and we shook hands like a pair of fuckwit business partners.

Just like most business deals, I continued to fuck over the other side, never complying with a single term. Although I did get some blood tests and I was clear of any STDs. When I showed it to her, she said that it didn't clear me of the sociopathy she thought that I was riddled with.

It took a long time for me to understand what June had

meant by trust. It was after the fire, after Dylan had changed, and I was showering and she was on her way out to the pharmacy, so she wanted to see if we needed any more shampoo.

When she opened the shower door, she flinched when she noticed the burn marks scattered all over my thighs.

"Did he do this to you?" she asked as she pointed to my thighs.

I didn't reply, so she asked again, "Come on, Max, you can tell me. Did he do this?"

Still, I couldn't reply, I just stood there under the torrent of water, the soapsuds trickling in to sting my eyes.

"I know that something's been up recently, I can tell. You always grind your teeth when there's something up. And you've been whimpering in your sleep."

I was starting to disappear, to where, I haven't a fucking clue, but I couldn't hear much of what she was saying anymore. I think she suggested a doctor, and like fuck was I gonna waste my time or money on one of those.

I remember her reaching for my arm, but I shrank from her touch. I could feel the water getting hotter, and it stung the open wounds like hell.

Suddenly, I was conscious of my nakedness, which was stupid when we still had sex and still got changed in front of each other. But in that moment, there was a danger that she was going to become someone else, where she had power over me, and the underworld would become a reality.

"Shut the door," I snapped. The steam enveloped her, made it look like it was holding her in place, so I reached for the shower door myself, and pulled it shut.

"Now fuck off," I shouted above the hiss of the shower head. It was cruel, I know that.

Fucking trust. It seemed simple enough, but it also carried a lot of fucking risk.

After the shower, I found her in our bedroom, staring out of the bedroom window at the smoldering ruins of the fortress site. I swear her pupils were dilated, and if I didn't know her better, I would've said she was high on something.

High on the power she was clawing from you.

Like fuck. She never bothered about power. She wouldn't even try hard with a board game when we had a power outage. From birth, her father spoiled her so much that she seemed like a fucking caged bird, or one with their wings clipped.

But she smelt it in the smoke drifting from the fire. She felt that writhing beneath the skin as much as you did, that greed that burned inside of her, and that made her forget about love and trust and anything remotely redeemable about you.

Fuck you. She's not like that.

You became an obstacle to her, an inconvenience. Just watch. She'll take everything from you and then abandon you, just as your mother did. Destroy or be destroyed.

Chapter Nine

~~~

Dylan

~~~

That night, when Paris crawled about the walls and ceiling, he held me with a look that he had always used. Every parent has one for their child. He crawled along that stare and slipped in through the gaps in my comprehension, those dark shadows of fear where anything can thrive. Now I see him, *it*, in the folds of the curtains, and it waits for me to sleep, so it can enter this world through my dreams.

I don't know how this really works, how the dead see life after they have gone, and how much influence they really have over their hosts. I'm guessing they use their eyes, choosing the people who share their genetics or some kind of attachment to them. Dreams are the easiest way for them to see things, and so I wince at the thought of him seeing my dreams of all those men writhing about as I plunge deeper into them, or they plunge deeper into me. How horrifying it must be for him to watch as his bloodline runs dry on the sheets or the chest of some police officer or Member of Parliament. Can this horror carry a force that is powerful enough to send radio waves that push abusive messages from an unknown number? Could all this disgust and shame (mine as much as his) plaster his skin so it suffocates and smothers him as the duct tape once did, leaving him writhing about in perpetual torment? I imagine he is probably looking for a way to burn down this family tree and incinerate what's left of it so the disease can't spread any further.

Tonight, I dream of Ania and she exists in a version of my life that might have been, had I really been Ares, that brave warrior that my mother assumed me to be. I found my sister in her bedroom, and she is still alive and smiling, with the same auburn hair as our mother, but without the fire and discord.

I reach out to touch her shoulder, but my hand slips through her image, and we both realize she is nothing more than a ghost because I never saved her. I was never that battle-lustful son. She turns her back to me, and she starts to pluck each panda pendant from her once-treasured silver bracelet. When it is bare, she tosses it aside and turns her attention to her cuddle panda bear. She picks out each stitch, letting it unravel completely so the stuffing, an aged-looking yellow and dirty brown, spills out like the opening stomach of a decaying corpse.

"Come on, Midget," I say to her, "you loved that thing." But she won't turn to look at me.

"I didn't know," I add, and I start to cry. All this guilt and shame, a thickened curdle to the blood that was given to me, implanted from the moment of conception. "I didn't know," I repeat to my sister, but still she won't listen to me. Why should she? I am of his seed, so surely there must be a similar kind of toxicity about me, something that makes me blind to what he has done.

There is movement from across the hallway, a creaking sound of the bedroom door in the dead of night and when the moon is shining full beam to wake the ghosts. They saw it happening, those ghosts of my forefathers who seized the land and built that fortress that couldn't keep out the ultimate danger. Perhaps they tried to warn me of the violence and I just didn't listen to them, and now they are rageful, now they want to trap me in this liminal state where I am permitted to exist, but I must not form a connection with any living soul.

I twist and turn with this guilt and shame. I twist so much that some of these strangers that I've met on hookup apps turn me inside out, and we are left with the stench of our innards, coating ourselves like we have been tarred and feathered. Sometimes I don't even shower it off before I coat myself in more of it, and I wonder if that sickening smell enrages the ghosts and makes them hate me more. They have a lot of rage, these ghosts, because the haunted are usually the ones who have been taken too soon, in unjust circumstances, so they remain on earth to seek out who wronged them. With all this shame and guilt coating my skin, plastering me to make me sweat, they must think that I am the one who meant them harm, so more and more of these ghosts are trailing me. In the corner of my dreams, I see the nanny who still tries to re-assemble herself on the charred patio in that backyard, and the passengers still swimming underground, trying to find a way out of that tube station since the second world war.

"You failed me," Ania says as she finally turns to look at me. Her mouth hangs with a gaunt expression, the flesh of her chin tearing from her jaw. Her eyeballs melt, leaving bloody pools that I fear I might drown in if I stare at them for too long.

"You failed me," she repeats.

I know some of what she is accusing me of. Like me, she had trouble making and keeping friends, and whilst I tried not to care, the loneliness was slowly suffocating her. All she wanted was for someone to claim her as their own and subjugate her, so she knew where she belonged. I can understand now how important that was, when her identity at home, as Paris' daughter, was such a violent and painful thing.

"Look at me," she cries as she shows me how she would stand alone in the corner of the playground. No one cared. The adults who worked at the school had arguments with other members of staff, and they would often complain that they weren't paid enough to do more than the bare minimum, so why should they intervene and help a girl who was crying?

From somewhere, I hear the sneering from the other girls. "Weirdo," they would call her. "Freak"

"You could've helped me," she moans. "It hurts, Dylan."
"I know, Midget," I say.
"It won't stop hurting," she says as she turns away from me. "I keep looking at those days, trying to reshape them. If I could do it over, maybe if I'd tried a little harder, maybe they would've liked me."
"No. It wasn't you that needed to change."
"Words. All those stupid words, and you never did anything. If you had tried to help me even once, then I wouldn't have had to…"

Her shoulders tremble as she remembers the tree.

"You let him back in," she whispers. "You didn't have to, but you did."
"Please," I say to her, touching her shoulder gently, but it is softer than it should be and I'm afraid that my hand might sink into her putrefying flesh, so I pull it away. She must have sensed my horror because she turns sharply back to me, and I think I'm going to see anger in her face, finally the anger that might have saved her life and made her defiant enough to stay. It was the anger and defiance that kept me alive before the fire, when I would stare at the same apple tree and run my hands over the same length of rope in the garage. And since the fire, it has got harder to resist taking too many drugs and letting strangers do what they want with me in dark places as I drift into an oblivion. But the anger and defiance keep my head above water, still fighting for the next breath. The trouble is, I never saw any of that anger or defiance in Ania, and she's showing me that the meek never inherit the earth, they just get fucked over so many times until it destroys them.

By now, Ania has no face, only a gaping hole that starts to pull me in. I can smell the putrefying flesh from here, and I hear the moaning of the underworld, and it is getting harder to fight it when I believe that I deserve to be in there.

The following morning, Viqaas is waving at me from across the crowded lecture theatre. For days now, he's been doing this at the beginning of every lecture, always mouthing "I saved you a seat" and refusing to let me sit elsewhere. I still haven't found a way to avoid him, so I end up next to him with our legs touching and his scent lingering in the air we share.

"I got the Calvin Klein one," he says as he slaps his cheeks with both hands.

"It smells good on you."

"Damned right. I've got all the right hormones. Besides, it smelled so good on you that I had to give it a try."

"Single White Female."

"Nah, I'm not that into you," he replies with a dazzling smile.

"I just like the scent. It *sent* me. You know?"

He starts to laugh at his own joke.

"Oh, come on," he continues, it wasn't that bad, was it? Well, if you can't laugh at my jokes, the least you can do is go to Ruby's party with me. Don't forget, it's tonight."

I choose not to reply, and instead I turn to the professor who has already taken her place at the lectern, cleared her throat, and launched into the requirements to create a prescriptive easement.

"She's inviting everyone in our class," Viqaas continues at the top of his voice, seemingly oblivious to the lecturer. "So that means you have to come. It would be weird if you didn't."

Still I ignore him, and still he persists.

"Come on, Dyls. I haven't seen you at any of the uni events. I'm worried you might be a little boring. What's wrong? Got a dark past that you're trying to hide? Or are you a vampire and out sucking people's blood at night while we're at the student union?"

The professor hasn't stopped staring at the two of us, even though she is still delivering her lecture and pointing to the slides.

"Come on, no excuses," Viqaas continues. "Prove to me you aren't a vampire, or just downright boring. And besides, Ruby lives in a really posh house in Kensington, so I'm gonna

feel right out of place there, especially if she invites some of her private school friends. Don't leave me alone with all that."
I shake my head in reply.
"Why not?" He stares at me with his big, brown eyes, and then he leans closer. The peppermint of his gum is so fresh that it starts to make my eyes sting. He's trying to show me a different world, far away from the stagnation of isolation, but he doesn't realize that the more he comes close to me, the greater risk that the two worlds will become one, where all manner of filth and contamination will spread and distort everything he once knew. I try to resist him, but the thing beneath my skin, this greed, burns too intensely.

"Come on," he continues, now with his face just inches away from me. "I'm waiting for the latest BS excuse about washing your underwear or ironing your hair or whatever else you do in that little room of yours."

"Why don't you guys go get a room," the professor finally says, pointing straight at us. There is an awkward moment when no one says or does anything, so the lecturer takes the initiative.

"I don't think I've made myself clear. I would like you to leave my lecture and return on another day, when you've had time to reflect on what manners look like."

Viqaas glances at me, dumbfounded, and I realize this might have been the first time he's ever gotten into trouble. In fact, this could be the worst thing that he has ever experienced. I laugh at this, and my dry cackle echoes around the walls and ceiling of the lecture theatre. I can see this is making the other students uncomfortable, and the ones sitting close to me lean away, unwilling to appear associated with me.

Shoving my notebook into my backpack, I help Viqaas to do the same and then drag him by the hand out of there.

Outside, the street is busy with the squealing brakes of black cabs and red buses.

"What the fuck?" he says, staring back at the faculty.
"Don't worry about it. She'll get over it come the next lecture."
"I've never been told off by a teacher."
"Oh jeesh, Vik, you really haven't lived, have you? If that's

the worst that's happened to you, you're lucky. Come on, let's get out of here."

I start to feel like my old self again, comfortable in the role of the unwanted and unruly. Eris gave me good training to embrace this with her sneer at compliance.

"Where are we going?" he asks.

"I don't know. We have the entire city at our disposal," I say as I walk down the street of dignified Victorian and Edwardian row houses. Each one has a lantern hanging above the entrance, an attempt to gaslight us into forgetting the horrors of British rule.

"This fine British Empire," I say with a sardonic bite, "it deserves a little attention from us. Besides, it's gonna be much more fun than falling asleep in a cramped lecture theatre stuffed full of sweaty students."

"Empire?" he gasps as he runs to catch up with me. "I'm not sure you could call this place that anymore. I'm not even sure your country deserves that status, either."

"I think a lot of Americans would disagree with you," I reply. *"The greatest nation on earth, the land of the free*, etc etc. That's what they say about it, what we're taught from the moment we start school. You know they call New York the *capital of the world*?"

"Jeesh, and you think us Muslims are indoctrinated?"

"I think some Americans would find it hard to view any place beyond the US as an empire."

"They probably don't know much about history," Viqaas said with a sigh. "People forget that there was a Russian empire, then for a few hundred centuries before that, an Ottoman empire, and a Mongol empire, and a Roman, Seljuk, Roman again, Frankish, Arab Caliphate, and…do you want me to go further back?"

"Not really," I reply. "I thought we were skipping the lecture today."

"You white guys think it's been the same for eternity, but your empire's hanging in a balance, and most people are on the side of the Ewoks."

"The…what?"

We catch each other's eyes for a moment and then we both burst into laughter, and I try to figure out when I last experienced this. Maybe it's my first time.

We spent the whole day together, and afterwards, he insisted I accompany him to his room. I stirred, as I'd never been there, and I still couldn't break the association between hanging out with men near their bed and having sex. But all he wanted was for me to listen to an episode of the Archers.

"What did you think?" he asked me when it was finally over.

"It's…interesting. I didn't really know who the characters were, so it was hard to keep track of what was going on."

I was in sensory overload. The musty, earthy smell of him was all over the room, and I couldn't stop staring at his bed and the pile of boxer shorts on the floor. To think of getting undressed there and sleeping there and doing other things inside those sheets left me unable to concentrate on anything else.

"Give it time," he added, "you'll come to love it. There's a whole world of drama set in an agricultural setting that's just waiting for you. I love the Grundys. I've been listening to them since I was a kid, with my sis. We grew up with Radio Four in the background spouting Woman's Hour, the World at One, Book at Bedtime, and when I couldn't sleep, I would drift off to the Shipping Forecast and Sailing Away. That's the theme tune to the Shipping Forecast."

I was smiling, and I think I managed to nod at all the correct moments, but I didn't have a clue about most of the things he was saying.

"Come on, Dyls, you haven't really told me anything about you. I mean, from the look of your clothes and watch and stuff, you seem like you're minted."

I don't know what to say in reply.

"I'll interpret that silence as a *yes*. So what else is there about you? Loving parents on the East Coast who have a yacht in Florida and a trust fund at the ready?"

"Both of my parents are dead. My sister, too. She died when

she was sixteen."

His cheeks flush with embarrassment.

"Oh, I'm sorry. That was clumsy of me."

"It's fine. No sweat."

He's too polite to ask about the circumstances of their deaths, so he allows me to change the subject.

"Where are your law books?" I ask him. I point to a flimsy bookshelf screwed into the wall over his bed, where I notice there isn't a single law textbook. Instead, he has lined up, in size order, an interesting array of literature including *We've Always Lived in the Castle, We Need to Talk About Kevin, Red Dragon, Future Home of the Living God, Migrations, The Picture of Dorian Gray,* and *High-Rise.* I make a mental note to gift him my copies of *Tell Me I'm Worthless* and *Boy Parts.*

"I actually wanted to study English Literature," he replies, "but my parents wouldn't let me."

He spots my frown and adds, "They're Pakistani parents, so it's law or medicine for me."

"Why don't you just switch?" I ask him. "I mean, it's your life, isn't it?"

He rolls his eyes at this.

"Oh, you white people and your independence. As a Muslim, I respect my parents. I don't scream at them that they don't understand me, or demand a car from them, or post on TikTok how abusive they are. They love me, they know better, so end of. Besides, I get to read law in Bloomsbury of all places, just minutes from Charles Dickens' house. So I figure it's a win-win situation."

He stares at me and then starts to shake his head.

"You still don't understand, do you?"

"Not really, no," I reply.

"Islam isn't just something you do once a week, like going to the Mosque and that's it. It's an entire way of life, and that includes doing as my parents wish."

He tells me about a father who never went to university, and who spent decades working late as a cleaner at the local high school. He would return home each night full of stories about the kids who would throw their trash on the floor right in front of him, and the teachers would watch and ignore this, or roll their eyes, or even laugh. Still, he went back to that school each day because he wanted to set an example to his children to work hard no matter what.

"So I'm gonna work hard at this law degree because he never could. I'm not going to throw it back in his face like it's some unwanted trash."

"Those bratty kids throwing their trash," I added, "and the teachers who don't give a shit. That sounds like where I'm from on the East Coast. It's a toxic place with so many opportunists trying to make a buck. Everyone is always marketing themselves, so it's all surface shit without anyone caring about what really matters."

"So what *really* matters?" he asks me.

"You know, misogyny, racism, homophobia, transphobia...," I reply.

"Maybe those *opportunists* are too busy trying to survive. Not everyone can afford to fight the good fight."

"Wait, what?"

"Survival. It's the most basic need for all species, isn't it? Like they say on planes that you should put your oxygen mask on first before trying to help others. Maybe some of those *opportunists* have got no oxygen to spare to help the others. So if they tried to take on a fight, even if it was against misogyny, racism, homophobia, or transphobia, they might not survive."

I feel powerless. He's just taken my rainbow flag of justice and stomped on it.

"Maybe. I don't know," I reply. "I guess I shouldn't single out the East Coast. Maybe it's all of us. Maybe we're all a bit toxic, with all our in-fighting."

"Who's *us*?" he asks.

"Humankind. We all do it, fighting amongst ourselves, fighting against nature and fucking up this earth with all our landfills of toxic waste. Plastic bags are just dumped without consideration so they tighten round the necks of birds like a hangman's noose, or they tangle round the legs of some other creature so they can't escape, and they starve or drown with the rising sea levels. Have you heard about the AMOC collapse?"

"Sounds like you need to stop your Extinction Rebellion newsletter," he says as he shakes his head.

"I thought it was established knowledge," I reply. "I can't tell you how often I've seen people idling in their cars outside the schools of their very own kids, whole lines of parents in their SUVs. It's like they've formed a suicide pact, and they've decided to take the kids with them."

"Okay, but you say it like we are all the same. Some of us are producing more waste than others, and some of us can't afford the SUVs you're talking about. You sound like this great environmental warrior, probably because you can afford to be. Meanwhile, the rest of us are just trying to survive. My dad gives me cash for food now and again, but I can never take it because that would mean less for him. It's that kind of push and pull tension that I know you've never experienced."

My cheeks ignite with a flush of shame. "But it's okay," he continues. "I'm not hating on you because of your privilege."

"I mean, it kinda sounds like you are. Maybe just a little."

"No, it isn't your fault if you have privilege, if you're white, educated, rich, American, or any of that stuff. But save me the environmental catastrophe soliloquy when your family probably got rich off the companies that pollute the most. It's not like we're all rolling up our sleeves and uniting against a common cause. Because we're not all in it together. It's gonna be the poorest who suffer the most from this climate disaster, and the rich will treat it like some form of entertainment."

"That isn't what I'm doing."

I want to tell him that I know some of what he is talking about. I want to share with him what Charles told me about the crisis response service to save the super-rich, and the conversations I've had with Katherine about privilege, but I know that Viqaas has more to teach me than I could ever teach him.

"You should understand a little more about this climate crisis than what the mainstream media tells you," he continues. "Especially when it comes to your own country. Did you know that race is the single most important factor when they decide where to locate a toxic waste facility?"

From my blank expression, he already has his answer.

"People of color have always suffered from racialized environmental policies, and your country is no different. Federal, state and local policies have intentionally located toxic facilities in communities of color. You have to know that. To you white people, our labor, our lives, have always been cheap. You've enslaved people of color, segregated society, and then you expect us to take up arms for you, fight this climate crisis with you, and yet you'll never see us as equals…"

"Okay, I get it."

I watch Viqaas flex his long fingers, and then he cracks each knuckle.

"The Dutch population live in flood risk zones but there's been a shed load of investment for flood protection measures. There won't be as many lives and livelihoods lost in the Netherlands, but there will be widespread devastation in Bangladesh because it's about poverty, not just flooding, not just climate change."

"Okay. I don't know what to say."

"It's fine. You don't have to know. As I said, I'm not hating on your privilege, I'm hating on your ignorance. I'm sure one weekend you'll go on one of your Extinction Rebellion rallies, and you'll fly your rainbow flag in June, but the whole year, not just a weekend or a month, there are people fighting."

I get up and pace the room like I am a prisoner who is counting down the time until my release.

"Aww, come on, Dyls, don't look so serious. We're just having a conversation."

"I didn't mean to offend you."

"You didn't. Did I offend you?"

"No," I reply.

"You aren't gonna be much of a lawyer if you can't have a debate every now and then."

To my surprise, he throws his arms around me and squeezes me in a bear hug. When he releases me, we stand staring at each other, and I can't figure out who either one of us is.

"Better?" he asks me.

I nod in reply and lean in, slowly enough to give him a chance to stop me, but he doesn't pull away. Our lips touch, the warmth and softness sending me wild with an energy that hums throughout my body.

"I can't," he says as he quickly pulls away. "Even if I wanted to, this is haram."

"Sorry."

"No, don't say sorry. I kinda felt it too. But… Anyway, it isn't an option. Ever. And if my sister ever found out, she'd kill me, and then kill you."

"Okay."

"I'm serious. She's been calling this war on Palestine a genocide on all Muslims. She's really afraid we're all gonna be eradicated, so she says we need to stick together and remember what being a good Muslim is all about."

"I get it," I say. "Listen, I'm gonna get changed before the party."

"Wait, you're coming?"

"Fuck, whatever. I don't have the energy to keep saying no to you."

He bounces excitedly, reminding me of some stupid tiger in a children's cartoon.

"Meet you at reception in half an hour?" he asks me with a beaming smile.

"Sure."

It feels weird when he walks me to the door, but then he leans in and kisses me lightly on the cheek.

"Still buddies, right?" he says, and I nod, not even realizing that this is what we've become. And I'm surprised to feel grateful.

On our way to Ruby's party, Viqaas points out Kensington Palace, or, as he puts it, "the birthplace of the chief hunter and pillager."

"Who?" I ask.

"Queen Victoria. You know she survived seven assassination attempts," he adds. "People were pissed at her because she was living it up while children worked their fingers to the bone on the docks. Some lived their whole short lives bare-footed and begging, and many starved to death. Sometimes ten would live in one room. Can you believe that? Diphtheria, measles, cholera, they were all rampant as hell. And how she loved her East India Dock Company because of how rich it made her and those fat white landed gentry. Meanwhile, street urchins in her own country, and the colonies she invaded, starved to death."

"I never knew any of this," I say as I curse the quality of my American public-school education.

"You talk about the environmental catastrophes of today, but back then Queen Victoria's greed, her quest for relentless progress, with her steel networks of train lines slashing scars into the English countryside, sounded the death knell for the natural world. Did you know that Britain really was once great because there were wolves and bears roaming wild and free? But they were wiped out with the factories and mills that old Vicky built."

He was starting to sound like an encyclopedia, but I loved seeing how passionate he was about all of this, so I just let him get on with his soliloquy.

"Churchmen called her industrialization *the advancement of the devil*, but I guess they just felt threatened. Finally, the church didn't have a monopoly on power. These church folk always condemn what threatens them, saying it's *the work of the devil* or *a danger to the young*."

I think of Pastor Pry and the hate she stirs up as her church attendance and donations dwindle. She would probably blame the popularity of social media as much as she would say it's the fault of the gays or the trans community, or even the world of commerce. There's an intense hatred for Max that crackles when I've seen her with him, probably a jealousy of the millions he makes without any kind of accountability. I'm sure the feeling is mutual. I wonder what Max would make of these stories of Queen Victoria. I feel a little sick when I think of his abandoned warehouses filling up with child laborers to make him another tidy profit.

"Always the friggin children," Viqaas continues. "*Won't*

somebody think of the children? Meanwhile, no one really thinks about the children. I mean, not really, not if it threatens profit margins. Ever heard of the match girls?"

"No."

"Kids as young as four years old were forced to dip match sticks into the toxic phosphorous, so the gentlemen could light their cigars, pipes and cigarettes."

We finally arrive at Ruby's home and Viqaas presses a large brass doorbell. The entrance is framed with gleaming white columns and a pair of miniature evergreens.

"They developed phossy jaw," Viqaas continues, "their flesh turning black and stinking to high heaven before they died a slow and painful death. But anything for progress, eh! Dear old Vicky, queen of relentless progress no matter the cost to any living thing, and now everywhere I go I feel her presence, that imperial, battle-hardy warrior with her big round face and double chin. Either that or there's a statue of her dearly beloved Albert whose death sent her crazy with grief. If you ask me, she always was a crazy old witch."

"They used to call my mother a witch."

I don't know why I tell him this. Maybe Eris has been listening, and she wants to push her way into this world through my words and action. I watch as my fingers flex back and forth, the writhing beneath my skin returning after having calmed down for most of the day.

"It wasn't fair to call her a witch," I continue, "when really she was just haunted by the death of her daughter."

"Oh gosh. I'm so sorry. I can't imagine how I would cope with that. You said your sister was sixteen when she died?"

"Yes. Eris, my mother, got really tangled up in her grief and I sometimes think that's what destroyed her. I mean, she was a complicated person even before that, but I think that's what pushed her over the edge."

When the door opens, we are greeted by a slender, fragile-looking man who seems weary of the world.

"Are you here for Ruby?" he asks us. He holds his head in such a way that makes my neck ache, like he has been straining to decipher what life is all about, and the print is only getting smaller.

"Yes," Viqaas replies.

"Then step this way," he says with a flourish of his arm. I notice he spills a little of whatever was in a fat tumbler in his hand, but he doesn't seem to care.

As we walk down the corridor, I hear ice clinking on the side of his glass. He tells us that many people have already arrived, and he asks us to please excuse his garden as he hasn't had time to tidy it up. I peer out of a rear window off the hallway and catch a glimpse of a long backyard filled with pots and bird feeders. Everything looks heavy under the weight of this relentless rain.

As Ruby's father opens the door to the living room, Viqaas leans in to whisper, "If you want to chat some more about your mum and sister, I'm all ears." He uses his hands to flap his ears like Dumbo, and I laugh as we walk into a room full of awkward-looking, skinny girls. Each one scans us from head to toe and then turns back to the person nearest to them to continue their quiet conversation.

"Ruby's preppy school friends," Viqaas whispers in my ear. He makes my spine tingle. "They're probably trying to identify you from some country club or polo competition."

I glance at the clock and try to figure out when might be a polite time to make a quick getaway. Viqaas notices and whispers, "Give it a full hour and then we'll make our escape."

Ruby greets us with a tight squeeze, as if we have been friends for years, and the way she staggers and leans on me suggests that she's already drunk.

Someone cranks up the music, some thick beats striking through the well-decorated living room, and a rapper shouts in what I now know to be an east London accent. He sounds angry about warfare and revenge, and it's all too much, so I tell Viqaas I'm going to use the bathroom.

I find the bathroom off the hallway and savor the quieter noise as soon as I lock myself in. I think of the bathroom of the buzz-cut guy, and how far away that now seems. This sink hasn't become a grotesque face of startled tap eyes, a hooked spout nose, and a plughole mouth that is ready to devour me. I realize it's been a while since I noticed the smell of putrefying flesh, so I think of what it might be like to allow Viqaas to become one of the points to my pentacle of protection. Maybe he is the only source of safety that I need, but is that as irresponsible as stealth breeding? For me to feel safe, to allow him into my life, am I exposing him to dangers he might never have encountered?

I try to pee, but nothing flows out. This usually happens when I've taken too many drugs, but I've been clean for a few days, so it's more likely to be the strange sense of unease that's niggling me and causing me stage fright. It starts as a hair-line fracture in the back of my mind, barely even registering, until I realize that something is off. There are footprints all over the bathroom floor, not unusual in itself, given there's a party going on, but the shower curtain is also closed. It would be very on-brand for Max to be waiting behind there, just long enough for me to have my pants unbuckled so he could jump out and fuck me while he keeps one hand clamped over my mouth.

I see the shower curtain sway just as I turn, and as panic rises through my body, I rip it back. All I find is a small rubber duck smirking up at me. There's also a tiny window above the bath and someone has left it open. It's barely big enough to let in a cat, let alone a six-foot tall American, but now I see how it's been letting in a breeze to make the shower curtain swish back and forth. I slam it shut.

Max used to like to play games, dabbling in some kind of masochistic foreplay. He'd hide from me in the shadows or in a closet, or beneath a table, and then jump out, sometimes with a ski mask on, and force me onto the ground with a knife to my throat. He didn't like it when I played with his ego, saying that if he hadn't held a weapon, he wouldn't have been able to overpower me. This only made him thrust harder into me.

Those days, when I watched him sleep, it felt right to be entwined like that, when I believed that he could protect me. But then the fire happened, and he started to shrink from me, and the last time I watched him sleep, I remember staring down at his thinning hair and viewing him as nothing more than an old and weakened bully.

"Fuck," I hiss, "fuck you for haunting me for so long."

Standing back at the toilet, I'm finally able to relax again and the pee flows out of me. The scars on my thighs start to throb. I feel them there each day, as if he is still burning his initials into my flesh. At that time, I wasn't anything to anyone, so why wouldn't I let someone burn their initials into me? I was his for the taking, to be subjugated and possessed by some one-man empire. But in the harsh reality of the bright lights of this bathroom, the softness that Viqaas is offering makes any life I experienced so far seem dirty and cheap. I was that idiot who believed Max would offer me something more. I judged June for being the silent wife, but I was even worse, and it makes me want to crush the memories and stamp on them like they are fucking pests crawling about this bathroom.

Branded like livestock, but I didn't squeal like you hear in some of those abattoirs, when their eyes are wild with fear, and they silently beg to be spared. When the glowing ember met fragile flesh, with the fizz, sizzle, and smell of such sweetly singed flesh, he squirmed. But I did not. At that moment, some special part of him was touched, and I watched him unfurl like a blooming flower. He realized he had a taste for it, and he wanted to inflict more. Or, at least, that's what I told myself. He probably did it to all the people he fucked.

I hear a knock. And then another knock. From outside the door, I can hear a muffled argument developing; one person says something about privacy while another says something about basic bodily needs. Then someone starts to hammer on the bathroom door. It isn't just a polite knock, it's a crashing that is reverberating so hard that there are splinters of white paint exploding from around the door frame. I hear someone curse from outside the door, and just when the hammering reaches a crescendo, it suddenly stops.

I flush, wash my hands, and open the door, only to find an empty hallway. I am just about to turn off the light when I feel a hand on my shoulder.

"Fuck," I shout.

"Sorry."

It's Viqaas.

"Was that you hammering on the door just now?" I ask him.

He shakes his head as he pushes past me into the bathroom. He turns on the tap and splashes some water on his face; the droplets glistening in the overhead light.

"Nah. I've been bored out of my skull chatting to someone called Cynthia. She told me Daddy cut her off last year when she got with an Indian. I think she thinks anyone looking like me is Indian. She didn't even pause for a breath before she went from talking about *the Indian* to talking about her daddy's thoroughbreds."

"Yikes."

"It certainly was that. I'd far spend the time talking to you."

He's smiling as he dries his face and then he stops, seems to weigh something up, and then throws the towel in the sink.

"Fuck it," he says, and slips both hands around my face, pulling me gently to him. Our lips touch, and so do our tongues, and we press our bodies into each other.

I don't know how long we stand there, kissing with more passion than I've ever experienced, but eventually he breaks away, out of breath and flush faced.

"Wow," he says with a gasp. "That was worth the wait."

I thought better of asking why this was happening, and what it might mean. I just let him take my hand and say "Hour's up. Let's ditch this party and head back to mine."

We ran from the party, and we kept running until we couldn't breathe, so we had to stop. We've stopped in a narrow street with a crooked pub that's hunched in the shadows of newer developments of glass and steel. The windows of the pub are thickened like the glass of a bottle, and I wonder if this is deliberate, to hide the rampant alcoholism that defines British university life and, from what I've seen at a certain minute past five, the British after-work culture.

"You think this place is haunted?" I ask, uncertain what I want to hear in reply.

"You believe in that nonsense?" he asks, for once not adding a smile.

"I think so," I reply. "I mean, things happen that I can't explain. Horrible things, sometimes, weird images or movements that can't exist without pointing to some kind of haunting."

We walk deeper into the alley and a spider scuttles up a drainpipe.

"Ghosts don't exist," he says. "It's all in your imagination."

I wish I could take comfort from his certainty.

"In the queer community, we've always known haunted houses," I say. "I think it's the shame that haunts us. All those forbidden desires and hidden temptations that come to us in the dead of night…"

I stop myself before I speak of secret rooms, hidden keys, and fake wall panels.

"And that's not to mention the straight-boy crushes in middle school, all that unrequited love building up inside of us. It's a wonder we don't howl at the moon on a nightly basis."

I can see from his face that I've stumbled into a territory Viqaas isn't ready to explore, and maybe he won't ever accompany me into that world. Nothing's been promised, and you hear about this sort of thing happening all the time in university, where kids try on new identities to see if they fit.

Viqaas guides me through the dark alleyway and out into an explosion of light and noise that is the West End. People are spilling out of theatres, all of them too smartly dressed for the trash bags they have to step around to flag a cab home.

"Here," he says, pointing to the underground station. I don't know if I'm ready to return home so soon, where Max might be waiting for me, or there's the scuttling of eight spindly legs that hide in the folds of my curtains. But Viqaas pulls me by the hand, his skin so soft and warm that I don't want to break away from him.

We ride the tube in silence. The motion of the train keeps knocking our legs together, but neither of us moves further apart. The carriage is packed full of commuters, so I can't stare at his reflection in the window opposite us. I'm longing to trace the contours of his soft, rounded lips and his beautifully toned body. I'm conscious that these thoughts, and the movement of the train, will stir something in me, so I stare at the tube map above my head, choosing not to share how many tube stops I recognize from all the guys I've hooked up with since I arrived in this country.

When we get off the train, I can smell the putrefying flesh again, so I hurry Viqaas along, certain that I might see an arachnid scampering up between the two escalators, my father's face distorting in horror when he sees me with a man and not a woman. "Not a little girl, either" I want to scream at him, indignant that he of all people could judge me.

There's a sticky residue on the handrail of the escalator, and as we glide up to street level, I can hear a train rushing into one of the platforms behind us. Already I can feel the movement beneath my skin as I imagine tumors are growing, stirred into life by the iron oxide air and maghemite. They stir and flicker like maggots emerging from their eggs, and I look to the other people on the escalator, to see if there are signs that they feel it too. But everyone's face is muted and distant, and I realize they are gaunt and swollen and water-logged. These bodies are lifeless, you can see it In their eyes. They stare through me and some of them even have their hands outstretched, reaching for me to save them when they are already dead. All around us, the tunnel has filled with water that rushed so suddenly; I didn't even notice, and so we are held in this watery tomb, and I'm scared until I look at Viqaas, and I realize he's still smiling as he knows nothing of this. So I start to laugh, a dry, hard gasp of laughter that pulls at my chest.

"You okay?" Viqaas asks me.

I shrug as I continue to laugh.

"What's so funny?" he asks me.

How can I tell him that my mind is filled with tumors and maggots and drownings when his is probably calmed by the gentle splash of waves against rocks at an Aberystwyth beach, or the fussing and soothing of his parents' chatter as they worry about every one of his present and potential needs?

To expel some of this nervous energy, I suggest to Viqaas that we walk up the rest of the escalator. I offer some nonsense explanation about getting in our daily steps.

"You're losing it bro," he says to me, as he climbs the steep escalator behind me.

As soon as we leave the station, my phone rings, which completely throws me because I don't remember ever switching it from silent mode.

"You should answer it," Viqaas says as we cross the chaos of Euston Road.

"It's probably the wrong number," I shout above the honking of an angry cab driver.

"Or it isn't. Might be something important."

"They'll leave a voicemail."

Viqaas opens his mouth to object again, but then the phone falls silent.

Finally, we reach our halls of residence and my phone rings again. Viqaas shakes his head in dismay.

"I could never ignore a call like that. What if it's my mom or dad or sister? They would whoop my ass if I ignored them. They'd think that I didn't care about them, or I didn't need them anymore, and that makes me kinda sad."

"Fine," I say with a sigh, "I'll answer it." I don't want to be cruel and remind him that my own parents and sister are dead, so everything he said doesn't really apply to me.

I snatch the phone from my pocket and turn away from him as I say, "Hello?"

"Finally, you answer," comes the voice on the other end. It's an unknown number, but it's a British voice, so at least it isn't Max.

"Aren't you going to say something?" they ask me after a moment of silence. "Are you even listening to me?"

"I'm listening."

"It's good to finally hear your voice. Are you alone right now?"

"Yes," I lie, realizing it's Robert, my not-so-friendly *bobby who's likely to beat me.*

"Good. So what the fuck? Why the radio silence? Didn't you get my messages and voicemails?"

"You know that I did."

"So, are you going to explain yourself?"

"No."

"I'm being very patient with you," he says. "But I don't have to be."

I let out a sigh, more of boredom than anything else, and I can see Viqaas gesticulating at me.

"If you want me to leave you to it, I can," Viqaas whispers, only he's a little too loud because Robert starts to curse at me.

"You fucking cunt. You lied to me. You're not alone, you're with that fucking brown boy. What the fuck is this? This always happens to me. I mean, I meet someone, and they say they like me, and they seem nice, and we hang out and have fun, but then they don't want to know, it's like they get bored. Have you got bored of me, Dylan? Is that what it is? Because if it is that, just say it, don't string me along like this…"

"Who's stringing you along?" I reply as I pace back and forth. I should just sleep with the guy to appease him. That way, he'd become pacified for a while, until he wanted it again. I can numb myself to most things, and it really isn't that hard. I know you might judge this as sinful, as Pastor Pry might have done, or you might label it as something diagnosable, but in another place or another time, this might be deemed to be a strength or a superpower. Don't judge it until you've tried fucking with the hand squeezed tightly around your throat, or the throat of another, and the fact that some call it a violation or the act of a beast makes it all the more exciting. We're all just a composite of nerve-endings, after all, so aren't we getting ahead of ourselves when the pastors and psychologists try to create a convoluted concept about the basic pastime of fucking, the animalistic urges that remind us that we are still, for now, part of the living.

"I'm sure we can work this out," he continues as I pace about the street. "Can't we give it a trial period and if you really are bored, if you think it isn't going to work out, then I'll respect that? I'll step away and let that Pakistani have you."

I'm afraid of what I might say or do if I don't keep pacing about this street, if I don't use some of the energy that is building up as it writhes beneath my skin. But I can only fight one person at a time, and with Max lingering in the background, waiting to pounce, I have no choice but to switch into fawning mode with this imbecile of a policeman.

"Trust me, you're hot," I lie, "and I really would like to make a go of it. There's so much going on that I just need to sort a few things out. Would you give me a day or so?"

There's a pause, and a crackling on the line, and I wonder if he's touching himself after I just called him hot.

"Fine," he finally replies. "I'll give you a day, maybe even two days, to figure it out. But then I expect a call."

When he hangs up, I imagine him going to cry on his mummy's shoulder, and she will complain about cancel culture, saying *you can't say anything about brown people these days*, not without getting into trouble, or having your job taken away from you. And she would know because she lost her job of fifteen years as a secretarial assistant just because she called someone an *angry colored woman* and refused to apologize for it. Maybe she'll stroke her son's hair and reassure him that he's a big strong man who's clever and a true hero when the real villains are the ones who sneak into this country and take everyone's job, the ones with the brown skin who could never look as pure and big and strong as Robert, who's so much like her in so many ways, this apple of her eye.

"Shall I meet you later?" Viqaas asks as I join him in front of our halls.

"No. Fuck that shit. It's nothing."

He doesn't wait for me to explain any more before he's leading me by the hand, up the stairs, and through the corridors to his room.

Once inside, he kisses me, and we crush our bodies against each other. Every time before him, I've been hasty, clumsy, drugged up or drunk, but this time, in full sobriety, with ease and softness, I follow his silent instruction.

Afterwards, we lie in bed together, and his long fingers trace the scars on my thighs.

"Does it hurt?" he asks me.

"Not anymore," I reply.

"What happened? You don't have to tell me if you don't want to."

"It's okay."

So I finally tell him about Max. I try to explain things as clearly as I can, but it's hard to encapsulate so much. Some things you only learn with age or hindsight, and some things are still too shameful to admit.

"That isn't love or lust," he says, "that's abuse."
I shrink away from Viqaas' arms, slipping out of bed and gathering my clothes.
"What's up?"
"I don't know."
"It's true. Whether you want to hear it or not. Max sounds like a fucking psychopath, and when he first, well, you know, you were way too young to know what was going on. There was a power dynamic that he took advantage of."
"Okay, we can stop talking about this now."
"I don't want to upset you. Sorry, Dyls."
"It's okay, or it's not. I don't fucking know. That's kind of how it feels now. I don't know anything. I mean, I've been the *slut*, the *queerboy* who fucked around, and now suddenly you're painting me as *a victim*. It's a lot to get my head around."
"You're not a slut."
"You don't know the half of it. I told you he was married."
"Yes. And I've seen you sneaking off from the halls most nights, and sure, you've probably been seeing many different guys. Whatever. Stop beating yourself up and stick to the point. That man, Max fucking West, was a creep, and you were young, way too young to know any better."
"It still doesn't sit right. Besides, you painting me as some victim leaves me feeling pretty vulnerable, and the last thing I can afford right now is a hole in my armor. He'll see it a mile off."
"So you're gonna meet up with him?"
I shrug my shoulders.
"I don't know. I haven't replied to any of his messages, not yet. I mean, I don't ever want to, but putting it off indefinitely doesn't seem like a long-term plan."
"I could come with you. If you really have to see him, I could be your moral support."

"I imagine you probably would, but the last thing I want is to drag you into this."

"I'm already in it," he says as he snakes his fingers along my cheek.

I wish I can end this day with just Viqaas and me, but I hear my phone ringing again and I see some messages flashing from Max.

"You should check those," Viqaas says with a kiss on my forehead.

"Fine," I say, reaching for my phone and unlocking the screen.

"I've been patient enough," one message reads. "I'm done fucking around and waiting for you," another one says. "St Martins church, Trafalgar Square. Tomorrow afternoon at one. Deal with me or I'll leave you to Sammy."

Chapter Ten

~~~

Max

~~~

They closed off the roads around my hotel. Some bullshit about flooding. I was meant to be meeting a new contact in Wapping to scope out a new development site, but with these closures, I won't have time for that and the meetup with Dylan. I opt for a video call to the Wapping contact, even though it's a shit substitute for the real thing. Via video, you can't stand over someone, threatening them with your silence. I mean, fuck, they can easily just end the call. Either that or they'll record it and share it online. Dan was threatening to do that if I didn't return his calls. This is years ago now, and I don't know why it's come back to haunt me like this. I guess business trips do that, where you sit in a soulless hotel room and stare at your memories like they are cheap souvenirs.

Before I replaced him with Dylan, Dan was besotted with

me, and I made sure he gave me his all. But when Dylan came on the scene, I didn't really have a use for Dan, so he started to threaten that he would post shit online about us. I don't think he ever would've gone through with it, not really. And before he ever got to upload anything, I would've taken him down to one of my warehouses to neutralize any threat he posed to me. But in the end, he neutralized himself by running in front of a truck on Route 17.

Dan told me to be at that gas station at that particular time. He told me he had something important to tell me, to show me, or whatever. I'm still trying to work out why I didn't send one of my boys to sort him out instead of playing along with his stupid games. I guess I became petty, bringing Dylan along for the ride. I kinda wanted Dan to see me with his replacement to get the message that we were done. I knew the kid was on the edge. I mean, Dan's messages were getting so fucking long and rambling; most of that shit didn't even make sense. I could feel that we were heading towards something weird, like we were both eyeballing each other with a gun in between us, just waiting for the moment one of us flinched and grabbed it. Well, he certainly showed me. I figure this is one of the few means left for anyone to get one over on me. Can't argue with a corpse, right?

After the incident, Katherine asked too many questions about the kid. I told her we were business associates, or maybe I said he had worked for me. I don't know. I was in shock at the time, so I was bullshitting on the fly. Whatever answers I gave her, she just stared at me with those big, wide eyes. She didn't share any of her conclusions, and maybe she hadn't made any. Maybe she was still trying to work out what kind of father I really was.

I still see his body cartwheeling through the sky, his intestines flying in the air like a tickertape parade. His blood sprayed like a can of soda would when I'd goof around with the workmen and throw one at them. Before the impact, before he exploded, I swear I saw him laughing, a full fucking belly laugh.

With those wild green eyes, he always looked hot when he

laughed. And that thick head of jet-black hair. The last time we'd fucked, I wanted to rib him for slicking it back, so I said that the Italian half of him was trying to play at being some kind of gangster. Only that time he didn't laugh, he just stared at me like I'd whipped him with a belt or something. It was then that I realized he was trying to impress me, trying to keep up with me and Sammy, and from that moment, I kinda lost interest in him. You can try too hard, you know?

I remember how Dylan cried when he saw the carnage, and he asked me whether he was the cause of it. He knew he was Dan's younger replacement, and until that moment, he probably felt like it was an ego boost. That might've been the first time Dylan learned that nothing is for free.

All I could think about was how some mother or father was gonna be torn apart when the cop turned up on their doorstep. I could picture the wailing, how they might even beat the cop a little with their helpless fists, but I didn't feel anything. I saw it; I heard it, but that was it.

Eat or get eaten.

With all this violence in my life, there's a danger that I might be accused of causing it all. Hard to argue with that, really, but I've never really cared until now. But Katherine is growing up, and she's getting wise to the dismissive explanations that no longer add up. She keeps asking me about people from her past, the ones who vanished, and I feel sick when I see, for a moment, a flash of fear in her face. Maybe I'm stupid to think that this was sustainable, that I could show her mercy and love while I inflicted so much violence everywhere else in the world. I knew I had justifications for all of it, but I doubt she would accept any of them.

Destroy or be destroyed.

If something happens to Dylan, this friend Katherine has grown attached to, then she'll blame me, and I don't know if she would ever forgive me for that. But if I don't do what those voices ask of me, that siren call urging me to bring Dylan back to Rotherwell, then they will go after Katherine instead. This time, I'm not going to let a woman I love slip away.

"The cycle of familial trauma."

That's what Katherine has been saying. She's been taking a psych class, and she's taken to diagnosing anyone who will listen. It's fucking infuriating when it's nothing more than a game of *blame the parents and grandparents*.

"Grandad was a brute," she declared.

"Enough," I snapped back. She was right, but I didn't want to hear it from her. I'd figured I could ease into it in my own good time, like, never.

"It's okay," she added. "There's no shame in it."

"Who said anything about shame? I'm just saying you need to zip it about someone who's dead and buried."

She widened her eyes at me in frustration.

"I'm just saying, if I can get a word in edgeways, that many of the best people are wounded."

"Okay. Cool. Thank you for your contribution."

Despite all my protests, I was fascinated that she could express herself with such confidence when her lookalike, my mother, was slapped down every time she opened her mouth. They had the same long blond hair and the same dimples when they smiled. The same laugh, the same crazy sense of humor. Same defiance. The only difference was that I still had Katherine to lose.

It was a mistake to share any of this with Dylan but, after the fire, something weakened in me. And then the words just tumbled out, like guts from a freshly sliced stomach. And that was the moment Dylan started to burn me. The first time, June had been at the shore house with the kids, so we had the house to ourselves, and after we spent the afternoon fucking, we lay there together as I watched the smoke rising from the rubble of Dylan's family home. The smokey phantoms lingered outside my bedroom window, spectators of our naked show, and I thought of how rough he'd been, how he'd bitten and clawed at me while we writhed about the sheets. I wondered if I was teaching him violence as my dad had, as his neighbor had when he forced me onto the ground in his basement, and I figured that if Dylan was developing a taste for it, he wouldn't stop at me to satisfy his hunger. I'd been careless to introduce more violence to pollute and threaten my family, perpetuating that fucking *trauma cycle* that Katherine always talks about.

Dylan didn't even ask me if he could light a joint, in my fucking bedroom of all places, but before I could say anything, he was sticking the glowing ember into my naked thighs. I heard the singe of heat at the same time I smelled my burning flesh.

"I'm not into that," I'd snapped, snatching hold of his wrist so he couldn't do it again. Instead of apologizing or putting out the joint, his mouth twisted in a sneer.

"Pussy," he hissed.

"What did you say?" I didn't really believe it, certain he'd never risk fucking around like that, but he said it again. I grabbed his throat and squeezed, his veins pulsated beneath my fingertips, and his hold body went rigid.

"Fuck you," he spat in my face as I felt the searing burn in my thighs. He was doing it again. The fucker was actually playing this game with me, even though he knew he would end up dead.

Over his shoulder, the smokey phantoms continued to dance outside my bedroom window, those toxic fumes from the fortress site. Maybe Dylan wanted to die. I mean, his, *their*, parents and sister were all dead, so maybe he wanted to join them.

"I'm gonna tell you one more time," I said, very calmly, and close enough to his face that I could smell the peppermint of his toothpaste. I knew he always cleaned his teeth before we fucked, even though the natural smell of him drove me wild.

Again, there was a burning sensation in my thighs, and that flipped the switch in me. I saw my father's face and his sneer, and I squeezed harder and I could hear Dylan choking beneath me, and I wanted to cry because I didn't want to hurt him, not him as well, not another one in the long line of losses and violence that just keeps happening over and over again. I felt trapped in a loop, a living hell that is the color of his blue lips and purple veins that bulge beneath my fingertips.

But he didn't die. Quite the opposite, in fact. I felt him rise beneath me, grow bigger and stronger, and he broke free from my grip, and I felt like there was a sideways shift because it had been so long since I had felt failure. It was a horrible, slippery loss that made me want to scream out "Stop" and try again.

Too quickly, he was on top of me, that rock-hard body that refused to let me go. Still he smirked as he kept me pinned to the bed, and I didn't let him fuck me, but he did it anyway. He had a power that overwhelmed me, pinned me to the bed so I was helpless. When I struggled and made noises showing that he was hurting me, it made him push even harder. He would probably say that this made us even, that warrior with his battle-lustful thrusts. Frozen there, held by some ancient force, I was locked in a mirror image of the life we had shared before, where we silently slipped into roles that opposed everything we had known.

When he was finished, I glanced down, and I saw the pale pink of fresh burn wounds on my thighs. They were clustered together in an orderly straight line down one side, and then curving back up to meet the starting point. It was clearly a *D* and *G* scorched into my flesh. Behind Dylan, I saw them watching us, those hooded creatures that stank of putrefying flesh. They were rocking back and forth in unison, nodding as they encouraged Dylan to do more.

Quid pro quo.

Since then, Dylan has claimed that I burned him. Even though I have the scars, he says I did it to myself after I burned him, and I used his joint to do it. He tells me the same story over and over again, that apparently when I did it, I sat there laughing like a maniac. After I burned myself and him, he says that I stuck my finger into each of the puss-filled holes, licking the stickiness as I smiled. When he told me the story, the hooded creatures were lingering behind him, and I don't know if he even knew they were there.

Those fucking hooded creatures won't leave me be, and now they've followed me to London. They're sitting behind me right now, crawling across the headboard in this shitty hotel room. To think that those childish fears were true all along; the creatures really do visit, and they wait for nightfall, when you are paralyzed by sleep.

I watch those creatures crawl about as they remind me about Katherine.

She's on her own, right? they whisper to me. *She's helpless to what might crawl across her face and mouth when she's paralyzed by sleep. She always hated spiders.*

So what are you going to do about it? Are you a man or a mouse?

My fuckup of a father used to say that to me. No matter how hard I try to ignore it, his voice is mixed in there with the rest of the hauntings. It's because of the bullshit he would say to me, about what makes a "man" rather than a "faggot" that I push my son, Smithson, away but allow Katherine to show me her love.

The last thing you want is a pussy of a son.

I can still smell my father, that stale liquor on his breath and the cigarettes staining his filthy fingers. Most days, he could barely stand upright and yet he would still question my strength. Mine, of all people. He thought he could make me feel small, that he could tell me what to do, and I wouldn't fight back. It didn't make me feel proud leaving him with that split lip and purple, swollen eye. It wasn't like this was a defining moment where we could right our relationship and have peace in his final years. He won again because he fixed me with that look that he always used, that disgust and disappointment that keeps burning inside of me.

He told everyone that some kids had broken into his house and roughed him up. When June saw my knuckles that night, she wouldn't look me in the eye. She had been the one to respond to the call from the hospital to tell her that my dad had been found by a neighbor in his doorway.

"He kept you alive," June said to me that night. "After your mom left, he kept paying the bills so you still had a roof over your head and food in your belly."

"Barely any."

"Sure. Okay, but... Look, I'm not going to ask you what happened between the two of you and how you hurt your hand. I'm just thinking about what you do going forward. He's your father, and he's old and vulnerable."

"You don't know the half of it." And I was never going to tell her.

"No, I don't, but I know that he's a very old man now, and you don't have much time left with him. So, you can either spend that time full of bitterness, harking on about the past, or you can make the best of what you have now."

I refused to put anything on my bloody knuckles, so she left the Neosporin on my bedside table.

You let him scar you; he branded you with his own initials. You let that faggot conquer you.

I still feel the torn skin on my buttocks. I still hear the swish of leather as the belt was whipped from his jeans. And that one moment I pleaded with my dad, I actually became a pussy and cried when he held me by the throat at the top of the stairs. I thought he was going to drop me.

Wash away your sins.

Isn't that what Pastor Pry would say? It seems so simple, when water is in such plentiful supply these days. Just look at the fucking rain right now in this dismal city. Just wash the blood and shit off the ground and pretend there's no violence, no puncturing of the skin. No scars in the shape of someone's initials.

Come one this afternoon, the roads must be open, and Dylan better turn up.

I bet the kid appreciates my choice of St Martin's church as a meeting point, where there's a statue of some queer author Dylan used to go on about. It's been shoved in the back, where, by night, drunks piss on it after the pubs have closed, and, by day, children point at it and ask who Oscar Wilde is. Parents often steer their kids' attention to a transphobic author instead, only I don't know if she's really transphobic. It's just what Dylan told me. Would you believe that Dylan tried to get our local library to remove her books from their shelves? When they refused, Dylan went off on a rant about Pride and the celebration of trans and queer rights, as if Dylan expected a medal for shoving their dick in someone's ass. They should be careful because it doesn't take much for the laws to change and you find yourself in jail for buggery. Tastes change. I mean, one minute they're throwing queers in jail where they starve to death, and the next they're putting up a statue to commemorate them.

Dylan and Katherine would say that there are churches like St Martins all over the world where preachers like Pry are waiting to pick on the carcasses of the next object of everyone's hatred. Those preachers have a story for every sin, and if Isla were here to see this kind of rain, she'd be flicking to the tale about Noah and how the floods can wash away the sinners. Or was that the sin? Either way, I'm happy to pair up with her if it means I'm gonna be saved.

Days before they left Rotherwell, I found Dylan standing at the fortress site and muttering to the smoldering rubble. When I touched their shoulder, their whole body seized up as if they were bracing for impact.

"What's up?" I asked them, a little irritated that they were taking up my time like this. Even though the air was still that day, the aconite stirred as if some invisible hand was stroking it.

I could hear the siren call and it reminded me of all that I was letting slip through my fingers, the way Dylan had burned me, and the force with which they could pin me to the bed. The voices were reminding me that if I could just give them Dylan, everything would return to the way it was, and Katherine would be safe.

Do it. Do it now.

I should've done it there and then. I should've given them the kid, but Dylan sensed something in me and slipped away from me.

I should have followed Dylan.

And now I hear laughing everywhere I go. Everyone's fucking laughing at me. My father, June, Dylan, that bitch pastor, they're all laughing at my weakness, the way I let people get away with things, the way I let people overpower me, turn me over, fuck me, and then burn their initials into me like the faggot I really am.

Chapter Eleven

~~~

Dylan

~~~

We walk out of the halls of residence and the clouds disperse. Despite the flooding, sunlight breaks through and it feels like someone has turned up the contrast on the picture. I feel disorientated because I only remember seeing such vivid colors in Rotherwell, so every person who passes looks strangely familiar. I imagine these could be ghosts of my former life on the East Coast, sent to warn me or even to drag me back.

As we cut through the park, watching people play tennis together, I notice that Viqaas keeps glancing over at me and laughing.

"What's got into you?" I ask him.

"What?"

"That," I say as soon as he lets out another one of his mischievous laughs.

"So I'm not allowed to be happy?"

"Sure you are, but something's up. I can tell."

"My Dyls, you need to try this happiness thing yourself some time. All that negativity is toxic."

"I laugh and smile, when there's a good enough reason. Doing it for no reason could be seen as certifiable behavior. Anyway, you still haven't told me where we're going. Is it something to do with that? A brand-new exhibit where there are dancing monkeys? A performing seal who can drive a car? Come on, how am I to know?"

Earlier on, as we were getting dressed in his room, he said he wanted to take me somewhere, but he couldn't tell me where.

For hours, we've been trapped in his room as we explored each other's bodies as much as the past we lived before we met each other. Only a matter of hours, but it feels like years, and I can see that he is falling just as fast.

"You just have to trust me," he says, but I'm still not sure I know how to.

"Why can't you just tell me?"

"Oh, come on, what's wrong with a surprise every once in a while?"

Once we are through the park and waiting to cross the road, he finally says, "Okay, my parents and sister are meeting me at the café down the road in about five minutes. I figured you might want to join us."

"You figured *what*?"

Of course he's rushing in too soon. I did the same with Max when it was my first time.

"Hey, easy," he says, obviously noticing how widely my eyes stare at him. "I'm not turning into a psycho. They just happened to be in London to visit me, and it's inevitable that I'm going to meet up with them."

"But it isn't inevitable that I'm going to join you. The things you said, about haram and stuff, and your sister being scary and wanting to murder me, and you."

"I'm not saying we need to have a coming out session. I'm not going to introduce you on the back of a Pride float with rainbow flags and Charli XCX playing on a loudspeaker. I just want you lot to meet each other and take it from there."

"Fine. No problem," I lie as the panic starts to rise in my chest. I feel like I'm being maneuvered into place, no more or less than when Charles told me to lift my hips some more and Max would tell me not to cry when it hurt.

Too quickly, we are walking through the flimsy door of a café I always passed and wanted to explore. The jingle of a bell hanging above the doorway rattles my nerves, and I become the incendiary device, a ticking time bomb ready to unleash carnage that his family never deserved.

I see them in the corner, an angry young woman and an equally angry but defeated looking older woman who looks vaguely like Viqaas. And the father could've been Viqaas, if it weren't for the dried out, wrinkled skin beneath his eyes and the thinned-out head of hair.

"Viq! Over here," the father calls to us as he waves. He's too impatient to wait for us to join him, so he races over like an excited schoolboy.

Already I am shaking the father's hand. He's a short man who smiles like Viqaas and nods his head at nothing identifiable, and all I can think of is whether I washed my hands after making his son orgasm just fifteen minutes earlier. I am the rot, a possession to haunt them, and I feel the contamination start to spread.

Viqaas' parents present themselves as good, tidy people of quiet conversation. They are so quiet that I can't hear them above the screaming in my ears as I'm haunted by my sister being torn apart by my father and my mother slashing and burning her way through to try to save what was already lost. This is what I understand a family to be, so I can't escape the horrors, and I look for signs of it inside Viqaas' father, writhing about beneath the skin of his smile.

Viqaas' sister and mother fix me with a knowing stare, as if they are telling me that they've seen me before, in their worst nightmares, and they know what I've been doing with their Viqaas. Still silently, they press into me the promise that they will keep me from him for as long as they can.

The pendants of a bracelet on the mother's wrist jingle about as she strokes her long, dark hair that is cascading all over her shoulders. I imagine she hoped that she would one day get a daughter-in-law to bully and give her gifts like this bracelet, or a neck scarf, and she would very much like to tether such a neck scarf around her own neck right now, or mine, or both, because she sees how her son's face flushes with excitement as he catches the eye of this strange white person she is being introduced to.

I take a seat at their table, Viqaas' sister refusing to move along the bench to give me room, and I listen to Viqaas' endless stories about his son's childhood.

"Vafia," Viqaas says to his sister. "Have you said hello? Have you introduced yourself to my buddy?"

She shrugs in response and stares back at her cell phone. She keeps her lips pursed tightly with disapproval as she hides beneath a heavy fringe. I'm wondering whether she always guessed something about her brother, whether his excessive jokes and enthusiasm about every damned thing under the sun made her search for things online. "How to tell if my brother's gay" and "What to do with a gay" and "Is gay really haram?".

"Ah, American," the dad smiles. "Very interesting. And what do your parents do?"

Viqaas blushes.

"Dad, I told you Dylan's parents passed away, and I told you it didn't happen that long ago."

His dad looks genuinely sorry as he shakes his head and apologizes.

"Too young to be on your own. So very sad and tragic. I am very, very sorry"

His eyes soften with sadness, and he places a hand on mine.

"Maybe one day you'll consider us to be your parents. Any friend of Viqaas is a friend of ours."

I listen as Viqaas' dad tells me stories of limited consequence. He uses this gentle tone that soothes me, and I can imagine he is content to let life slip by as effortlessly as the turning leaves. He doesn't seem haunted by violence or ghosts, otherwise his breath would come in shorter gasps and his tone would be sharpened with fear. To realize this makes me scared for him because he isn't dried out and hardened, not shell-like to make him impenetrable to the dangers that linger around me. Caught in a gravitational pull, it would be so easy to drag him into a nightmare world where he's washed far away from the safety and comfort that he once knew.

I make our meetup as quick as politeness can permit before I make excuses about studying and tiredness. Viqaas gives me a *Yeah, right* wide-eyed look, but he says nothing as I leave the café.

Back in my room, I wash my face at the sink, trying to get rid of a sticky feeling of shame. I try to forget for a little, and yet all I hear is the chattering of the jawbone beneath my bed. If I look under there, I'm afraid of what I might find; hooded creatures, an arachnid with my father's face and its eight legs crawling all over Viqaas' sister.

Bad things happen to bad people.

Max has been calling. He's probably making sure that I'm not going to stand him up because his ego probably couldn't take it. He's used to people doing what he tells them to do. He once told me that the last time someone let him down was when his mother walked out on him. "So," he said, "imagine the rage that might be unleashed if anyone made me feel that worthless again." I could see that he was scared of this happening as much as I was.

I hear a knock at the door. I freeze, careful not to make a sound. After another knock, I hold my breath. I try to figure out how long I can do this without passing out. Already I am seeing stars and the room is starting to shift about before my eyes.

"I hope you're not wanking in there. Don't want you tiring yourself out."

Viqaas.

When I open the door, I can tell that something has shifted in him. He's not smiling anymore. He lunges for me, pressing his lips against mine as he pins me to the bed. Every one of my senses is heightened and I can see and smell and hear and taste and touch things all at once, in the present but also in the past, where the fortress stands tall, undamaged by any fire, and I feel hope. But then I feel something plunging into me and it hurts, and I am afraid, and I feel hot, so hot that there is sweat breaking out across my forehead and trickling down to sting my eyes. I'm burning, and I see the fortress burning, and Max is on top of me, not Viqaas, and he's inside of me, but then we switch, and I am on top of him, and inside of him, and then I see that it is Viqaas again and not Max, and then the fire is out, it isn't smoldering, there's nothing but a cool breeze stirring about our sweat-stained skin.

We lay naked in the bed together, still and staring at each other, and Viqaas seems to be trying to figure something out. I guess I am too, and perhaps our thoughts are in sync as I wonder what version he's going to get from me, and how this will end. Despite the stillness that has descended upon this room, there's still a monster that sleeps inside the closet of my fears. It's a monstrous tree that stretches far and wide, so at night it bursts out of the closet and penetrates me, through my mouth and my ears and every orifice to reach the heart of me. I've stood at that tree so many times, watching Ania grow swollen and heavy as she hanged there, ready to drop with the very next breeze.

Nothing more haunting than a person's greed.

As I watched Ania sway on that tree, I felt more roots growing up from the ground and through the veins in my legs to puncture every internal organ as it charged up through my throat, spouting words I didn't understand but I felt it invading every inch of me, this contaminant, this invasive species; the rot that is my family tree.

I can't remain trapped by these fears any longer. I don't know whether I am the contamination or whether something or someone contaminated me.

You can get the answer.

I'm caught in this loop and I'm sick of it. I'm sick of shrinking in on myself and hiding from my own reflection, out of fear that I might see my father and his sickening desires.

Only one way to find out. Come back home.

I want to know whether I can look Viqaas' parents in the eye. I want to know whether this is just a trauma cycle that needs to be broken, so I can exorcise myself of any shame that was never mine in the first place. Or, if I am rotten to the core, at least I will know that I should keep my contaminants away from Viqaas and his family, so I don't drag them down to the underworld with me.

Return to Rotherwell, you'll find out for sure.

Last night, I dreamt of Robert in a tunic emblazoned with swastikas. I was helpless as he frog-marched me across Trafalgar Square. He opened up the back of his police van, and there was my father, still sprouting the eight legs of an arachnid. Robert seemed nonplussed about this, he just wanted me to stop struggling and fighting him. If I could just go limp and let him fold me up like a little package, he could slot me neatly into the back and go about his day.

"There's a good boy, or girl, or *girlyboy*, or whatever you call yourself these days, while you touch yourself and put your penis between your legs and pretend you have a neat little vagina. Isn't that what deviants like you do, dirty deviants who make the place all untidy when we have nice boys' and girls' bathrooms, nice orderly clothing sections of department stores, and you can see it in the older school buildings, etched in stone to weather all elements, to last longer than you and I, it says it right there, right above the doorways, that there is one entrance for the boys and one entrance for the girls. So why do you insist on confusing things, just as your sort will confuse your body parts, you'll do things with your back entrance which is only built for pushing things out not pushing things in, even though you and I know that I do it too, and quite like it, but that doesn't count because I wear a uniform and you do not. I don't want a vagina and also a prick, and you probably do, although I don't really know what you do want or do when you're left alone, so it's best that deviants like you are cleaned off the streets of London, and maybe if you're good, we might put up a statue of you years down the line, after we've thrown you in prison and left you to starve and rot."

Robert gave my father a quick *Seig Heil* before he shoved me into the van, muttering something about my father being a pillar of the community and how I am the apple of the eye of this honest, hard-working man. He told me that he wished there could be more apples to grow on such a mighty tree, and he wanted there to be whole orchards of these trees to regrow and flourish no matter how often the diggers came and tried to tear them down.

Chapter Twelve

~~~

Max

~~~

As soon as I left the hotel, making my way to Trafalgar Square, this cop, a young, skinny guy, kind of a cute geeky twink, tried to stop me.

"Sorry, sir," he began, his voice breaking with the tension. It amazes me that the British hate conflict so much that even their cops aren't comfortable handling it.

"You can't go that way," he continued. "The roads are closed because of the flooding."

"Dude, I have things to do. I can see to the end of the street. I mean, we're talking deep puddles, not rivers."

"I'm sorry, sir. My orders are to keep the road closed for now."

I figure this is why this empire fell so hard; they got caught up in so much red tape that they were helpless when their kingdom was plundered. And now this twink of a cop is trying to use a bit of blue and white police tape to stop me, which is about as effective as the rubber truncheon he's been given.

"Later, dude," I wave to him as I duck under the tape and step around the deeper parts of the water.

I see a pair of rats scurrying from behind some trash bags, but they have nowhere to go, so they freeze, staring up at me as I walk past. I have boots on so I could bring the rubber soles down on their tiny skulls, listening to the squish as I watch their death twitches. I glance back to see if the cop is watching, and I see that he's talking to someone who seems familiar, someone with the same stooped body that I've seen before. Something alerts the old guy's attention, and he turns around to face me and then I realize I know him and that sniggering as he staggers in a drunken stupor. He's still so far away from me, but I can smell his rancid breath and the stink of beer and vodka. I want to crush his frail, tiny skull, so I turn back to crush those rats instead, but I'm too late. They've drowned and so they just float in front of me, their thick, fleshy tails swirling as the water is stirred by something unseen.

Katherine would say that I'm displacing my anger.

Destroy or be destroyed.

I'm getting closer to Trafalgar Square and I'm flicking through different scenarios that I can play out to get Dylan back to Rotherwell if he won't cooperate.

Package him up in your suitcase. Bodies can be folded in all manner of ways.

I heard about someone doing that not far from here; he folded himself up into a suitcase, even locking himself in for extra thrills, only he got stuck. I don't know if he suffocated or starved in there, but it took a number of days to find his body locked in a duffel bag. Initial reports were that he was found in the crawlspace of some attic, but that was later corrected to be a bathroom. Creepy as shit. What made it more suspicious was that he was a spy who was working for the British equivalent of the NSA. You can't make this shit up. My betting is that he found out something he shouldn't have, like some backroom deal between the government and the ultra-rich, the *green wellie brigade* who look practically destitute but sit on fortunes.

The rain is starting to intensify again, and people are looking panicked because it doesn't seem like the water is going anywhere. I see an elderly woman start to cry, and she slows my pace as I work over the idea of stopping to help her. Already I've seen her stumble twice, and one of those times she was knee-deep in water. I think of hidden glass or wire cutting her open, and I wonder how long it would take for her to bleed out. But still, I walk on towards the lions and fountains and pigeons and column of Trafalgar Square.

Already I see in the distance the spire of St Martin's church.

Chapter Thirteen

Dylan

"I am generous," one message begins, "do you know how generous? I've let you live. I've fought the urge to cut you from ear to ear and make you smile about the sordid little things you do with that dick of yours."

I don't think these are from Max because it isn't his style. I keep thinking about Robert, that annoying British cop and his unending frustrations about life; not least the impotence of his rubber truncheon.

"I know you still have a dick," the message continues, "under those clothes that you like to tear off with strangers. You might claim you're not a man, but you're still as dangerous as one, more dangerous when you pretend not to be one. A wolf in sheep's clothing because you really want the women, you're just playing at this queer shit so the women

194

won't suspect it until it's too late and they see your ugly little dick. Isn't that what you like to think about when you're home alone at night? I've seen your internet searches and the filth and gore you like to watch, illuminated only by the glow of your cell phone and touching yourself because you have that dick that gets hard when you look at that filth, doesn't it, and you want others to like it too, don't you, and even if they don't have willies then you want them to get wet when they look at that filth, that sick filth that you want everyone to do, to stick things up assholes and spit roast and choke and get choked and orgasm and then choke again. You want that as much as you want everyone to cut their willies off and pretend to make vaginas like you are children playing at dressing up, even though this isn't a game is it, this isn't something you can just get bored of and switch to another game, you degenerate filth. Don't you get it? Didn't you hear about those detransitioners who were even more fucked up than they were before, because you told them to chop their willie off or carve out their Adam's apple or chop their breasts off or take drugs to make their facial hair grow, even though they can't take any of it back because their wombs have been scooped out like kumquats, and you probably ate their wombs because you'd heard somewhere that it prolonged your life, as you ate their tiny fetuses that were trying to grow in those scooped out wombs because you thought those embryos would make you live forever, and maybe that's what you're trying to do with all that, you're trying to live forever when you should take a dressing gown cord and tighten it around your neck until you can't see straight, until you feel the warm piss leaking down your legs that you shaved only this morning, I mean, what a waste of time that was when you could've been watching more of your fucked up tranny porn where they fuck and piss and shit on each other and it makes you hard again. Well, this time you won't get hard, or you might, that one more time, because you like getting choked, even when you are doing it to yourself and dreaming that it is the big hand of some big business owner who treats you like shit and burns you, but you still keep coming back for more. You're imagine it is his hand, and maybe you're trying to kiss it, trying to get some kind of acknowledgement that this was all worthwhile, so you use your final few breaths to wait for a kiss that is never going to come when your lips only make contact with the fabric of your dressing gown cord, so you won't shrivel and lose the feeling down there, and you wonder if you are dying, because you might as well be dead if it all shrivels up down there, if you can't be a fuckboy or fuckgirl of a fucktheythemtheirs, I mean, have you really thought this all through, do you know what you're doing right now, or is it all going to become clear in those dying gasps, too late, when you realize you got it wrong and this world was the underworld, and the one you were so angry at, the one you would fight when you played dressup as that rainbow warrior, was actually safer and more nourishing than you gave it credit for. You got it wrong, you silly little asshole, you silly fucktheythemtheirs, and now you're going to die alone in that filthy little room of yours in a city you barely know about, where no one will notice if you're gone, especially when you've changed your name, you're untraceable, as if you never existed in the first place. You might as well do it now and die by your own hand, just as your fucked up little sister did, only strong enough to hack it for sixteen poxy years before she got into choking too and choked herself so hard in that orchard at the back of your house that her parents found her swinging by some piece of rope from the garage. Die a horrible death, where skin flaps open and you feel every nerve-ending poked. I want to rub salt on those nerve endings, so you know who you are dealing with, so you think twice before you spread your disease and filth around this city. Fuck off back to your disease-ridden country, you fuck. And if you don't leave, I'll bury you underground with all the other rotting queer pig corpses and hold your head under water in a torrent of filth."

If it is Robert, I want to know how he knows so much, as if he's been watching my nightmares. I could've said things while I slept next to him, that one time I made the mistake of letting him in my room to fuck. It was a momentary lapse in judgment, but maybe that was all it took.

The underground has been suspended, so I walk all the way from my halls to Trafalgar Square. Usually this isn't a problem, but the flooding has caused so many road closures that it took me double the amount of time. I'm surprised Max hasn't been calling to harass me about keeping him waiting. I glance behind my shoulder, just in case, and I feel foolish that the thought of him still scares me.

There's a screech of brakes and I flinch, still expecting to see that kid cartwheel across Route 17. It's been years, but it still haunts me. The way Dan's blood sprayed majestically like a flower in its final bloom, I don't think I'll ever get that out of my mind.

That afternoon, after it happened, Max and I just stood and stared at the traffic on Route 17. The motorists slowed down so they could take a closer look, and some even recorded the carnage on their cell phones.

After the ambulance had taken away Dan's body, I watched as Max filled the tank, paid for the gas, and then drove me back to his place. That whole time, we didn't say a word to each other. I felt complicit and seedy because there was a part of me that wanted Dan to be out of our lives. In the last week or so before he died, Dan had been trailing us around Rotherwell and sometimes he'd appear drunk or drugged up. He'd call me a "Slut" or a "Whore," and sometimes he just cried when he saw us together.

Finally, two days after the incident, I asked Max about it, and he just shrugged and said, "His choice."

Only now do I realize that was just a week after my sister's death. Her fucking suicide. All that death, and he just shrugged and said nothing about it. All that death, and he just continued to fuck me, and I continued to let him. Limp, lifeless, nothing more than a lump of putrefying flesh.

"That's it? A twenty-one-year-old threw himself in front of a truck. His life is over, and all you have to offer is *His choice?*"

He seized a hold of my chin and pulled my face so hard that I thought my head might rip from my shoulders. During times like this, I knew it was best to just let him do whatever he needed to work out the frustration. Usually when he ended up fucking me relentlessly, I'd go light-headed, but at that time, I didn't care. I would just let the rhythm carry me, imagining how a parasite occupies their host and moves the carcass across the ground, making it look like the walking dead.

"We aren't talking about this. Got it?" He said it with a growl, a final warning.

I wondered if I would ever end up cartwheeling across Route 17. If Max left me and I had to see him around the area with my younger replacement, would I end up like Dan? At the time, I assumed that death would be a form of escape from the pain of *not* having him in my life, whereas now it seems like a way to escape the pain of having him follow me around forever.

"Dylan," I hear someone call from behind me as I climb the final stone steps of the church. "Where have you been?"

I braced myself for Max's powerful hands on my shoulders, but I feel nothing, so I turn around.

"Robert? What are you doing here?"
"You still haven't called," he whines. "You promised me."
"We agreed two days," I reply. "Let's chat on Monday."
"You're a liar. You're never gonna call me. Ever."
I think he's crying. Despite the rain, I can see that his eyeballs are glistening and bloodshot.

"You're gonna keep fucking that brown boy, aren't you?" he screams as spittle flies from his lips.
"Did you follow me here?"
"You promised me," he repeats.
"You didn't answer the question. For fuck's sake, don't you Brits know about privacy? I really am sick of this."
"*You're* sick of this?" He races up the steps, so we stand at the top together, and I realize he's taller than me. I shouldn't be standing so precariously close to the edge as I imagine how hard the stone would feel as it smashed into my skull. I put my hand up to steady myself on the wall of the church, the cold of the stone making my bones ache.

"*You're* sick of this?" he repeats. "I haven't been able to sleep. I've been fucking up at work. You were already fucking me around in the first place, and I was patient. But then you promised, you said you'd make contact. But you haven't called."

He's trembling, and I can't help but feel sorry for him, so I reach out a hand to touch his cheek. But then someone else calls my name from behind me, making me wince and pull my hand away.

"Is he bothering you?" I hear someone ask. Now I recognize that voice.

"Fuck off," Robert snaps, without turning to look at Max. My stomach braces for impact, as if I'd been the one to show Max this disrespect.

"Dude, you have five seconds to get away from Dylan," I hear Max growl.

"Oh wait, is this another one of your fuck buddies? How many do you have, Dylan?"

The police officer's voice has become whiny, and I know Max enough to know that Robert should run away now.

"Maybe you didn't hear me." Max is still using a calm tone, but I can see his fists are tightly squeezed.

"Look, I don't know who you are," Robert says with a sigh of irritation, "and I don't really give a shit, but I'm a police officer on official duty. So, fuck off."

Max snorts with a dry laugh, giving the copper one glance up and down, and then swings the back of his hand into Robert's face, toppling him backwards down the steps.

"Let's get out of the rain, shall we?" Max says to me as I feel him gripping my arm and guiding me down the steps. I can see that Robert is still alive, which is a relief, and the rain is washing the blood that leaks from his cheek.

"What took you so long?" he asks me as we walk through the rain.

"I had to walk here. Where are you taking me?" I ask, half-expecting to see Sammy waiting in a nearby car.

"That café," he says as he points to the warm lights of a place just next to the church. I'm surprised it's even open with all the panic about the flooding.

When we shut the door behind us, the cafe feels strangely

safe and calming, even though I have no reason to feel either.

"You look tired," I say.

"That's nice of you. You don't look so fresh yourself."

We are both trying to reprise old roles, but it's futile when we know that we can never go back.

"You alone?" I ask, the panic rising in my chest when I realize he could have someone who is behind the counter of this café, ready to jump on me and throw a sack over my head.

"You think I'd tell you if I wasn't?" he says with a snort.

"You know I'm carrying a weapon," I lie.

"Let's not make things complicated," he says.

"So, what are we doing?" I ask him.

"Taking the first flight back to Newark."

Even the name makes my stomach twist.

"Or JFK," he continues. "Whatever flight's available to get us home. You know we have to do this."

"No, I don't," I reply.

"You know how fucked up it got back there," he continues. "You know something is going on at that fortress site."

"There's more you're not telling me. What else has got you so spooked? You always said that nothing was going to scare you into doing anything you didn't want to do."

"I told you not to make things complicated," he snaps.

I watch as he clenches his fists, and I wonder whether he is going to hit me.

"We have to do this, Dylan." His tone is softer now, barely a whisper. "It said it would hurt Katherine."

I see the legs scuttling. I hear the creak of the bedroom door. And then I see Ania, trapped inside an attic inside a fortress that has been rebuilt. This time she screams, when before she wasn't given the chance because at night, she had a hand over her mouth, or was instructed not to tell. That scream will haunt me forever, and remind me that I never saved her, despite the letters I found and showed to my mother. It never changed anything, and he will keep coming back, for Katherine this time but after she has thrown herself from the next regrown apple tree, there will be more bodies to pile up in a ditch at first, but the ditch will spill over, like a swollen river to wash through Mount Pelion Way. And it won't stop there, the rivers will rise with these bodies to flood Rotherwell, and the rest of New Jersey, and the whole of the East Coast because I didn't do anything, I saw all the warning signs and heard it, but I still did not stop it.

"You should see some of the things they show me in my nightmares," he whispers, "the things they will do to Katherine. Horrible things."
I thought he might cry, but he just snapped his gaze away so I couldn't see his face.

I can still smell the vinegary tang of formaldehyde that made me want to retch. Eris, our mother, had used this to keep my sister as fresh as she could; reborn only in fantasy, only in some sick nightmare that made me doubt who was desecrating and haunting who. Eris moved her body without permission, but who should grant or withhold permission from someone who has carried her body for nine months and done everything in her power to keep her alive? A woman has a right to her body, and from her body Ania was born, so she could return there, if Eris wished. When the fortress collapsed, I imagine their bodies becoming one again, only there was a contaminant, the bones of Paris Brown, collapsing onto and into them. As intertwined as we are to Mother Nature, a pollutant as intractable as microplastics.

I wish I could see my sister again. I dream that she is back with me, that we are scheming against our fucked-up parents, united as it should be, even complaining about them, as we watch them deteriorate with old age, slipping into a time when we can finally take charge of them and get our own back. But it never happens because Ania remains stuck as a sixteen-year-old, which keeps Paris and Eris fresh and full of life in their middle age, a time of self-satisfaction when they have all they need, so they look for ways to distract themselves from their boredom.

I still hear the hiss and pop of her flesh. I still taste the sickly sweetness, the pungent aroma that could be a delicacy if I didn't know it was so wrong. I don't know if I really smelled that at the time, or whether the depths of my horror made me think that, made me retch at the thought of it, when really all I could smell was smoke.

"They won't leave me be," Max continues, as if it were my own story. "Even when I get away from the fortress site, even when I leave the fucking country. They come for me in my sleep."

I see his bedroom and the sheets that were twisted after our violent, biting, clawing moments together. I see myself in the twilight, staring out his bedroom window at the smoldering ruin, and I watch as he walks over to me. He is naked, and the moonlight bounces off the curves of his biceps and buttocks, and I remember the sex again, only then I feel the burn in my thighs. He was down there, and the pleasure turned so sharply to the pain of the joint as he pressed it in. His lips tightened, intent on finishing what he started. He was always intent on finishing what was started, whether I wanted to or not, as he'd thrust in harder, as my writhing beneath his grip made him even more excited. I could see it in his body as much as his face, that excitement over this violence, my terror, his power over me to do whatever he needed to do to get the job done.

"Who? Who's been interrupting your sleep?" My tone is flat, and I feel like I am separating from my body, trying to no longer care about Max. I remember the cold of the church wall and I imagine sinking into that stone to become a gargoyle so I can scare off the things that are malevolent, things like Max, maybe even me, and I can keep the kinder people safe from this malevolence, people like Viqaas and his family.

"Those fucking hooded creatures," Max says, almost in a whisper. "They keep coming to me just when I think I can finally slip off to sleep. You know what it's like not to sleep for days on end? They appear at my bed, and they show me fucking horrifying things. You have to do something."

"Like what? Perform an exorcism?" I start to laugh. I don't know why, but it feels good to ridicule him.

"You're fucking laughing?" he snaps. "Watch your mouth."

"Why? What are you gonna do to me? You just said that you need me."

"Because if you don't, I'll give you a present made out of

human skin and bone. You've seen enough of those dark web clips to imagine what kind of torture inflicts the most pain. If you don't cooperate, if you do anything to put my daughter in danger, I'll take the one thing that is special to you. I've had eyes on you this whole time. You should know me by now that I don't let anything go unnoticed. What's his name again? Vistash? Viqaas?"

After Max burned me, I saw in the twilight his look of disgust, and it's still a familiar expression when I've hooked up with guys who are still in the closet. As soon as they scratch that itch, they want nothing more of me or the part of them that desired me in the first place. In that twilight, he threw a towel at me and told me to clear myself up, even though he had made the mess of me.

From outside the café, a car screeches, its tires slipping in the wet, and I see it slam into a car in front.

Max is going to keep doing this, isn't he? He's going to keep invading and plundering and destroying, and I have no way to stop him.

"You know it's spreading wider than Rotherwell. Just look around you. This whole planet is fucked."
Since when did Max West ever care about the planet beyond his business kingdom? I could argue this, but instead I just nod as we watch the torrent of rain rush down Charing Cross Road, sweeping umbrellas and trash and the occasional unsuspecting person.

"Please, Dylan. We can do it together; we can finally end this."

Chapter Fourteen

~~~

Mother Earth

~~~

During Dylan's absence, the malevolence, all that wrath and vengeance from the fortress site, has been growing stronger. Beneath the hands that claw through the rubble, there is anguish and filth as much as toxins and contaminants. You can see the various layers of it, all the leakage throughout the generations, and it is combustible, sparking a hatred, a writhing greed that burns beneath the skin. It doesn't just disappear when someone dies, in fact when you bury a body or scatter their ashes, you just add to it all, rotting the soil to poison anything that grows from it. And anything that is built upon it is doomed from the beginning, just as surely as generations of loved ones are destined to perish. There's nowhere safe, no stable footing, and so soon you can see the cracks appear, the footings buckle, and mighty empires fall as surely as another one rises to take its place.

Think of the building you are in right now. Can you hear the cracks and groans under the weight of it all as the land shifts and pipes rust and crack and leaks more filth and contaminants? As surely as the ghosts groan and wail as they look for a way back home. It wants to give in as much as Dylan wants to, and the building you sit in right now could easily collapse upon you as it surrenders itself to the weight of all those decades.

But that won't happen, will it? There's always one little spark inside that makes you keep going, stand up and breathe again, even though what you are breathing in is riddled with stuff that will rot you from within. That's existence, that's the daily walk across shifting soil, knowing what has been built around you was put up by people who don't really care about you, and how could they when they never even met you, especially if you didn't even exist when they first put spade into soil And they only care that they get paid, it isn't down to them to make sure this thing they put up will stay standing and not crush your skull like popping a cherry.

One night, it was just Paris' head that rolled about the fortress site. It had veins trailing, and those hardened, becoming tiny legs that looked like a spider's. He used these legs to scuttle across the dirt as he screeched in pain, his eyes unseeing but fixed open, and he left a trail of drool on the ground until the sunrise dried it up.

Sometimes he just looked hungry, and he would lick his lips as he anticipated savoring every part of someone's body. He seemed intent on conquering, but he had no way of doing it without human form. He longed for a body, and he'd watch them writhing about in the other houses on Mount Pelion Way. Some, he thought, might even be creating a third body, as two were fused together in those fleeting moments that he watched with delight.

You think the horror is just in that arachnid and what he might do to the other people. But think of the horror that Mother Earth feels, as she sees more and more of you spewed out like sputum. Multitudes of people, a never-ending line of mouths to gobble and tear and chew at her dwindling resources. She watches as you strip skins from my animals and discard them in a long line of pointless, endless production, reproduction, and wastage.

And yet you still believe that she won't fight back. Already her sea levels are rising, and large swathes of her land are swallowing you whole. She was never this beneficent parent who was ready to sacrifice herself so you could grow. Every droplet of blood you spilled, she counted so she could seek recompense in time.

Quid pro quo.

She knows that none of you asked to be born into this world where you have to hit the ground running and fight for survival. But some of you, and you know who you are, still aren't satisfied when you are already surviving, when you should reach out a hand and pull someone onto your life raft before they drown. But instead, there is that writhing greed beneath the skin that makes you think about charging a small fortune for their survival, and when that small fortune isn't enough to satisfy the aching need, you double the cost to increase your profit.

Mother Earth tells Ralph that Max West is returning to Rotherwell. She whispers it to him in the breeze when he tries to think of other things, and she places it on his pillow when he sleeps.

Ralph goes straight to the fortress site, where he's sure he can still feel his sister there. He climbs an apple tree and as he waits for Max; he etches into the bark a spear and shield; motifs of war for Ares, the battle-lustful one.

Chapter Fifteen

Dylan

Max wanted to go straight to the airport, so I could only tell Viqaas over the telephone. He asked me if I was sure, and then he told me that he understood why I had to do this, which I didn't believe. Everything is happening so quickly that even I don't fully understand it.

When we checked in, I could see the confusion on the face of the customer service agent. "No luggage?" she asked, glancing over at her colleague. There must be some kind of protocol for this, especially since 9/11. Regardless, she handed us our tickets, and we passed through security without further questioning, so it seemed there was nothing left to stop us.

As we waited to board, I stared at the plane through the big glass window, unsure how I would cope with being crammed into such a pressurized container with all that combustible fuel. When we race down the runway, will all this energy that has been writhing beneath my skin just launch out of me, so I infect everyone on board? Or will I finally become that incendiary device, finding relief as I disappear in one final spectacle?

We board the flight on time, and I try to get comfortable in the cramped space. Max can see that I am nervous, so he offers me a Xanax.

"Sure, I really want to be drugged up sitting next to you on a flight," I snap at him.

"Suit yourself," he replies. "Feel edgy if you want."

"I'm surprised you have them in the first place. You never like to chill out."

And then I realize he probably has them to keep other people pacified.

A fire is bad enough, but the destruction of a family home creates such a nightmarish scene that makes people uncomfortable when they think of their own home and the memories that were locked up inside of it. Most people wouldn't want to think of their own bedroom in flames, to have to watch the fire take hold of their curtains and their bed and the boxes of the things they have accumulated over the years, all in the hope that someone might want all of that crap instead of adding it to another landfill. But what would they think if you told them that the family home was filled with horror and pain that made the structure ache and contaminated everything and everyone that sat within it? Would you say that it was better to create a funeral pyre of it all?

The firefighters said that the fortress should not have collapsed, despite the fire. According to their report, they reached the building when the fire still seemed pretty contained in the attic space. Between them, they had decades of experience of fighting fires, and from their calculation, they claimed that there should have been damage to the top level, but the entire structure should not have collapsed. So, they believe the fortress was already weakened by age and other things, but what these other things are, nobody knows. I have my suspicions. There is something rotten about the soil on which the fortress was once built, the fortress that failed to keep its inhabitants safe, the place that was more of a prison than a place of refuge. Whatever toxins were in the soil soaked into the materials they used to build the grand house. Timber and brick are porous enough and so, in time, every inch of the fortress was riddled with those contaminants.

They say that the workmen who were employed to build the fortress became sick, and although most could carry on working, because they had to, so their families didn't starve, some collapsed and a few even died. They also say that the other workmen carried on working around these corpses, burying them in the concrete foundations.

I was an asshole pre-teen, so whenever we were in the basement together, I would take delight in telling Ania about those bodies that were buried beneath our feet. I even told her that the fortress was alive, and the gurgling of the pipes was its stomach that was hungry for more bodies, and Ania's looked particularly appetizing. How her eyes would bulge with horror. I made things worse when the roof timber groaned under the weight of age, and I said it was stirring from a slumber, ready to devour her. In the end, it did swallow her whole, but that was not the fault of the fortress, any more than it was responsible for all the horror that was perpetrated inside of it. The fortress was an unthinking, unfeeling vessel to carry the horrors that others created. Just because it creaked and groaned and even moved a little, as the land became less firm with the intensifying storms, didn't mean it was an intentional being who meant us harm. Movement isn't always a sign of life because even corpses can sit up as they are cremated, because of the heat that is breaking down the muscles.

All that being said, just because trauma and violence are repeatedly inflicted in the same home by different generations of the same family, doesn't mean that family is evil. I know many would say that there was so much spite burning inside my family home that it spontaneously combusted. But what if we were all sickened by some kind of contaminant that was rotting everything that lived within that fortress? It might have been the same impurity that forced my grandmother to drive far away from that home. By placing a plastic bag over her head and switching on the exhaust of her car, she was never going to cleanse her mind, but perhaps she thought she could bring the contaminant, or the distortions it created, away from Eris, her daughter. And what if it was that same contaminant that twisted my sister's mind so much, she threw a noose around her neck to escape it, leaving my mother tangled with grief?

I'm ashamed of this next part, because how can I defend a father who inflicts so much violence, but the idea of a contaminant allows love for my father again. No matter how much I try to numb myself with drugs or men, there is still a childish voice inside of me that cries out, *"But he's my dad, and he didn't mean it because he was sick."*

Already I see something scuttling about between the folds of the curtains to the business class section of the plane. There are eight spindly legs, and then his face appears, and he looks confused. He seems hungry, longing to taste and feel flesh again, and I wonder whether he might have forgotten that he's dead. Is that what happens when you die, and parts of your skull decay, the shifting brain matter dislodging the memories along with it? What terrifies me the most is that he will eventually remember and then realize the part I played in his death.

Paris looks sad, as if he is the one who has been abused, and for a moment I believe it too. I feel a gravitational pull towards him, and the crazy notion that I can help him in some way. To think that I was terrified when I saw him crawl out of the rubble of the fortress in Rotherwell, and now I can watch him and not run.

I watch him peer over at me, weighing me up as he tries to decide whether I am of use to him. Stuck in the jailhouse of his own purgatory, with no girls available to him, might he turn to me for his comfort, tearing at me and making me bleed? What would happen if he penetrated me and he found the thing that writhes beneath my skin? It feels like a life force so would it give him power so he could transform into human form, so he could inflict more violence through my own body?

These could be my own fears, but they could also be

contaminants from Ania and Eris; familial legacies passed down like genetic quirks, whether I believe them or not.

The drive from the airport is the last time I see Max as his certain, silent self. The closer we get to Rotherwell, the more he starts to ask me, "You feel that?". He could be tricking me, but I think I feel it too, an aching, sickening pull towards the fortress site. I start to wonder if there is another way, that I can make a run for it and hide again, in another faraway place, but then he turns the car onto Mount Pelion Way, and something else washes through me, a flood of the siren call crashing through my mind.

You came back. You are here.

The fortress is defeated. During my absence, I'd rebuilt it in my mind, recreating the imposing stone and brick features to sit high on the hill and look down on the smaller, newer constructions. But now it is crushed by something and turned inside out, one of the turrets still reaching from the rubble as it might in a final plea for help. How pitiful do they look when empires fall.

Stay here. Don't run away again.

Pulling into the driveway, Max flicks off the engine of the car and the cicadas fill the space where silence could be.

"Go," he says as he points towards the smoldering ruin. "And what? Find a sacrificial goat?"

I should've known better than to make light of things that involved his daughter. He grabbed my throat and snapped my head back against the headrest.

"Don't fuck with me," he spits, leaning his body weight onto me so I think he might crush my windpipe.

"Okay," I gasp. "I'll go take a look."

I climb out of the car and slam the door behind me, hoping he will drive off so I can work this out on my own. But I can feel him watching my every move as I walk up the winding path that could lead to so many memories if I let it. Instead, I stare at the translucent smoke phantoms that are reaching from the rubble. As soon as I look closely at them, they seem afraid of me and disappear into the night.

When the fire took hold, did the people of Mount Pelion Way peer out of their windows and hope for this land to be cleansed? Aside from drowning, what better way to dispose of a witch?

When I make my way round the ruins to the backyard, I feel the darkness thickening so it holds me, turning me this way and that so I see things that it wants me to see. There is the aconite, a hidden breeze stirring their purple and blue flowers, mysteriously coming into bloom when they aren't even in season.

If I ever escape this place, if I manage to make it back to London and Viqaas, will I ever find a way to explain any of this? The violence that was inflicted within this fortress, violence at the hands of people who were supposed to love and protect each other. If I tell him about Ania, and what our father did to her, Viqaas might dismiss this as one bad apple experience. He might say this doesn't mean the whole cart must be burned, and the tree that produced the apples cut down and burned, and the land that grew the tree concreted over by way of some advanced form of remediation. Not that this would ever stop the toxins spreading, they would just soak into the concrete and break free, become airborne, and line the nostrils of every living being that exists as far as the wind carries it. But he could never understand how this thing beneath my skin that he must surely feel from the heat of my forehead, and the stirring within the blue grey in my irises, continues to burn, and that scares me the most. Not the horrors that crawl from the rubble of this fortress site, but the malevolence that I now carry, and that seems to be getting stronger.

I feel foolish when I look for Ania and Eris, allowing myself a childish hope that the siren call had been them all along, even though by now I am sure it was a trick.

With each step, dread weighs heavily on me, and I glance behind me to see if there is a trail of blood, in case Max has pressed something sharp into me and it was so deep that I barely noticed it. There's nothing on the path, so I walk on until I reach what used to be the back door, but it's now a gaping hole of broken timber, glass, and rubble. From there I see the apple trees still growing, flourishing fruit as if nothing ever happened. I tell myself that I am seeing things when the shadows form arms and legs and a head of someone perched on one of the boughs. I can't afford to let myself believe in any ghostly visions of my sister, at least not while Max is waiting for me.

Come closer.

The tone is harsher than before, and it presses so hard that my ears begin to hurt. It makes me think of the way Eris' words would slam around my head, around this place that used to be a home. I see her broken pots of herbs scattered around the backyard, like tombstones reminding me of all her failed attempts to nourish and nurture.

You're the one who failed.

The voice crackles in my ears.

You could've saved this family, but you stood by in silent sentinel and watched it crumble.

There's a distortion, and the voice deepens.

Call yourself a warrior, you're nothing.

And then I see the eight spindly legs emerging from the rubble. My father's face leers at me, silently pleading with me to step closer. He scuttles towards me, so quietly that no one would ever know, not until you feel the after-effects, that sticky residue left by him.

There's a moaning of the voice again, only it has deepened as it resonates throughout my body. Somehow, I know it to be something ancient, cursed, something integral to my existence.

You want to know, don't you? You want to discover the truth about that writhing beneath your skin. You want to know if you are the rot, the contaminant that just keeps spreading.

I take a step closer to the glowing rubble. I could look upon these embers as a womb ready to grow something new, to ripen until they are as swollen as the apples that mysteriously regrow, no matter how many times the trees are torn down. New offerings from Mother Earth or Eris or a combination of the two.

You took more than I was willing to give you.

Regrowth can be a cancerous tumor or a process of healing; it's the same multiplication of cells, or at least I think it is. And you can grow something beautiful to live beyond your years, or something hideous that turns on you and devours you.

As you have done to me.

"Is that you, Eris?" I ask. "Are you angry at me for some reason?"

There's no answer but instead I see the world turning inside out and instead I stand in a place where I peep through a gap in the brickwork of the attic and I spy on the neighbors, envying and detesting them at the same time, and I am suspicious of my son so I turn against him, and I wish my husband would do the same, although we all keep secrets from each other, because I can't let go of my daughter, who gives me a sharp intake of breath as I feel the wounds still deep inside my womb, and I become her, for she came from me, and as I, Ania, am alive, there is no flammable formaldehyde and no pentacle of candles attempting to protect me when the danger had already been and gone, and so the fortress never burnt down, and the contaminants are still locked inside its foundations, lying dormant until they can find freedom again. But I know too much, so I feel the noose fall around my neck and suddenly tighten, before I even had a chance to change my mind, and maybe it was the wind that I felt pushing me from behind, and then I try not to think of him because I don't want to become him, so I think of becoming anyone but him, so I become Max and I hate myself as much as the pastor hates all queers, and Max and I join forces in a business deal, becoming rainbow warriors together, and we recruit whole armies of warriors to slash and burn any queer we see, because we don't want to look at them and keep pretending we don't desire their bodies, pretending we don't grab them when no one is looking and do it quickly, only to feel sick straight away, when we smell the shit on our dicks, so we take it out on them, and because we are rich and Christian and white, no one suspects anything of us, and we stand by when we let others take the fall, blame the guy who looks different, throw him in jail and hang him while we watch online, while we touch ourselves over it and condemn others for doing the same.

I don't know what is real anymore. I need someone to remind me who I am, where I am, and what's safe and unsafe. Nothing makes sense anymore because with a ripple in everything I see, I am back standing in the moonlight and looking at the ruins of my family home.

I hear movement from behind me.

"Who are you talking to?"

It's Max.

"No one," I reply. "I thought maybe...But now I'm not so sure."

He stands too close in an attempt to intimidate me. Fear and hatred crackles in the pit of my stomach as I stare at this clench-jawed and overblown fool. I feel the writhing under my skin, an aching need to claw and tear at his dried-out skin, but instead I just stare at him, a sudden hatred congealing in my throat and making me want to spit at his gleaming white-collar shirt. Those bright blue eyes have seen so much in those abandoned warehouses filled with people he could misuse in any way he chose. Bitcoin payments on the dark web, kids brought in to lure business opponents, to blackmail them, to eliminate the competition. He's never going to stop because of the threat of consequences; he won't ever be on the receiving end of violence or prison time because he knows too much.

You can stop him.

"What did you say?" Max asks. I've been edging towards him, still with this writhing greed burning through me, and now I'm so close to him that I smell things on him that I can remember, when we were covered in each other, smeared with it, and it was terrifying and exciting at the same time.

"You heard that?" Max asks me.

"What?"

"*That.*" Max jabs his finger at the smoldering rubble, sounding increasingly frustrated. "Quit playing games with me. You heard it as much as I did."

"I don't know what you're talking about."

"Yes, you do. It was probably you all along, doing some kind of fucking projection of your voice, some secret speaker planted on me, or in me."

"Now you're sounding paranoid."

"It was probably you making those threats about Katherine, making me see things."

The land shifts. There's a ripple, subtle enough not to topple us over, but enough for us both to notice.

"You feel that?" Max asks, his eyes so wide the whites shine in the moonlight.

Just when I am about to answer him, the land flexes again, and something is pushed to the surface, as a splinter might work its way through the skin. We both see it. A broken bone, still with skin on it. And then the land shifts again and more bones rise to the surface. Skulls, too, and some with hair. The earth wants to vomit some more, so I see other body parts emerge, and they aren't just of human form. Mammals, birds, even aquatic life, they are all churned up in this dirty pit of death.

"I have to give it what it wants," Max says, his voice suddenly so close to my ear that I freeze.

The ground splits open, a dirty mouth waiting to be fed, and he pushes me towards the gaping hole. I feel something stirring deep beneath the surface of this land. It infects the body parts, so they come to life, possessed and now being moved by this writhing, stirring thing beneath the surface. I know how it feels, how it aches with this greed, and I want to help it.

Destroy or be destroyed.

Max grabs my wrists, pulling me now, and I can feel him trembling. I see his father in him, over him, whipping him with a belt and getting beaten by him. He is locked in this, a dance of trauma and hauntings, seeing his mother over and over again, loving and hating her, and then seeing his mother in his daughter, and knowing he could lose her too, and there is fault, and he feels guilty and shameful, so that the whole fucking world is in his grip, that is actually quite small, as if his hands are shrinking, so he can't even get his fingers round my wrist.

He won't do it, or he can't, he's finally lost his potency, so we both stand there, at the edge of that gaping hole that is getting bigger, and I'm sure we both feel it, this locked, frozen state where we feel so much power, we know too much, and yet we have no way of making any kind of change to any of this, all our furious learning, recycling of theories and knowledge and concepts and discoveries and all that we built, as tall as the sky, and we explore further, through space and time until it all amounts to a bundle of cells that implodes at a certain point, as if we never existed in the first place.

Something distracts him, and he lets go of me, throwing himself onto the rubble.

"Katherine," he screams. He throws bricks aside and I imagine he thinks she is buried under there, just out of reach each time he gets a little closer to her. He might also be searching for his mother in there, the one who left him all those years ago. In his panicked state, I wonder if he can still distinguish the two, so he becomes with each inward breath a father searching for his daughter and then, with every outward breath, a young boy searching for his mother who looks so like his daughter, so he is stuck in this eternal loop of torment.

"She won't be able to breathe," he gasps, "help me, for fuck's sake."

He hasn't noticed that he is precariously close to the fissure in the ground.

Fools. You thought you could create an empire and subjugate me.

I see the hands clawing their way to him; dirty hands with flesh hanging from the bone and stinking of putrefaction. The hands have him, and they are pulling him into the hole, and he tries to hold on to me, but this writhing beneath my skin now culminates in an almighty power that pushes him away. This strength is not mine, and it seems to vibrate in sync with whatever force has a hold of Max.

Bad things happen to bad people.

"Help me," he tries to plead, but his voice is swallowed by the darkness of the night, a darkness that feels so solid that it presses into the two of us, locking our eyes in a joint stare. I see what he fears, the stubble on his father's cheek as sweat trickles down it after he had whipped that belt so many times as Max's mom watched on, as she took another drink, as she lit her cigarette, all of which Max had been refusing to see since the day she left.

Dirt and rubble and body parts fold inwards to fill the hole with Max trapped in there. I watch as his legs and then torso sink further underground. Every time he struggles, he sinks deeper, and he starts to scream, sounding like a helpless little boy, so I suddenly want to help him. I reach out, but there is a force that holds me back. I strain so hard my head feels like it will pop. But still, I can't reach him.

There's no stopping this. And besides, isn't this what you wanted? Relentless progress, no matter the cost, no matter the pain and suffering.

This isn't the voice of Eris or Ania, or even my father. It never was. It's an older voice than any person who remains alive, much older than all of life.

You foolish thing. You thought that this was about you and your family and your lovers and the things you hold dear. Selfish and vain, as all humans are. You think you are the superior beings, deserving of my kingdom while you try to become king of me. But you're nothing more than vermin, beasts from other beasts, and you spread your diseases and filth and toxins to distort and taint all that is pure about me.

"Give me your hand," I tell Max. "Let me help you."
"Fuck you," he gasps and then gurgles, making me think that something is gnawing at him from underground.

"It hurts," I hear him say before he starts to make retching and choking sounds. His head twists so far that I can't believe he's still alive, and then his voice takes on a different sound, an ancient groan that terrifies me.

"You let your sister get fucked by your daddy," he spits. "You dirty little whore. You probably watched through the gap in the doorway, didn't you?"
"Stop it," I say. I would throw my hands over my ears, but something holds my arms at my side.
"You got off on it. No one wanted you, so you jerked off over the people in your own fucking family tree. The same tree your sister swung from by the length of rope around her dirty whore neck."

"Fuck you," I spit.

I watch as dermestid beetles crawl around his face. They burrow in the corner of each eye, and I can see the red of blood tears snaking down each cheek.

"Your sister was a freak, just like your bitch of a mom. That gargoyle, that witch bitch who should've been winched up to hang from one of the apple trees. She probably fucked her daughter, too."

The ground moves again, and bits of debris from the fortress of my family home fall about him. Parts of the rubble are glowing hot like embers, and they land on his cheeks to sear his flesh. I can smell the sickly sweet aroma of burnt skin, like the barbeque Charles told me about. And then I see my initials emerge on his cheeks, only this time they are D.B. for Dylan Brown.

"No better or worse than your dear daddy. Right, Dylan? Faggot fuck, sticking yourself into every orifice in every part of that city. Don't think I didn't see you whoring your way around London and spreading your diseases. I can smell the shit on your cock. I see the herpes blistering all over your lips. Ass full of cum, dripping between your legs, you little freak show of a whore. You think this is over…"

And then he begins to laugh hard, so hard it sounds painful as his head thrusts back in the dirt, and his mouth widens so violently that the edges of his lips begin to split open.

"Oh god, it feels good," he continues, "this pain, this pleasure, stretched beyond the limits. That's what you've done, isn't it, you whore? Got every guy you know to split you open as they shoved it deep inside, and then you flipped them over and did it back to them."

Then, with a new sound, one that sounded closer to Max's true voice, he splutters "Kill me. Please. Kill me, Dylan."

I watch as roots snake around his face. Roots whip around Max's wrists and ankles, much like the duct tape Eris used to tether my father to the bed frame, and still he struggles. With every movement, the roots tighten, squeezing him so hard that I hear things start to pop and crack. Then thicker roots emerge, exploding up from somewhere inside him and out of his mouth and nose and ears. I see the glistening white of his eyeballs, and those beautiful blues that had lured me in that very first time in the woods, right at the end of this very street. He lured me in so many times since that I became numb to it, lost from myself, but I start to see it all now, all he took from me when he didn't give me a chance to say no.

And now I'm glad that the roots are holding him in place as his body starts to dissolve. All that toxicity from all those contaminants after all those years of waste selfishly discarded about the place.

Max stares at his body, surprised that he might be giving birth to all these tree roots, as if he has become a surrogate of Mother Earth, or a host to her parasitic intent.

Excrement, I hear echoing all around me.

To fertilize, to bear new growth. Nothing less than you deserve.

I watch as Max dissolves into the soil. His skin and bone bubble and there's the final twitches of life before he soaks into the soil, without leaving any trace.

This is justice. This is the wrath and vengeance you've been seeking for all this time, with that greed that could not be satiated. Look at it. Know how much you longed for it.

My skin cools and I feel calm again, and the land settles too.

And now what? What is to become of you?

Chapter Sixteen

~~~

Mother Earth

~~~

I told you that empires fall. It was inevitable that we would see the end of Max, this one-man empire, as inevitable as the decline of the empires on either side of the Atlantic. Yet some refuse to see the truth, some are too preoccupied with the thought of seizing more to realize that there are dangers that are approaching. Instead, they sit and drink tea out of a bone China cup and saucer and emphasize the *great* about a nation that has been dying for a long time now. I wonder if they think that the ghost of Queen Victoria reigns over them, and perhaps they think this mother of commerce might feed them some more. That could be why they keep so many statues of her, as a grieving child might keep the body of their mother in an attic somewhere. These greedy pigs, never satisfied, always suckling at the teat of some mother, any mother, as long as they can get some more. They don't care that she is running dry, that she has started to bleed, they just want more.

We hurt the ones closest to us.

Didn't I say that these ant-like people, these greedy terrorists, have inflicted their violence on Mother Earth for too long? Caught together in this vicious cycle of trauma and violence, their relentless pursuit of progress, they claimed her as one of their subjects, a whole world of them believing that they were the empire, and Mother Earth was somehow inferior. Hasn't this always been the case? Haven't you always claimed superiority over each other and the natural world? You point to scientific knowledge that you have created, to skull measurements or skin colors, and you believe each other when you talk of a master race. You create an echo-chamber of ignorance to justify more invasions, rapes and pillages of other people as much as Mother Earth's resources.

From the moment you first tore the skin from one of her animals, using it to cover up your genitals, you claimed that this set you apart from everyone else. You claimed superiority because of the homes you built and the territories you reclaimed as your own and renamed and carved heads of your presidents into the sides of mountains, just to prove that even nature agreed. (Nature did not agree.) Humans, the ultimate imperialists, rageful as you plunder all that you can seize, and anyone or anything that tries to resist is contained in a fortress that is kept under lock and secret key while you send in your tanks and tear up their land and use other ways to concentrate their mind on what you are trying to convince them about, so they believe in your superiority, because if they don't, you will use the camps again as all empires have before you. And still, you call your subjects the barbarians, savages, or the unevolved.

But fortresses can crumble; it was arrogant of you to believe your concrete would hold for an eternity. All that is made can be unmade, all that is created eventually deteriorates and crumbles, setting free all manner of wrath and vengeance. You've seen what happens with every successive empire. Mother Earth will never be subjugated.

From his position in the tree, Ralph saw everything. He wanted to call out, to try to stop things that were happening because he wasn't a bad person, and he didn't like to see people suffer. But the darkness held him in place. It wouldn't let him move a muscle, and so all he could do was watch.

When it ended, when Max disappeared, Ralph didn't feel satisfied. He knew that nice girl Katherine was going to be upset when she heard the news. Upset? It was going to tangle her up in grief and burn through her veins for an eternity, and he feared that she might spend the rest of her life seeking vengeance with her wrath. No, this was not something to feel satisfied about.

When the darkness finally let him go, he slipped from the branch of the tree and ran through the backyards to where he'd parked his car earlier that night.

Fool.

He hears this just as he gets into his car, so he checks the rear seats to see if anyone is hiding there. Nothing. He starts to feel calmer, and he feels smart for checking before he started to drive. He is clever and smart, as his husband always called him, and Ralph decides that he's going to call his husband during the drive home. He's going to promise that he will put aside all thoughts of fortress sites and apple trees and Max West, and he doesn't have to explain why he can so easily do this now. He never has to explain this to anyone, and that's the easiest way to live, in denial, with all the horrors locked safely away in a trunk at the far corner of his mind.

Already he's feeling better, and the thick darkness of the night is now broken by the flashing street lamps as he drives faster and closer to the border of Rotherwell. He vows to himself that he'll never return here again, and just as he does that, Mother Earth flips his car just as it bounces over the railway tracks.

He rolls down the embankment and crashes into a ditch.

Because he is still alive, Ralph believes that someone is still watching over him. He is thankful, and he promises to be a better person.

Just as he reaches for the door to make his escape, he sees

that he has been impaled by a downed utility pole. It pins him to the seat like a butterfly in a museum.

He knows he is dying because he can see the amount of blood and the internal organs that are peeping from an opening in his stomach. He thrashes about, trying to get himself free, even though he knows it is futile. But he doesn't want this yet, not when he can't see his sister. Surely, by now, at the end, she should be stroking his hair.

But then he sees the hooded creatures as they climb in through the broken window. They have scalpels and claw hammers and bone saws to glint in the moonlight, and they place a forefinger to their sack-covered face in a silent plea for him to keep quiet. They have work to do.

Satisfied, Mother Earth switches her attention back to Dylan, and she sees them jumping into Max's car and driving back to the airport. Dylan probably thinks they have escaped any further harm. They probably think this is over.

Chapter Seventeen

Dylan

~~~

There are words, phrases, whole sentences threading through my mind and yet none of it forms a coherent whole. I can't stay focused because there's still this writhing, an itch that can't be scratched. I thought it would die when Max disappeared, but still it squirms beneath my skin, swimming through my bloodstream with all the other pollutants, trauma, and genetic quirks. You might call it a haunting, an evil spirit, perhaps, or a curse, and others have tried to blind themselves from such a fearful explanation by slapping a diagnostic label over it, calling it psychosis or some other mental health condition. But still, the only word that really fits is *greed*. Only now I don't feel so alone to acknowledge its existence. This greed is a universal condition, as intrinsic as the constant companion of a beating heart.

For the three weeks I've been back in London, June and
~~~

Katherine have been calling and asking where Max is. Even the Pastor and Sammy left a voicemail for me. For now, I can ignore their calls. I'm not sure of what will happen when he's been missing for long enough for the police to take it seriously.

Viqaas still hasn't asked me what happened, but he did say that I might need to talk to someone about it, even a trained professional.

"I'm fine," I lied. "I just needed to see you."

We stood at his doorway for a moment, and I wondered whether he was weighing it all up, trying to figure out whether this amount of drama was worth it in his first year of university.

"Wanna come in?" he finally asked me. "I mean, we could catch you up on any missed lectures, or listen to the Archers Omnibus. Maybe even laugh at Eastenders?"

"Sure. All of the above."

"Well, we should start with the lectures because you don't want to get kicked out in June, do you?"

I shrugged my shoulders.

"And tomorrow you're coming with me because I'm meeting up with my parents and sis."

"Again?"

"What can I say? They like to visit me."

When I made the decision to return to Rotherwell, I had a question to ask the fortress site. I had to know if I deserved a life with someone like Max or someone like Viqaas. Now Max has gone, and Viqaas is still here, I realize I have the answer. Perhaps that's why I no longer hear the siren call or the chattering of my mother's jawbone. And perhaps that's why I no longer see the scuttling of eight legs or the swaying of the hooded creatures.

There must have been hundreds of people packing into the underground station. No one had seen rain like that, even after the recent storms. I don't know why they kept allowing people in to pile up like we were carcasses being dumped. Come to think of it, I hadn't seen anyone in the ticket office, and at the time I assumed it was because the whole world was shifting over to automation. Now I wonder whether the workers knew something that we didn't, and they'd left us there to fend for ourselves.

I can smell the damp everywhere, and I see it running down the walls, and it feels like the world is overflowing. More and more people are pushing us, and for a moment, I lose sight of Viqaas and his family. I could be swept away from them, and I feel calm thinking of this, being carried far away by something beyond my control. Finally, it wouldn't be my fault, and I'm curious about the feeling of just letting go.

But something makes me fight against the crowds to join them again, and as I bounce from shoulder to shoulder, I find Viqaas' father smiling at his son.

"Is this where you meant to take us?" he calls to Viqaas. "No, Dad, as I said, this is Balham. We were meant to get off at Morden, so we could walk to Morden Hall, but they've closed that station, so this is as far as we can go. We can either try to take a bus from here or give up and find somewhere else to go."

"Let's go home," his mom snaps. "We can get some fish and chips on the pier."

"Home as in Aber?" Viqaas asks.

"Yes. You should come too," she replies.

"I've got lectures this week."

"You never come home anymore," she complains.

"I was home the other weekend, Mum."

She doesn't sound satisfied with his answers and tightens her folded arms across her chest.

There isn't enough air so we are all starting to feel a little irritable about how closely we have to walk together, so close that I can smell the pot on Vafia's clothes as she glowers at me. I wonder if her parents, or even Viqaas, know what that smell is.

Someone collides with me, which makes me knock into Vafia, and she drops her phone. I bend down, scrabbling amongst the various shoes, and I manage to grab the phone before someone steps on it.

When I hand it to her, I see that it's unlocked, and her message app is open. The first message I see includes the words "Pussy ass" and "faggot."

She snatches the phone from me and stares into my eyes for a moment as I imagine her sending all those abusive messages to me. She could've found out about us by trailing us around London when she claimed to her parents that she was visiting a friend. Or she might have sneaked into his phone and seen the flirtatious messages Viqaas and I exchanged at the beginning, and then the blatantly obscene messages as our relationship intensified.

As quickly as the thoughts form in my mind, the crowd separates us again as I hear Viqaas' dad deliver a brief history lesson.

"You know," he shouts across the crowds, "this station was bombed in the Second World War."

"Don't talk of such nonsense when we're down here," his wife snaps back at him.

"Balham, right?" Viqaas asks.

"Yes, son, well remembered. 14th October, today's date, in fact, but it happened way back in 1940. The Gerry bomb fell on the road above the northern end of the platform tunnels and drowned so many people down here. How sad to think of how many lost their lives in that watery tomb."

Now he has spoken about them, the ghosts emerge from the shadows, these translucent figures of passengers from decades ago.

I can hear an air-raid siren, maybe another one of those stupid cell phone alarms, or perhaps it has leaked through with the ghosts, carried by the violence that once tried to eradicate them.

"To think how much the world has changed since then," Viqaas' dad muses as I manage to join them again. "How much suffering the Jewish people were put through back then," he continues.

"Yeah, and now look at that murderous Zionist regime doing exactly the same to the Palestinians," Vafia snaps. She says it a little too loudly as some nearby passengers flinch at her words.

"Vafia, that isn't a nice thing to say," Viqaas' dad snaps. "You have to think of how something sounds to the other person."

Vafia says something else to her father, but I'm distracted from their argument by the sight of the ghosts who have started to run. They jump onto the train tracks and their eyes are wide with terror as they stare back at something in the tunnel.

I follow their gaze, and then I hear it before I see it. A thundering roar of water rushing towards us. This nightmare, this ripple of time from sudden violence that traps someone in fear for an eternity, and it's such an intense fear that others can see it for generations to come.

The water rushing towards us, this haunting, seems so lifelike, and then it crashes into me and Viqaas and his parents and sister.

And then I realize the water wasn't just a haunting but reality.

Time's up.

I can't see his parents or sister, but I've been pushed by the other passengers onto Viqaas, and we cling together as the water continues to rush in.

You thought you could keep yourself safe with your mythical charms and rituals and your pathetic faith in your gods.

There's no time to think, so we just grab at things in an attempt to stay buoyant.

"There!" Viqaas screams as he points to a hatch on the side of the wall.

We struggle over, half-swimming, half drowning, but we are quick enough to make it to the hatch.

We hold on to something metallic, maybe the handle to the hatch. There's too much chaos to figure it out. The water keeps rushing in, and Viqaas and I know not to let go, even though I wondered if he wanted to, so he could try to find his parents and sister.

I stare at him, hoping he won't blame me for whatever decisions we make in that moment, even though there isn't any forethought, no ability to use our rational mind as we are swept up in all that fight and flight. And the water keeps rising.

I turn the metal handle that I am holding onto as I repeat in my mind the rhyme my father taught me, *Righty tighty, lefty loose,* and the metal hatch gives way and opens up into an adjoining tunnel.

We don't hesitate, climbing through it, and fall to the ground.

I see movement ahead of us, and I realize other hatches have opened up into this tunnel from other parts of the flooded one. I see that people are running in a certain direction, so I decide we have to follow them, and I pull Viqaas' arm. At first, he resists. He screams something about his parents and sister. And that's when I lie to him. I tell him I saw them ahead, that they seemed to be okay, and so we run.

When we finally emerge into daylight, we see helicopters above us, all a uniform brand color with a *Crisis Response Ltd* sign on the side of each one. The streets are blocked by unmarked cars and armored vehicles with the same company logo on the side of each, all with tinted windows and armed guards. No truncheons in sight, just big, powerful guns.

"Fucking Charles," I hiss to myself.

At first, I didn't know what happened to the other people who were in the station that day, the ones who didn't see any of the hatches, who might have been swept too far down the platform that they couldn't escape before the water got too deep.

But slowly things came back to me, like the panic and confusion on their faces and the thrashing about in the water, presumably because some of them could not swim.

And when the water got so deep that they were submerged, I imagine the twitches they made at the end, after they tried in vain to take breaths under water. There are multitudes of them, all swirling around down there, trapped in a horrific aquarium where drowned humans are the exhibits. Their faces became pale and swollen, their eyes bulging with asphyxiation. And in that wide-eyed death stare, did they see the hooded creatures who swam to them and stroked their hair and reassured them that this was the end, no matter how hard they fought it? I wonder, though, what happened to them next, in that darkness that we all try to avoid.

Chapter Eighteen

~~~

Mother Earth

~~~

Dylan and Viqaas check every hospital they can reach, but the doctors and nurses are overwhelmed by the flooding. For decades now, the national healthcare system has been pillaged so the resources could be redirected to privatized initiatives set up by the spouses of politicians. Even so, Viqaas remains hopeful that his parents and sister made it out alive, and they are okay, and they haven't called yet because they dropped their phones, of course. That would explain it.

Finally, at the end of another day of searching, Viqaas finds his sister in the first hospital he'd checked, only they couldn't locate her because of the chaos. Who has time for accurate paperwork during a crisis like this? Besides, the nurse, a white woman in her sixties, born and bred in Dagenham, didn't like these strange names that sounded foreign, so she didn't really try hard with the spelling.

Vafia was pleased to see her brother, and she was too worried about her parents to give Dylan a second glance. She urged her brother to go back out and look for them, checking twice, three times and more, just so he could find them. But just as he turned to walk out of her ward, a nurse asked to speak to him. She was a different nurse than the one who couldn't get Vafia's name right. She was kinder, so she expressed her condolences, a little too hastily, when the bodies hadn't yet been identified.

Viqaas tries to comfort his sister, but she screams at Dylan that all of this was their fault. She tells them both to leave her in peace, and after they have gone, she hears something sweet and melodic. It is a voice urging her to listen carefully because it has a tale of vengeance to tell. In this tale, she can become the main character where she rampages through bodies using knives, shards of glass, and guns. This siren tells her that she deserves to do this, and the people who get hurt deserve it. *They were your parents, after all.*

As she feels the wrath burning beneath her skin, she sees the hooded creatures scamper along the floor of her ward and leap onto the bed beside her. They feel her greed, that need for vengeance that burns beneath her skin, and they want to help her.

And Mother Earth watches on, satisfied, for now, that things are going according to plan. These foolish, greedy, ant-like people. Hearing voices and seeing images of who they love and fear the most, when all along they should see that it was her all along. Mother Earth was the one they should love and fear the most.

~~~
~~~

Acknowledgements

~~~

Special thanks to M, L, and W.

~~~

Learn more

~~~

To learn more about this book, and others written by BB
Clifford, use the following link to receive updates:
https://www.bbclifford.com/signup.html

~~~

Preview of Malevolent Fairy

~~~
~~~

Malevolent Fairy

~~~

The Tale of Ania, A Troubled Soul

BB CLIFFORD

A Zero Labels Book

ccxxxvi
~~~

Prologue

~~~

Misogyny and its accomplice

~~~

It came in the night, as all destructive things do. When I awoke, I was no longer a child. It took what he needed from me, without any respect or care, carving deep inside me the shape of misogyny.

The first I knew, there was something shuffling in the hallway outside my room. My childish fears tried to make me believe that there were eight legs of an arachnid scuttling up the walls, but I was growing too old for myths and legends. It was probably one of my parents or my brother.

The door to my bedroom creaked, and my body locked up, trapping the breath in my chest. I was frozen in space, powerless to stop what was about to happen. You see, the moon was shining full beam, breaking through the gap in my curtains, so I could see who it was. And I knew that he was going to do it, skewering his flag to claim me as his own. Just because he could.

I fell asleep shortly afterwards. I've since heard that this is often what happens because our brain, our body, can't comprehend any of it. So we just give up and slip from consciousness. We play dead.

I wanted it to be a nightmare. I wanted to laugh at how ridiculous it could be to think of something so terrible that it locks you up in the paralysis of sleep. But when I awoke, I felt it, and I still feel it now, as I sit in the stillness of the early hours before dawn. Before the ravens take flight.

I waited until sunrise to leave my bed. It felt like the right thing to do, to follow the same routine for fear of attracting someone's attention.

From those first footsteps into the bathroom, pretending it was just another day, I realized it was possible to split apart what was on the inside from the veneer I showed the rest of the world. I could smile and place one foot in front of the other like a normal person who had not felt the sweat and weight of someone upon me. I could split off the part inside that was scampering on all fours, possessed by the horrors that tore apart my night. In that tear, the old me, that younger, untouched self, just leaked away like bodily fluids. It was absorbed into the mattress and disappeared without leaving a trace, as if it had never existed.

Ever since, something has started to grow. For the last six weeks, since the idea penetrated my mind, the ugly truth has germinated. And there is no going back. The horrors divided, multiplied, as rapidly as cancerous growth. Only, it is the kind of growth that is revered and protected by laws. Men in suits constantly try to prohibit me from doing anything about this, and they expect me to transmute this violence into some kind of holy mission, to deliver a life to them, fully formed and intact. And then? What then? I'm not sure the men in suits have given this much thought, and even if they have, they probably don't really care.

In its existence, it is monstrous and incredible at the same time. I, barely sixteen, could create another life? When I am barely navigating this one. When I am not considered responsible enough to drive a car or drink alcohol or vote. And yet I can grow something that will let out the throb of a heartbeat, and kick me from inside, making certain that their presence is not forgotten. As if I could forget about this constant companion. We are reluctant roommates who compete for the same resources, and fate sits back on their haunches and waits to see if love or hatred grows out of this little arrangement.

Powerless. Isn't that how they want us? Girls and women alike, we are supposed to just lie back and accept all this. Dutiful, diligent, and silent. Dylan could never suffer this fate. No matter how many times they claim that biological sex is less important than gender identity, my brother could never end up trapped in this liminal state for nine months, with something that is the makings of a horror story.

Every morning, I wake up to the same thought of walking down the stairs and faltering in my footing. I imagine what it would be like to tumble down those hard wooden steps. Would I notice you dislodging from me, producing no more blood between my legs than a nosebleed?

I could never do that to you. So instead, I glide down the stairs as carefully as I can, and I am greeted each morning by my mother, Eris, who still insists on making my breakfast.

"She'll never grow up," Dylan says with a hiss to our mother. "You're infantilizing her for your own sake, just so she doesn't outgrow you. What are you gonna do, lock her up in the attic for the rest of her life?"

Eris ignores my brother, pushing past them so she can embrace me. Her body vibrates with a restlessness stirred up by Dylan, and I feel her gravitational pull. She needs a comrade, someone to defeat this battle-lustful warrior that has occupied her home, but I refuse to turn against my brother.

"So you're finally up."

I don't know why I didn't jump at the sound of my father's voice. He was standing so close behind me that I could feel his hot breath on the back of my neck.

To stay upright, to stay conscious, I stare out the kitchen window. There are reports of a hurricane heading towards the East Coast. Already the wind is picking up, so I watch the aconite flicker as if it's stroked by a hidden hand. *Wolf's bane for the wolf pack*, mom once said about her favorite flowers. In an unguarded moment, I told her about the cruel girls at school, the ones who have been calling me *Freak* and *Weirdo* for so long that I refer to myself in the same way. Eris promised that she would crush up the poisonous flowers and sprinkle them in their Stanley cups. I keep telling myself that she's all talk, but the older she gets, the more tangled up she becomes in her wrath and vengeance.

Something calls to me from the orchard. It could be the wind creaking the limbs of the trees, but I would rather believe it is a siren warning me of greater dangers ahead and promising that there is a way to escape all of this. I feel pathetic to hope for something like this. I can't muster up enough malevolence to do my own dirty work, so I have to project it onto some kind of spirit. I mean, is there really any kind of freedom that could be found in a row of trees? Am I supposed to become some kind of woodland nymph where I brew concoctions to poison the ones who torment me? No better or worse than Eris, goddess of discord and strife.

"I'm glad to see you wearing that at last." Paris gestures at my bracelet, the one he bought for my recent birthday. I'd forgotten I was still wearing it, and who gave it to me. Otherwise, I would've flushed it down the toilet.

I play along with his game and smile at him. I am the good child, obedient to a fault, yet all along I want to scream at him, "Just wait until I fuck you up, you rapist conniving cunt!". I can feel the words writhing about deep inside my body. They start to move in unison, forming the sentence that burns so hot that I think they might scour their print into my skin.

As he stands too close behind me, I feel him watching my every move. I want to fold my body into a smaller package, so small that he can't see me, but still existing, so I can inflict damage on him. Like a tiny shrapnel from an incendiary device whizzing through someone's skull and felling him before he even notices he has been hit. Of course, I can't do this, so my big, long limbs collide with the fridge and the counter as I move clumsily away from him. Every movement makes the panda pendants jingle, and Dylan points at them, smiling at me.

"You sound like a fairground ride."
The analogy makes me flinch, so, without thinking, I snap back, "I like to think they are fairies approaching."
I don't know why I said it, and it instantly made me sound younger and more foolish than I really was.
"Aww, midget," he said with a sigh. "You really are a little cutey!"

He views me as a little fairy, a sparkling highlight to his tale. But I have my own story to tell.

I turn to face my father, and that's when I see them. The hooded creatures that are standing next to him. They sway in unison, hypnotizing me with their gentle presence. My father doesn't see them, only they see him, and they watch his every move as he lingers around me.

Even though they make no sound, I can hear their messages, and they make promises of scalpels and claw hammers and bone saws. They want to see violence as much as I do, and they don't care if it happens now, in this brilliant morning light, or later tonight, under the glare of moonlight.

Each one places a forefinger to their sack-covered face, in the place I imagine their lips to be. They issue their silent instruction to keep this a secret, and if anyone tries to speak of them, these hooded creatures will snip their tongue with a razor blade and stitch their lips together. Isn't this the way families work? They keep their secrets locked up in the far corner of the attic of a fortress of latches and bolts. No one can know, so we are left to distort in that darkness of ignorance, and in such conditions, shame multiplies like spores of mold to contaminate us.

I stare at the knife block and the siren call gets louder. It is so loud that it hurts my ears, but I can make out words now, as clearly as if they were being etched on my father's bare skin.

Bad things happen to bad people.
This seems simple enough, something that I can justify. He hurt me, so I can hurt him back. The whole world never went blind with this eye for an eye vengeance. Nations of warriors

use the concept to justify the violence and torment they inflict across borders, so what harm would come from one young girl using this to eradicate her predatory father?

I step over to the knife block, glancing over to the hooded creatures as I expect to see their encouragement, but they are pointing past Paris to someone else.

I turn back to stare out at the orchard. I feel the restlessness of these hooded creatures from behind me. They want me to see.

I shut my eyes, and yet now I feel their sticky fingers peeling back my eyelids. They stink of rotting flesh and apples and bark, and they try to show me more.

I should run from here, but I know they will find me, and they will continue to make me see the truth.

Order your copy of Malevolent today –

https://www.bbclifford.com/

243

If there is a problem with any order, please send a message here –

https://www.bbclifford.com/contact.html

Other books by BB Clifford

~~~

Tangled Knot
The Tale of Eris of Suburbia

~~~

Like the whisperings of a ghost, this is a hellish tale of grief, isolation, and revenge. See how this family tree has become tangled and haunted by trauma, and learn whether anything can grow from this beyond poisoned fruit.

Eris once believed that she could keep herself safe from the suburban beast that slithered around the swampland of a small town on the US East Coast. She hid herself away behind latches and bolts and locks, making a fortress of her family home. They called this recluse a witch, and if she had lived in another age, this suburban misfit would have been hanged or burned at the stake.

Despite her fortress, the dangers still found Eris. As if myths and legends were true all along, her family was torn apart one snowy night when her teenage daughter was found dead. Ever since, Eris and her husband, Paris, remain tangled in a marriage knot riddled with grief. Every move Paris makes to free himself of this grief only tightens the knot like a hangman's noose around Eris's neck. For either of them to cut themselves free means they will fall into the unknown, which could mean a landing on softened soil ripe for regrowth, or a plunge into an abyss of hopelessness and despair.

Two years on since her nightmares became a reality, Eris thinks she has discovered the truth about her daughter's death. She stirs concoctions of poison and vengeance, but will this kill off all hope, proving herself to be a witch who should be condemned to isolation in a fortress that is haunted by grief? She fears that such a fate might leave her exposed to horrors that still haunt her: What good are locks on a fortress if the greatest danger threatens her from within? Anything is possible since the unnatural occurred and the bond was broken between parent and child. All manner of natural things has become unnatural as her life has become an underworld.

Compelling, poignant, and deeply real, Tangled Knot is an account of grief, isolation, and revenge that grabs you by the throat from the outset and will not let you go until you resolve for yourself whether the greatest threat is from the haunted world outside or the dangers that lurk within your own family—or even within the tangled knots of your own mind.

About the Author

~~~

247

BB Clifford has written *Rainbow Warrior, Tangled Knot,* and *Malevolent Fairy*.

BB Clifford is a queer author based in northern New Jersey. They live with their children, partner, and two cats. BB Clifford is greatly influenced by Shirley Jackson, Alison Rumfitt, and Thomas Harris.
~~~